Mack Bolan pressed himself agai̶̶̶̶̶̶ hand fisting the Beretta 93-R, the other clasping the stone ledge. When the sentry finally moved away, the warrior waited a minute, then resumed his climb to the top.

He hiked himself onto the stone lip and started to rise, his silenced pistol aimed at the guard's back. The hardman turned suddenly, as if he sensed a dangerous presence.

The Beretta coughed once, and a 9 mm round drilled into the man's heart, putting him down. Bolan dragged the corpse behind a boulder, then knelt to scope the enemy stronghold. More than two dozen men stood on the parade field, most of them staring at the MiG fighters streaking across the sky. The big radar dish was mounted to the side of one of the buildings.

The warrior nodded with grim satisfaction. He had found the Aggressive Concentrated Radar device responsible for so many deaths and for driving the world to the brink of war. Yet the ACR technology wasn't to blame. The men who used it for their evil purposes were at fault, and it was time for them to pay.

The Executioner had arrived to pass judgment on the enemy.

DON PENDLETON'S

MACK BOLAN®

STONY MAN™

BLIND EAGLE

A GOLD EAGLE BOOK FROM

WORLDWIDE®

TORONTO • NEW YORK • LONDON
AMSTERDAM • PARIS • SYDNEY • HAMBURG
STOCKHOLM • ATHENS • TOKYO • MILAN
MADRID • WARSAW • BUDAPEST • AUCKLAND

First edition September 1994

ISBN 0-373-61896-4

Special thanks and acknowledgment to William Fieldhouse
for his contribution to this work.

BLIND EAGLE

BLIND EAGLE

CHAPTER ONE

Pontic Mountain Range, Turkey
Sunday, 0320 hours

Stanley Fell missed the "good old days" of the cold war. It was hard to believe that one could feel nostalgia for the shadowy business of spy versus spy, but Fell thought the world seemed to make more sense back then. At least his job had seemed easy enough to understand. There were good-guy Americans and their allies, and bad-guy Soviets and their Communist comrades. The concept was simple to grasp and seemed to justify anything and everything Fell was required to do.

Perhaps he relished this black-and-white philosophy because nothing else about being a case officer for the National Security Agency was uncomplicated. The technology used for reconnaissance and surveillance became more sophisticated every year. The cloak-and-dagger days when Intelligence was gathered by agents in the field had been replaced by spy satellites, radar detection and laser transmissions.

Fell had never been part of the old school of espionage. By the time he'd joined the NSA in 1980, the agents who specialized in slipping back and forth across the iron curtain were already anachronisms. Fell was involved in SIGINT, or signals Intelligence, which collected data by electronic eavesdropping and photo recon from satellites.

His expertise consisted of evaluating information on the monitors, transmitted by the high-tech spies in the skies, computer enhancement of photo imagery and telemetry analysis to determine the guidance system, speed and fuel consumption of missiles. Pretty tame stuff compared to the fictional adventures of James Bond, but the fancy gadgets in the movies paled next to the high-tech equipment of SIGINT.

They had pinpointed the locations of every major missile base and silo in the former Soviet Union and detected the incredible Russian civil-defense system with massive underground shelters, complete with networks of tunnels and enormous food-storage sections. Thanks to photos, videos and radio transmissions from satellites hundreds of miles above the earth, they had acquired a great advantage in the cold war.

But the cold war was officially over. There was no longer a Soviet Union to compete with. The Communists were out of power, and the former Soviet Union was known as the Commonwealth of Independent States. The great red menace Fell had known all his life had simply dissolved. Although the Soviet satellite and electronic surveillance technology had been inferior to that of the U.S., the Soviets had presented the only serious challenge in the global game of chess. So what were NSA and SIGINT to do now?

Stan Fell didn't have to apply for unemployment. The government still had plenty of work for him. In fact, the situation seemed more complicated and demanding than before. The USSR might have transformed into the CIS, but thousands of nuclear weapons remained on Russian soil and the territories of the other former Soviet republics. They were still arguing about who ought to control the arsenal and what to do with the weapons. The democratic reforms hadn't gone smoothly, CIS was suffering serious economic problems, and political experts worried a new totalitarian regime could take over.

The NSA case officer stared at the rows of monitors that were operated by his team members. They manned the recon system twenty-four hours a day. Fell's post had to constantly gather and evaluate information because they were concerned with covering a wider range of territory and activities than before. Numbers and abbreviated terms in the jargon of SIGINT rolled across the screens. Enhanced, multicolored images of topography appeared briefly, replaced by other scenes unless something of special value had been detected by the computers.

The world had changed, and no one was quite certain who was friend or foe. Different countries seemed to change their status in the eyes of Washington from one year—or even one month—to the next. Fell's post at Mountain Balloon had formerly concentrated on recon of Iran, Libya and Syria as the major concerns next to the Soviets and their East European satellite nations. This had changed shortly prior to the Gulf War, when attention shifted to Iraq as the bully of the Middle East.

Concerns also extended to the potential nuclear capability of Pakistan, India, South Africa and elsewhere. China, North Korea and Cuba presented the remaining Communist threats to world peace. Yet these countries weren't within Mountain Balloon's task-

ing—a term used for targeted areas of reconnaissance—assignments. The Pontic Mountains placed
Fell's station in an ideal position to receive transmissions from spy satellites that covered a third of the CIS
and most of the Middle East. That was plenty. Fell
would happily give part of his burden to anyone willing to take it.

Fell was almost bored as he strolled from the coffeemaker with yet another cup of the hot black brew.
He had elected to take the graveyard shift because he
figured that was when the most serious conflicts or in-
vasions were apt to take place, but the data on the
screens suggested it was fairly quiet. An operator
named Darryl Osmond was seated by a monitor for
Space Eye 12. Fell recognized the data on the screen.
"Arme 40/45" and "Azer 40/45" referred to the Ar-
menia-Azerbaijan border. The two former Soviet republics had been involved in an on-again, off-again
war for almost five years.

"Any change in troop strength or arsenal on either
side?" Fell inquired.

Osmond looked up at him with a weary expression.
He punched the keyboard to summon information
from the memory banks. Numbers filled the screen as
the computer made a tally faster than a human could
manage. The answer appeared as the count was completed.

"According to heat level and optics, the situation
hasn't changed in the past forty-eight hours, Mr. Fell."

"That's nice. Let's hope it stays that way. A truce is
always best when both sides keep it."

"Yes, sir."

Fell smiled. It still seemed strange to be called "sir." At thirty-four, he was the "old man" at Mountain Balloon. The crew was comprised of young men and women, products of a generation that had grown up with the microchip. They possessed fewer phobias about computers than most people Fell's age or older. The future of Intelligence operations didn't rely on skills of infiltration, smuggling microfilm across an obscure border or besting some heavy-handed secret-police goon in a karate fight. It would depend on artificial intelligence, high-tech equipment and knowing how to use it.

"What the hell's this?" Osmond remarked in a startled tone.

The comment drew Fell's attention, and he glanced down at the monitor. The screen was filled with black-and-white waves of static. Osmond placed a hand to his headset as he fiddled with the tuning dial by the keyboard. Fell saw the rest of the crew also faced blank monitors. SE-12 had suddenly ceased to transmit data.

"No laser digital or radio transmission," Osmond stated.

"The Space Eye model is designed to switch to radar digital if anything happens to the laser system," Fell said. "Check for those transmissions."

"Already did. Nothing but static's coming through."

Fell glanced at the wall chart. It was a euphemism because the chart was actually a large radar screen that tracked progress of satellites in orbit above the . -signed area of Mountain Balloon reconnaissance. The screen was covered by a wash of wavy lines and static. The base radar tracking was out.

"There's a KH in orbit up there," Fell announced. "Maybe we can establish contact with it."

A "KH" referred to a Keyhole satellite, a forerunner of the Space Eye model. The others were familiar with the technology employed by the KH, which used radar digital rather than laser. Even if the SE-12 failed to transmit by either system, the KH might be operational.

"You, you and you," Fell began, thrusting his finger at personnel without wasting time with names. "PF-40 and clear your screens. Then punch in the codes for the KH. Double-time, folks!"

Fingers danced across keyboards. Yellow numbers appeared on green screens, followed by more displays of mocking static.

"We've got squat," an operative named Alvin stated.

"Everybody's radar is down," another voice added, "including ours, Mr. Fell."

"I noticed. Okay. Radio scan. See what broadcasts we can detect. Very high, ultrahigh, modulations on any frequency. There's got to be something coming in from somewhere."

Fell headed for an international transceiver and switched it on. He turned up the volume to discover the crackle of static. Others still struggled with their monitors, either trying to contact the SE-12, the KH or any other communications source. Fell changed frequencies, every effort in vain. He couldn't even find an AM broadcast from the radio station in Ankara.

Suddenly voices penetrated static from another speaker.

"Isminiz nedir?"

"Biraz Turkce biliyorum. Ingilizce biliyor musunuz?"

"I speak little English. What your name, please?"

"George. I'm calling from a boat in the Black Sea."

"No understand..."

Fell abandoned the transceiver and headed for Alvin's monitor. The operative had found the only available transmission, but it appeared to be idle chitchat.

"What the hell is it?"

"Shortwave radio broadcast," Alvin replied. "Got us a couple ham radio hackers. Sounds like an American tourist and some Turkish guy, probably in Trabzon or Rize or somewhere else along the coast."

"Useless," Fell said with frustration.

"What's going on?" Osmond asked. "Has anything like this ever happened before, Mr. Fell?"

"Not to this degree. Not since I've been at Mountain Balloon. All we can do is keep working at the monitors. Stay open for SE-12. Those assigned to the KH, keep on it. Alvin, try some other frequencies. Not much point in listening to those hackers."

"Maybe we should record it for background sounds. Could be something hidden in the small talk."

"Hell, go ahead. I'll scan for other radio broadcasts."

"How long do we do this, Chief?" Alvin asked.

"As long as it takes."

This proved to be nearly half an hour. The blanket of static lifted as abruptly as it had begun. Suddenly images appeared on every monitor, and Fell received a jolt when an FM broadcast blared from the transceiver. He sighed with relief as he stared at the radar blips on the wall chart. The satellites were still in orbit.

"God Almighty!" Osmond exclaimed.

Fell rushed to the monitor and stared at the display. The digital print images were virtually the same as those of a television broadcast. The SE-12 used a multispectral scan, with a photomultiplier, as well as infrared lenses for superb night vision. The images on the screen were very clear. Uniformed figures exchanged fire with automatic weapons. Yellow fire ejected from the muzzle of a tank cannon as an explosion erupted near a row of sandbags.

"Armenia and Azerbaijan are at it again," Fell said with a shake of his head.

"No, they're not," Osmond corrected. "Look at the ID on the screen. The battle is being fought along the border of Armenia and Iran! These are real-time imagery, sir. This fight is going on right now!"

"Iran and Armenia?" Fell repeated, checking the information on the screen to confirm this claim. "How the hell did this happen? We've never observed any aggression between these two countries before."

"It must have happened when our systems were blocked."

"No shit?" Fell replied, the remark more caustic than intended. "We have no idea which side started this or why."

Moscow, Russia

GORKY STREET was one of the few sites in Moscow that hadn't changed its name since the transformation in 1991. Yet the street itself looked different. The biggest avenue in the city had never been clogged with traffic jams, but the number of vehicles in the ten lanes had dropped dramatically since the Communists' fall from power. Most Russians who used to own cars had been in the Communist Party. Now there were fewer Communists, fewer drivers and an economy that prevented most from owning private vehicles.

Of course, there was hardly any traffic at a quarter after six in the morning. The buses transporting workers and an occasional produce truck traveled the lanes as the black limousine rolled along Gorky Street. A small American flag labeled the vehicle as a U.S. Embassy car. Ambassador Whiteside sat in the front seat as Stan Fell drove the limo. The ambassador was bleary-eyed and surly about having to go to work so early on a Sunday.

Colonel Amer Narek had obviously been awake for hours. The Armenian officer appeared apprehensive, uncomfortable in the official vehicle. Sharing the back seat with Valery Zaystev didn't improve his disposition. The head of the Russian Ministry of Defense didn't seem very happy, either. The man's round face was lined by stress, and he nervously drummed fingers along his knee.

"This is a pretty incredible story, Colonel," Whiteside began. "You're claiming the Iranians attacked you without any warning or provocation?"

"Provocation?" Narek asked with a frown. He seemed to mull over the term, comparing it to more familiar words in his lexicon of English. "Provoked? Of course we did not provoke the Iranians."

"Well, Mr. Smith is from a certain listening post that monitors satellite surveillance," Whiteside said.

Fell nearly forgot he was "Smith."

"Like I already told you, Ambassador," he replied. "We didn't detect the border battle until it was already in progress. We can't verify which side initiated the conflict."

Whiteside stared at Fell. "I expected more from NSA. You guys are supposed to have the best equipment in the world."

"We do, but something happened just before the battle occurred. Everything was blocked by static. Never saw anything like it before."

"I can verify what happened," Narek insisted. "The Iranians launched rockets at us. Something like RPGs. I was there."

"Unfortunately the Iranians claim your country started the conflict," Zaystev declared. "They are already making accusations. It's the major news story on radio from Tehran. Virtually the only story. The Iranians claim you Armenians started the fight. They're also accusing us Russians of being involved. Just for good measure, they're also saying the Americans are probably connected with it, as well."

"How did they come to that conclusion?" Whiteside asked.

"The United States is still the 'Great Satan' to most Iranians," Fell explained. "They'll blame us for just about anything. If they haven't already added Israel to the hate list, they will soon."

"Oh, yes," Zaystev said with a nod. "They mentioned Israel in the broadcast. I suppose that's what one can expect from fanatics."

"It wasn't that long ago the U.S. and the Soviet Union accused each other for just about everything that went wrong," Fell reminded the Russian. "I take it your spy satellites didn't cover the beginning of the border conflict, either?"

Zaystev shrugged. "That's really not my department, Mr. Smith."

"Sure. When you get in touch with whoever is responsible for Russian satellites these days, you might ask about this."

Zaystev coughed, seemingly to clear his throat. The Russian official was embarrassed, aware his tainted version of the truth hadn't fooled anyone.

"I'll contact them," he began. "Of course, if they had discovered any vital information from the satellite scans, I assume they would have already told me."

"So whatever blocked our satellites did the same to your Russian space gear in perigee at the time."

"Perigee?" Whiteside inquired, unfamiliar with the term.

"That's when a satellite descends to the lowest level of its orbit and thus gathers and transmits Intelligence to the most effective degree."

"Fascinating," the ambassador said dryly. "So our most recent Intelligence isn't much help. What about prior data gathered before the border clash? Any evidence Iran was preparing anything like this?"

"We went over records of recent recon across Iran," Fell replied. "Nothing suggested the Iranians planned anything like this. Frankly I can't see any reason why they'd do it. What would they hope to gain by such a stunt?"

"I assure you they launched the attack, Mr. Smith," Narek said in a defensive tone. "Armenia certainly has nothing to gain by starting a conflict with Iran. We've had enough problems with Azerbajdzanskja. I believe you call it Azerbaijan?''

''It's easier for us to call it that,'' Fell admitted.

''I'm certain you are aware Azerbaijan is predominantly Muslim,'' Narek began. ''We Armenians are mostly Christians. It could be that Iran has decided to side with a fellow Islamic country in a so-called 'holy war' against a small and vulnerable Christian neighbor.''

''That doesn't make much sense to me. Iran has been trying to establish a more palatable public image since the death of the Ayatollah. Iran might not be the favorite nation in the Middle East, but they haven't been threatening to carry out any jihads lately.''

''You're dismissing this matter rather easily,'' Zaystev commented. ''Perhaps because this is a threat to a country of the CIS and not the United States of America.''

''No one is dismissing anything,'' Whiteside assured him. ''We can't jump to any conclusions one way or the other. I urge you and your government not to do anything hasty, either.''

''Twenty-three brave Armenian soldiers were killed this morning,'' Narek declared. ''Twice that number were injured. Perhaps you should talk to the Iranians about 'hasty' actions.''

Fell had slowed the limo to a bare crawl during the conversation. He glanced at the buildings. Everything seemed dismal and grim. He realized this was probably his imagination and the knowledge that Russia was gripped by a terrible economic situation. Of course, no stores were open so early in the morning. The overcast, gray sky did nothing to dispel the impression of despair.

"No one is minimizing the importance of this incident," Ambassador Whiteside told Narek. "We just have to be careful about making any definite claims at this time. Please understand, it isn't up to me to make decisions concerning what position the United States will take in this matter."

"Russia is faced with an even more serious situation," Zaystev stated. "We don't want to get involved in conflicts concerning the other CIS republics, but we can't allow Armenia to be invaded by Iran, either. Whatever action we take will make us very unpopular with large segments of the population. If we do nothing, the Armenians will regard us as unfit leaders of the CIS because we offer no protection from outside forces. If we send troops, many Armenians would see us as oppressors instead of protectors. The other republics will almost certainly have that opinion. Especially Azerbaijan."

"We Armenians may have to accept whatever proves necessary to ensure our survival in this case," the colonel said glumly. "Iran is a large country with approximately fifty million people. It's obvious we can't fight them by ourselves."

"Before we start planning the possibility of war," Fell began, "I'd like to know what happened to our equipment. It's one hell of a coincidence that happened while this border conflict occurred. I don't know what could have caused all of our equipment to draw blanks at the same time."

"Maybe it was some sort of weather condition," Whiteside suggested.

"I've been involved in SIGINT recon for more than a decade, and I've never seen any kind of weather conditions that could cause such total blocking of transmissions."

"You think this might have been caused by some sort of scrambling device or force field or whatever?" the ambassador asked. "Sounds like something out of science fiction to me."

"A great deal of modern technology sounded like science fiction just a few years ago," Fell replied. "I don't know how someone could block satellite transmissions or who could be responsible, but I think it's worth considering the possibility this was a deliberate action."

"We Armenians certainly couldn't have done anything like that," Narek said. "We don't have any technology of that sort and wouldn't use it if we did. What could we gain by doing this? No matter what happens, it will be bad for Armenia."

"Yeah, but Iran is in the same situation, and I doubt they have the technology to do anything like this, either," Fell added. "Frankly I don't know who could have done this or why they'd do it."

"Or even if this conjecture is accurate," Zaystev said in a weary voice. "I don't mean to offend you, Mr. Smith, but NSA is no doubt embarrassed by this situation. Are you certain you're not trying to find some rationalization for SIGINT's apparent failure?"

Fell glanced over his shoulder at the Russian. The guy was blowing smoke, and they both knew it. The Russian Intelligence forces were faced with the same concerns Fell had already mentioned. Zaystev could pretend otherwise, but he wasn't fooling anyone by such remarks.

"Well," the NSA officer began, "I sure hope it turns out there's some other explanation because we've got one hell of a problem if someone has developed an effective way of blinding spy satellites. If they could do it to us this time, they can do it again. And God knows what might happen the next time."

CHAPTER TWO

Sunday, 1315 hours

Hal Brognola shoved the plunger into the sink basin. He was glad Helen was visiting a friend in Baltimore. The big Fed didn't like to look incompetent in front of his wife. This didn't happen often, since Brognola was a man of truly exceptional competence in many fields.

However, as a plumber he couldn't justly claim to be more than an awkward dilettante. Frustrated, he looked inside the cabinet under the sink for something that might succeed in unclogging the plumbing. Brognola spent so little time at home he wasn't sure what might be stored there.

The strident ring of the telephone drew the big Fed from the task. He was relieved to get a reprieve, and headed for the den to take the call. Brognola dropped into the swivel chair behind his desk and plucked the telephone receiver from its cradle.

"Yeah," he offered as greeting.

"I'm afraid we have a problem."

Brognola immediately recognized the voice of the President of the United States. "I'm listening."

"A skirmish occurred between Armenia and Iran along their border," the President explained.

"Armenia and Iran? That's a new one. What caused those two to start fighting each other?"

"That's a good question. Unfortunately we don't have any answers. Right now that's our major concern. The SIGINT satellites failed to detect any sign of aggression because something happened to the transmissions. You're familiar with SIGINT recon by the NSA?"

"I know a little about it, and I've got people who can make up for any lack of knowledge on my part. You think the failure of the satellite transmissions was caused by enemy action?"

"That's what it looks like."

"Well, those high-tech gadgets are just great as long as they work," Brognola declared. "And high-tech Intelligence isn't flawless. You recall what happened with the *Baton Rouge?*"

"One of our subs that collided with a Russian sub in international waters in February 1992," the President replied, a trace of annoyance in his voice. "One of my advisers already reminded me of that embarrassing little incident."

"Good. We have to remember that even the most state-of-the-art machines can fail to do what they're supposed to do. As I recall, neither the American sub nor the Russian vessel realized they were about to crash until it was too late. They had the most advanced sonar systems, radio scans and I suppose somebody could have looked out a window—so to speak. They still banged into each other."

"That situation was different from what we're faced with now. The failure of the spy satellites is potentially far more serious. I wouldn't have called you otherwise."

Brognola was aware of this, of course. He was the director of the Sensitive Operations Group and Stony Man Farm. The man in the Oval Office wouldn't have contacted him unless the problem was serious enough to merit going to Brognola's unconventional organization.

"If someone can blind SIGINT satellites, our country has a major threat to our national security. The Soviet Union might be dead, but there are still hundreds of nuclear weapons on CIS soil and in several other nations. If we're going to have successful arms reduction, we have to be able to verify what these countries have and whether or not these arms are being destroyed."

Brognola listened to the President. He already understood the magnitude of the threat, but he allowed the Commander in Chief to continue the lecture.

"We also have reason to be very concerned about the border clash between Armenian and Iranian forces. You know the history of problems with Iran since 1979. The hostage situation, the rise of Shiite extremism under the Ayatollah, the Iran-Iraq war and the clashes U.S. forces had with the Iranians during the Reagan administration when American naval forces escorted oil tankers through the Persian Gulf. Iran was also involved in state-sponsored terrorism, much of it directed against the United States."

"Yeah," Brognola said dryly. "I remember."

A pause revealed the President realized he was talking to a man who had been instrumental in stopping some of the most ruthless and dangerous terrorist schemes to occur during the past several years. Brognola and Stony Man Farm had dealt with terrorists of dozens of different nationalities, including Iranians.

"Well, our sources tell us the border conflict has already caused an outbreak of anti-American demonstrations in Iran. For some reason they think we're responsible for the incident between Iran and Armenia."

"A lot of Iranians don't like America. We supported the Shah for about forty years. He wasn't very popular with his own people. His SAVAK secret police kept law and order by using torture chambers and firing squads. It's not surprising we were associated with that horrible oppression, and a lot of Iranians still resent us for that reason. Of course, the fanatic Shiite element also hates Israel and they're not pleased that we supported the Jewish state, as well."

"I'm surprised you're making excuses for them."

"I'm just trying to look at things from the Iranians' point of view," the big Fed explained. "Because there are some demonstrations, it doesn't necessarily mean the government in Iran agrees with them. You might recall there were anti-American, anti-British and anti-Israeli demonstrations in Tehran when the troops were in Saudi Arabia for Desert Shield. Iran had been at war with Iraq for eight years. You know that the government in Tehran and probably most of the population hoped we'd kicked the living daylights out of Saddam and his military."

"So you don't think the most recent demonstrations are anything for us to worry about?"

"I don't think we should jump to any conclusions based on them at this time. All it means is a bunch of Iranians want to complain about Uncle Sam whenever something goes wrong. Have you contacted the president?''

"Our diplomatic relations with Iran are still unconfirmed. Of course, we're trying to make contact by less formal methods. We have been mending a few fences with the Iranians in recent years. After that terrible earthquake in June 1990, we offered some assistance and the Iranian government accepted. That was the beginning of an effort to establish better relations. Of course, that progress will come to an abrupt halt if Iran is mixed up with some sort of new jihad.''

"That doesn't seem very likely to me, Mr. President," Brognola said. "Why launch a holy war against Armenia?"

"The Armenians believe the Iranians have formed some sort of secret pact with Azerbaijan, and that the two Islamic states might have decided to squeeze out Christian Armenia.''

"Well, it seems that these so-called holy wars are almost always political, with religion used as an excuse for the conflict. Even Saddam tried to stir up a jihad during the Gulf War, although his government was very secular and a number of Muslim countries were among his enemies. Saddam had definite political and economic goals. What would Iran gain by attacking Armenia?"

"I don't know what sort of logic would justify such an action, but there seems to be even less reason for Armenia to start a fight with Iran. Either way, this incident is a major concern because it could lead to the downfall of the Commonwealth of Independent States. There are elements in Russia that would welcome an opportunity to prove the CIS is a failure and demand they return to strict, absolute control over all the states once more. Possibly reestablishing a Communist government or some sort of neofascist regime that could be even worse.''

''How is the situation between Armenia and Iran right now?''

''Tense. The battle lasted about half an hour. When neither side advanced, both ceased fire. They've reinforced troop strength on both sides of the border. Armenia and Iran blame each other for starting the skirmish. It's a powder keg that can explode if anything happens to trigger more violence.''

''I'll get my people on it immediately, but I'm not sure what we can add to what's already being done by NSA, CIA and whoever else you have on this case.''

''Stony Man has the best track record of any outfit assigned to this problem. I want the best people on this. That means you and your organization. Stay in touch. Good luck.'' The President hung up.

Brognola placed the phone in the receiver and sighed. There were always problems somewhere in the world. One of them had just been delivered to him personally by the Commander in Chief.

At least he had an excuse to abandon the struggle with the sink. Brognola reached for the telephone book, hoping he could find a plumber who worked on Sundays.

Stony Man Farm, Virginia

AARON KURTZMAN WATCHED the information flash across the screen. Meteorological reports flooded in, some from Turkey, Greece and Russia. Kurtzman keyed the board to have the messages translated by the computers. The foreign reports were compared with those from the U.S. weather-information service. Kurtzman heard the phone ring but ignored it, his concentration fixed on the results of the monitor.

"Nothing," he muttered with disappointment.

As Kurtzman powered his wheelchair to the coffee-maker to help himself to a cup of the thick black brew only his stomach seemed capable of accepting, the coded steel access door slid open, and Barbara Price stepped into the computer room. Blond and beautiful, Price looked stunning even clad in a baggy jumpsuit. But the woman hadn't been chosen as Farm mission controller because of her appearance. Price was good at her job. Stony Man only used the best.

"Hal's on the phone," she announced. "He wants to talk to both of us."

"I think I know why," Kurtzman replied.

He wheeled to his desk and punched buttons to the phone to patch the call through the speaker. "We're here, Hal. Tell us about the shooting match along the Iran-Armenia border."

"How did you guess?" Brognola asked.

"Well, we monitor news reports and decode Intelligence transmissions routinely. The reports on that border skirmish were acknowledged by our system as a possible trouble spot. It's programmed that way. Anyway, things are a little quiet right now, so I decided to take a look into this incident."

"So what did you find out?"

"The interesting part is what I *couldn't* find out. I patched into the computer systems at NSA, CIA, ONI and a couple of other Intelligence sources, and they don't have any more information than UPI. At least two modern U.S. spy satellites orbited the area and probably one or two Russian models, as well. None of them saw a damn thing. All that fancy laser and radar technology, and they couldn't get so much as a snapshot.''

"That's the problem. Any idea what could have caused this to happen?''

"My first guess was Mother Nature might have canceled the broadcast. I ran analysis on weather reports, but there's no evidence of sunspot phenomena, aurora borealis or any other natural condition that can affect electronic communications.''

"The President thinks this might have been caused by some man-made device. Do you know of anything that could do that?''

"Not offhand, but we've got all sorts of stuff stored in the banks here. I'll see what we can come up with.''

"Okay. Double-check any Intel that might have come in concerning recent activities in Iran or Armenia. Look for any connections between Azerbaijan and Iran. Seems like a long shot to me, but I don't think we can overlook any possibility at this time.''

"What about the teams?'' Brognola asked. "Where is everybody?''

The big Fed referred to the special commandos of Stony Man—Able Team, the three-man fighting unit that specialized in operations within the United States, Phoenix Force, a five-member squad that conducted missions in other lands, and Mack Bolan.

The legendary one-man army had been involved with Stony Man Farm since its inception. Though now very much the lone wolf, the Executioner worked with the top secret organization when a mission needed him.

"Able Team wrapped up business in New Mexico," Price began. "They're due to report in tomorrow. We can tell them to put the R & R on hold and come in pronto. Phoenix is a little scattered, but I can get them together within a few hours."

"Okay. You can leave a message for Striker, and we'll get him as soon as possible."

"That won't be necessary," Price explained. "Striker is already here, testing firearms with Cowboy."

"Great. Call him in and brief him ASAP. I got a feeling we'd better be at full force for this one."

"Getting the teams together won't be a problem," Price said. "But what do we assign them to do at this point?"

"Start at the beginning. That means the NSA base that was tracking the satellites and maybe Armenia or Russia."

"The NSA base is in Turkey," Kurtzman stated. "I scanned over a file on the case officer in charge. Looks like he's smart, competent and well trained. His record looks good. Mountain Balloon has a history of being one of best SIGINT posts in operation."

"Mountain Balloon?"

"That's kind of an inside joke with the NSA. Seems the Air Force launched hundreds of reconnaissance balloons from Turkey, Greece and Italy back in the 1950s. These things were disguised as weather balloons and equipped with cameras and radio gear. The idea was for the wind to carry the balloons over the

Soviet Union and Eastern Europe. Sort of a low-tech forerunner to spy satellites.''

"I've got to hand it to you, Bear," Brognola said. "When you research a subject, you don't miss many details."

"If you overlook details, you could make mistakes. Mistakes cost lives."

"That's a fact," Brognola agreed. "Grimaldi is going to fly me in. I'll be there in an hour. We'll have a sit-down conference and figure out our next move."

CHAPTER THREE

Jack Grimaldi expertly piloted the Bell helicopter above the treetops. Hal Brognola, the only passenger, sat behind Grimaldi. He glanced down at the familiar conifers and oak as they flew over the Shenandoah Valley, best known as the site of General Stonewall Jackson's greatest military victories during the War Between the States. The big Fed had made the trip numerous times in the past, yet he still found the view spectacular.

Grimaldi radioed ahead to announce they were coming. It was standard procedure, as unidentified aircraft that approached the Farm would be fired upon.

A casual observer—given the opportunity—wouldn't have paid much attention to the property. It appeared to be a large, apparently successful farming enterprise with a large main house, two outbuildings and a tractor barn. Even the landing field didn't seem out of place. Numerous workers, dressed in denim, labored in the orchards and collected crops of strawberries, potatoes and snap beans. In fact, it was fairly successful as a farm and produced a large quantity of food for market.

When the helicopter touched down, Brognola immediately headed out the sliding door and walked quickly to a Jeep. One of the farmhands slid behind the wheel and drove the big Fed to the main house. Brognola got out and headed for the steel door at the front of the house and punched in the access code.

Price met him at the entrance. They didn't waste time with social niceties.

"Is Striker in the War room?"

"He's with Aaron and the computers," Price replied. "We've got something interesting. Could be our first lead."

They entered the computer room. Kurtzman was seated at his horseshoe-shaped desk. Mack Bolan stood beside him. Both men studied data on the wall screen, barely glancing toward the door when Price and Brognola entered.

The big Fed looked at the dot-image shape on the screen. A dish with a trio of prongs in the center rotated slowly across the screen, displayed in detail with 3-D enhancement.

"What is that? It looks like a radar scanner."

"Yeah," Kurtzman replied. "It's a variation of regular radar. See, the parabolic reflector is designed for greater intensity for transmission."

"Oh, yeah. I should have noticed that right off."

"One of the prongs is a radiating element. Same as you find on standard radar. The other two are extremely powerful transmitting devices that intensify sound vibrations to an incredible level."

"Sort of like a superbullhorn," Price added. "Only this concentrates the vibrations, not noise. At least not at the pitch heard by human beings. What we're looking at is the design for an aggressive concentrated radar unit."

"Aggressive concentrated radar?" Brognola asked with a frown.

"ACR for short," Kurtzman confirmed. "We didn't know about it until about an hour ago, either. ACR is one of those projects the military had high hopes for a few years ago, but they weren't that happy with the results. So ACR has been on the back burner ever since. In fact, it's more like they put it on a hot plate that's barely lukewarm."

"Okay. What's the purpose of this ACR technology?"

"Well, standard radar operates by detecting objects by reception and timing of radio waves," Kurtzman began. "Objects that pass through the radar beam can be judged as to height, size, distance, direction and speed. The information is read on a plan-position indicator, generally called a radar screen."

"I more or less understood that," Brognola assured him.

"But aggressive concentrated radar not only detects objects, it can also transmit a very powerful radio wave. It concentrates sound in a manner similar to how a laser concentrates light beams. Only the pattern is much wider and expands as it shoots from the ACR dish."

"Powerful enough to block the high-tech surveillance equipment of the SE-12 and KH satellites?"

"Possibly. ACR wasn't designed for that purpose. They had planned to use it as part of the technology for the Stealth bomber, but the ACR units were too large to be incorporated with the systems of an aircraft.

More compact models of the ACR proved ineffective."

"Another problem was the fact the ACR waves affect radio wavelengths in such a wide pattern they would block or scramble the transmissions of any bomber with such a device," Price added. "Of course, they wanted to make the Stealth bomber 'invisible' to radar, but they didn't want to render it incapable of communications."

"I can't imagine they scrapped ACR programs entirely," Brognola said. "The Pentagon and military store vast caches of obsolete gear and merchandise. They're not going to abandon something that could be a useful technology for offense or defense one of these days."

"Like I said," Kurtzman replied, "they put it on low priority, but work is still being conducted on ACR. Mostly by the AFTAC."

"Is everything an acronym these days?"

"The Air Force Technical Applications Center," the Bear explained. "Their leading expert on ACR research is a guy named Joshua Collins."

"You ran a check on him?"

Kurtzman nodded. "His background looks okay. He's one of those wonder boys with a genius for things mechanical. Graduated with honors, specializing in acoustics and communications. He worked in radio broadcasting for a while, then looked into getting a government grant for some research. That brought him to the attention of the Pentagon."

"And to work on ACR development for the military," Brognola concluded, guessing what happened.

"That's right. According to his profile, Collins has a weakness for the ladies—something that doesn't sit too well with his wife—and he spends money a bit freely. Still, he isn't regarded as a serious security risk, and it seems unlikely he'd sell out to some sort of enemy conspiracy."

"Maybe," Brognola said. "But we have to consider every possibility until we start finding some answers. Barb, you've had a chance to consider how we should handle this mission. Any ideas?"

"We need to contact Collins," she replied. "He's the leading U.S. authority in this field, so he's the best choice to evaluate whether it might be ACR technology used against the satellites. We should keep this with our own people as much as possible. This is very low-profile work, and we want to keep it that way. I say we send Able Team to get him. They'll bear in mind the guy might be a goat instead of a sheep."

"Agreed," Brognola said. "You said Collins is the top 'U.S. authority. Have other countries been working on ACR technology?"

"Yeah," Kurtzman answered. "The Russians were working on it, too. I'm not sure how far they got with it, but they seem to have scratched ACR projects entirely even before the fall of communism. There's no evidence the Russians or other CIS countries have been involved with it since. The British and the French have had limited success with ACR experiments. Some of the Soviet work on the subject was conducted in East Germany and involved some of their scientists. Of course, there no longer is an East Germany, and the present united German government hasn't been involved in ACR technology."

"What happened to those scientists?" Brognola asked. "We've kept tabs on the Soviet nuclear experts because we were afraid they might seek employment with other governments after the fall of communism, which also cut off their most-privileged-citizen status. I doubt if the same kind of care was taken with authorities in research programs everybody pretty much lost faith in."

"We'll try to find out what happened to them," Kurtzman replied.

"Russia has to be considered a possibility," Price said. "Regardless of what has happened in the past couple of years, they still have a lot of high-tech weaponry and some extremists who would like to reclaim control of the region. Phoenix Force would be the best trained people to send there. They're certainly familiar with how the KGB operated in the past, and Katz speaks Russian fluently. If nothing else, they'd be our best team to enlist cooperation from the Russian authorities. That's probably our best way to find out what the Armenian military might be up to, as well."

"Okay," Brognola confirmed. "That leaves you, Striker. Which side of the ocean do you want to operate on?"

"We've discussed this and think we should have someone in Turkey," Price explained. "Whoever is responsible for this might have known about the orbit patterns of the SE-12 because they knew about Mountain Balloon. If nothing else, it would give Striker a base of operations with the NSA."

"Makes sense to me," Bolan replied. "I'd also be close enough to team up with Phoenix in Russia if they need me."

"And you'll be right in the middle of a very dangerous portion of the world if full-scale war erupts between Iran and Armenia," Brognola remarked. "You know, Iran borders Turkey, as well. God knows what could happen if this thing really blows up."

"Yeah," the Executioner said with a nod. "Let's just hope it doesn't come to that."

CHAPTER FOUR

Ural Mountains, Russia
Monday, 0710 hours

Heinz Giessler finished cleaning and oiling the disassembled Bauer pistol. The small .25-caliber automatic didn't have much stopping power, but it was easily concealed and cobra quick. Giessler had used this "hideout" piece on three occasions and taken out opponents with the diminutive weapon. It was only effective at close quarters, but it worked.

He carried the pistol in an unconventional manner—in a special holster just below his nape, which required a small harness hidden under his clothing to support the holstered gun. It wasn't the most comfortable way to carry a weapon, but few of his opponents would suspect he'd be reaching for a gun while appearing to scratch the back of his neck.

This was one of many tricks Giessler had learned during his twenty-year service in the Staats Sicherheits Dienst—SSD—the East German state security service. Giessler had enjoyed a special status as a top agent with this shadowy Intelligence agency. A boy wonder, he had been groomed for his profession when state educators recognized his intelligence, near-photographic memory and a streak of ruthlessness.

Giessler excelled in language studies and learned to speak and read English, French, Russian and Arabic, as well as German, acquiring the proper dialect and colloquial vocabulary to pass as a West German Bavarian for missions across the border. The SSD worked with the KGB and generally served the interests of the Soviets. The "Russian uncles" appreciated Giessler's talents and enlisted him for some of their most ambitious projects.

The East German became a very valuable operative for both the SSD and the KGB. He gained more authority and power, and his standard of living and personal wealth far exceeded that of the majority of his countrymen. Giessler was one of the most important Intelligence operatives in all of Eastern Europe by the mid-1980s. At the age of forty, he no longer took on high-risk field assignments and spent most of his time as a go-between for Soviet–East German operations. There was little doubt one day he would be promoted to head of the SSD.

But then the world changed.

Giessler didn't believe the German Democratic Republic would end. The demands for democratic reforms, the threats to Communist Party rule and the intentions of the East European nations of the Warsaw Pact to break away from the Soviet Union all seemed to be elements of a nightmare. Even when Honecker resigned in October 1989, Giessler still thought the tide would somehow change. After all, he had been taught since childhood that the West was corrupt, weak and doomed to fail. Certainly those raised with Communist doctrines and the dream of socialism throughout the world wouldn't surrender to the whims of traitors.

Events occurred rapidly—much faster than most would have believed possible. On January 8, 1990, the East Germans dared to raid SSD headquarters. They destroyed records and documents, smashed equipment and demanded an end to the state security agency. Giessler was horrified. He fled the country, bitterly disgusted and disappointed by what he considered betrayal by his own people.

A man without a country, he lived in hiding, moving aimlessly throughout Europe. Giessler had managed to accumulate a small fortune during his career. Despite his hatred of capitalism, he had covertly put these funds in a Swiss bank account. He didn't need to worry about money, but he didn't intend to retire to a luxury resort.

The East German had discovered that power was better than wealth. Money hardly mattered when he had been at the peak of his career. Anything he'd wanted had been given to him. He'd been feared and respected by all but a few superiors, could have his pick of women, live where he wished, eat whatever he wanted without paying for it and have subordinates executed with the stroke of a pen. Losing all of that had been a crushing blow. The end of Communist rule in East Germany had destroyed his godlike power and forced him to run, fearful his countrymen would seek retribution for his role in the oppressive regime.

Giessler recalled these events as he assembled the little Bauer pistol. His present quarters were less than opulent, but that was a temporary situation. He glanced about the small room as he sat at the metal desk. The other furnishings consisted of a bunk bed, wall locker and some makeshift shelves for his books. At least he had a room to himself. Most of the others at the stronghold had to share their quarters.

Someone knocked at the door. Giessler put the .25 auto in a desk drawer and closed it, then called out in Russian.

"Enter," he said bluntly.

The door swung open. Ivan Suslev stood on the threshold. The stocky Russian had been with the KGB before the iron curtain fell. He'd worked with Giessler in some of the missions to the Middle East in the past and had eagerly joined in the German's new scheme.

The German rose from the chair and stretched his long arms and lean torso. The expression on Suslev's broad Slavic face suggested he wasn't the bearer of good news. Giessler wondered what had gone wrong this time. There always seemed to be some annoying glitch in their operation, usually some minor matter that didn't really threaten the success of their plans.

"Perhaps you should talk to the Arabs, Comrade," Suslev began. "They're arguing with one another about something, and none of them are terribly happy with you right now for some reason."

"You speak Arabic," Giessler said. "What seems to be the problem?"

"They won't tell me. You're the head man here, and they know it. I'm an underling, not fit to discuss serious matters with. I did gather Gahiz disagrees with Kadafadem and Mahdi about what we should do at this point. That's about all I can determine from their squabbling."

"Arabs tend to be argumentative," Giessler said with a sigh. "They're never happy unless they have something to complain about. How is Bukovsky holding up?"

"Still excited about the success of the ACR assault on the satellites. Right now he thinks we're invincible."

"Let him enjoy the euphoria while he can," the German replied. "When he realizes the dangers we face have increased along with the success of the ACR launch, Bukovsky will start fearing and brooding again."

"Right now he's not our problem. Don't forget Gahiz's top commando is in charge of that team in Iran. If he establishes radio contact with Nimeri, it's hard to predict what nonsense he might order his man to carry out."

"All right. I'll talk to them."

He followed Suslev into the corridor. They marched by the rows of doors to the billets. The mercury bulbs shone down from the ceiling, reflecting along the white walls. Giessler once again wished he had considered the color schemes with greater care. The corridor reminded him of a hospital ward, which wasn't an atmosphere he found agreeable.

They slipped into their parkas before venturing outside. The mountain air was cold, the wind bitter and often blowing hard enough to bite into skin. Outside, Giessler noticed men on guard duty, armed with AK-47 rifles. Sunlight splashed across the sky to create a canvas of blue and gold, but the German hardly noticed it as he trod across the hard, rocky surface to the main building.

The Arabs waited for him at the conference room. Abdel Gahiz wore the fatigue uniform he favored, a side arm on his hip and a beret canted by his right eyebrow. Gahiz's thick mustache was clipped and styled in the manner favored by Saddam Hussein. Giessler thought it odd Gahiz emulated the man he hoped to one day overthrow.

"Good!" the Iraqi declared in curt Arabic. "I'm glad you're here, Colonel Giessler."

"So am I," Ahmed Mahdi said. "Perhaps he can talk some sense into you. Musa and I have not been able to do so."

Tall, slender and quick to argue, Mahdi glared at Gahiz. A Syrian who still felt distrust and contempt toward his Iraqi ally, Mahdi always seemed upset about something. His sharp features reminded Giessler of a desert falcon, although Mahdi's balding pate, remaining hair laced with gray, softened his appearance.

Musa Kadafadem bowed in greeting. The Libyan was less apt to voice complaints. His black beard failed to conceal his stubby chin and narrow face, yet his dark eyes expressed intelligence and a toughness that one ignored at one's peril.

"What bothers my friends this morning?" Giessler asked. "The first phase of our plan has unfolded as we hoped. This is a time to enjoy the good news, not quarrel among ourselves."

Mahdi fixed Giessler with a hard stare. The German realized the Syrian didn't like him. Giessler was big, blond and Aryan. That was enough reason for Mahdi to resent him. The former SSD agent would have happily done business with someone else, but the man was necessary for the operation, and they would all have to tolerate one another.

"I'm not convinced this aggressive concentrated radar has been as successful as you promised, Colonel," Mahdi began. "The battle occurred between the Iranians and Armenians as planned, but that was thanks to the actions of our troops. The news doesn't mention the failure of reconnaissance satellites to operate during the clash at the border."

"You didn't expect this to be discussed on radio broadcasts, did you?" Giessler asked. "Obviously no one is going to admit to this problem publicly."

"Then we really have no proof," the Syrian insisted.

"I disagree," Gahiz declared. "If either the Americans or the Russians had filmed the clash with their laser cameras, they would present the videotapes to prove the conflict was started by independent attackers who triggered the battle with a couple of well-placed rounds. I am satisfied, Colonel."

"Tell him the rest," Kadafedam quietly urged.

"I also believe we should bypass other targets and move immediately into Iraq. Hussein is vulnerable, unpopular with many factions within his country. The Iraqi people will suspect Iran may present a threat that could draw them into war once again. Despite what they say for the media, my people don't want that. The time is right to remove Hussein from power."

"It is too soon for anything that drastic," Giessler replied. "I know you are impatient to return to your country and to free it from Hussein's rule."

Every person in the room realized Gahiz didn't want to free Iraq of an oppressive government. He simply wanted to be in charge. None of the others criticized the man because his goal was similar to their own ambitions.

"The fact no photographs or videotape have been made public does not prove anything," Mahdi insisted. "We previously discussed how this operation would be conducted. First the ACR technology had to have been proved beyond any doubt as successful. Iran, the only Middle Eastern country that might present a problem when we seize control in Syria, Iraq and Libya, has to be preoccupied with conflicts with other nations. Finally we must conduct our revolutions very close together in order to ensure success. The ruling governments will certainly increase oppressive restrictions if they see revolution in neighboring countries and fear the same could happen to them."

"Also the nation first under control would be better able to assist the others," Gahiz replied. "And that country is Iraq. Assad does not have the same widespread opposition as Saddam Hussein faces, and Khaddafi is not that unpopular in Libya."

"There are many factions opposed to Khaddafi within Libya," Kadafadem stated. "However, it is important that he appear to be assassinated by an outsider. Otherwise, we'll make a martyr of him, and his people will remain in control. They'll probably be backed by the bedouin. Khaddfi himself is a bedouin, which explains much of his popular support. If I don't have support of the bedouin when I take command, Libya will be plunged into civil war. That is a situation I wish to avoid at almost any cost. The Italians learned how difficult it can be to fight those desert warriors when they occupied Libya."

"That's exactly the sort of thing we want to avoid," Giessler assured him. "It's important the revolutions appear to be smooth, internal revolts against the current regimes in all three countries."

"I still believe we should make Khaddafi's assassination appear to be the work of the Israelis," Gahiz declared. "That would unite the Arabs of all nations faster than any other action we might attempt."

"Forget about Israel," Giessler warned. "Let the Jews have their little postage-stamp country. They don't have oil, and their harbors don't have the potential of the combined shipping interests of ports of Syria and Libya along the Mediterranean and Iraq's access to the Persian Gulf. Israel might hold Jerusalem, but none of you are truly religious Muslims, so you really don't care about the location of a holy city. Save that Islamic-jihad rhetoric for the ignorant masses. I know you men too well to believe it."

"As a German, you've never had the Israeli air force attack your country or clash with them in desert combat," Gahiz stated. "In fact, your father's generation had a far more agreeable manner of dealing with Jews under Adolf Hitler."

"And Hitler was defeated because he was too obvious, too clumsy in his strategy for power," Giessler replied. "If you're going to study history, you should learn from the mistakes others have made. Especially recent history. If we bring Israel into the conflict, that will ruin all our plans. The Americans are Israel's protector. They will back Israel and probably bring in the forces of Europe as they did in Desert Storm. I don't need to remind you what happened when Hussein's rash behavior brought about that disaster for Iraq."

"Colonel Giessler is right," Kadafadem agreed. "The greatest advantage our revolutions will have is the fact Khaddafi, Assad and Hussein are despised by the Americans and the West. They will welcome the downfall of those three tyrants. Probably even offer us foreign aid and cheer our victories."

"You'll be the greatest economic power in the Middle East, my friends," Giessler reminded the Arabs. "Your countries haven't been able to develop this sort of growth because the Soviet Union is dead and the West has been reluctant to grant you free trade and diplomatic relations. When that changes, you will be the ultimate force in the region. Kuwait, Oman, Egypt, Qatar, Bahrain and eventually even Saudi Arabia and Jordan will turn to you for leadership. You will control the oil and banking interests of the entire Middle East. That is far greater power than anything you can gain by military forces in the region."

"What you say is true," Mahdi admitted. "Even Gamal Nasser did not appreciate this fact when he tried to unite the Arab nations. Yet these are simply retelling the dreams we've spoken of so many times in the past unless the aggressive concentrated radar is as efficient as you promised."

"You will be satisfied with the results," Giessler replied. "Although you might not be convinced by the border clash, I assure you events in the next few days will dispel any doubts—events that will change the world forever."

"YOU HANDLED THAT quite well, Comrade," Suslev remarked as he and Giessler marched from the main building entrance. The Russian followed his commander, puzzled by the man's apparent aggravation.

Giessler glanced about the compound, his gaze resting on the huge reflector dish and trident prongs in the center. It resembled a giant metal flower. Yet the enormous blossom carried no scent and projected a mighty beam of sound waves. They had developed the ACR device beyond anything those narrow-minded bureaucrats of the Kremlin or Washington had attempted. But so much could go wrong, and all their efforts could end in failure.

"Comrade?" Suslev said. "Something troubles you?"

"We should have followed the schedule," Giessler said grimly. "I shouldn't have allowed the others to talk me into beginning this operation before we eliminated those technicians."

"The events in the former Soviet Union and the Middle East made this an ideal time to carry out the mission. You said so yourself."

"I remember," Giessler admitted. "I was eager to begin this operation, too. Eager to finally take this mission from the planning stage to action that will reward us for these past three years of effort."

"But you assured the Arabs everything was going well."

"What did you think I'd tell them?" Giessler replied, his tone harsher than he intended. "I spent every cent I had to lay the foundations of this operation, but the Arabs have actually financed building this installation. Of course, we won't have an empire unless their revolutions in Libya, Iraq and Syria are successful. We can't afford to have them lose confidence in this project and decide to withdraw.''

"We have teams hunting down those technicians now,'' the Russian said. "They'll soon take care of that problem.''

"We should have had this done before. There isn't much documented on file concerning ACR technology. No one has pursued it with much gusto recently. The greatest source of information on the subject is still in the minds of the scientists involved with ACR.''

"Even they don't know about the advances accomplished by Bukovsky. I don't really think they're a threat to us.''

"We can't afford any mistakes,'' Giessler insisted. "Even potential mistakes. Let's hope our people in the field do their job and make damn sure everyone here does theirs correctly. We have too much at stake. If we lose, we will lose everything. They'll either put us in prison or kill us. Personally I'd favor the latter option.''

"Think about what we'll gain if we succeed,'' Suslev urged.

Giessler smiled and nodded. If they succeeded, he would have greater wealth and power than he had had during the peak of his SSD career. More power than most could imagine.

CHAPTER FIVE

Atlanta, Georgia
Sunday, 2035 hours

The dark blue van carrying Able Team turned down Martin Luther King, Jr., Drive, Carl Lyons watching for the sign for Northside Drive as he drove.

"I still don't see why they had to send us to get this guy," Lyons commented. "This is the kind of milk run anybody with an IQ over fifty and some street smarts could handle."

"Maybe I'm getting old," Rosario Blancanales remarked, "but I wouldn't really mind an easy job for a change."

Lyons snorted, aware Blancanales would never be content to take on easy jobs. The tough Puerto Rican had spent most of his life involved in highly dangerous missions, including military service in Vietnam. He was too much like Lyons for the other man to believe he wanted a quieter life.

"Have you ever heard of this aggressive concentrated radar Josh Collins is supposed to be working on?" the big ex-LAPD detective asked, his gaze still locked onto the road.

"No," Blancanales replied. "I never thought of radar as being sinister. Even 'aggressive, concentrated' radar doesn't sound very threatening."

"Well, they sure hustled our butts down here in a hurry," Lyons remarked. "It must be important. We didn't even get a decent briefing."

"I'll admit it was a brief briefing," Blancanales acknowledged. "Cheer up, Carl. Maybe Collins will turn out to be an evil mad scientist."

"Is it my imagination, or have we been getting more of these 'go-fetch-it' jobs?"

"It's a high-tech world. It's not surprising that men and women of science are important and sometimes play a role in our missions."

"Sometimes I miss the good old primitive days," Lyons muttered, "when the most advanced device I had to worry about was the police radio in my car."

Hermann "Gadgets" Schwarz slid open the door that separated the cab section from the back of the van. As his nickname suggested, Schwarz was more at home with electronic devices than the other two Able Team commandos.

"Did you guys hear the clicky-clack of the fax machine above the yakity-yak?" he inquired.

"I guess we'll get to hear you yakity-yak about the clicky-clack instead," Lyons replied, annoyed because he thought they might be lost. "So what did HQ have for us this time?"

"Apparently Bear turned up another item of information about this Josh Collins guy. It seems the Air Force is sort of suspicious of Collins after all."

"Really?" Blancanales asked with interest. "They consider him a serious security risk?"

"They're not sure how serious it is, but they're suspicious of his loyalties. Nothing official. That's why Aaron didn't catch it right off. The AFTAC cut Collins's funding for the ACR research and put him on a lower salary, working on radio communications systems. Needless to say, he was pissed off about that."

"Seems logical," Lyons admitted. "That's not all they'd be concerned about. Collins has a right to be a bit ticked about something like that."

"Well," Gadgets continued, "Collins contacted a couple of representatives from the Saudi Arabian embassy. They were identified as high-ranking officers in the Saudi military."

"Last I heard, Saudi Arabia was still regarded as an ally by the United States," Lyons remarked. "That still doesn't mean Collins can sell them military secrets."

"The Air Force isn't accusing him of that. At least not yet. Of course, they generally think ACR technology has been a white elephant so they probably figure Collins doesn't know anything that he could tell the Saudis that would jeopardize national security."

"Why are they handling him with kid gloves?" Blancanales asked. "Why not confine him to quarters until they have a chance to investigate the matter?"

"Collins isn't military," Schwarz reminded his fellow Able Team warrior. "They can't enforce military justice on a guy who works for them as a civilian employee."

Lyons saw the turnoff for Northside Drive and hit the turn signal. He glanced in the rearview mirror as he changed lanes. "I'd say we'd better assume there's a chance Collins is a wolf instead of a sheep. Wouldn't hurt to check our weapons and crack out the Kevlar just in case."

"I already did," Schwarz assured him.

JOSH COLLINS'S HOME was a pleasant two-story house with a well-groomed lawn, surrounded by a short fence of stones and mortar. An aesthetic rather than practical barrier, the wall appeared to be an effort by Collins to cling to some threads of his New England heritage in the heart of the South. There were no watchdogs, security lights or any other overt evidence that the place was protected.

It was an upper-middle-class neighborhood, which meant the police patroled the area more often than in the sections of Atlanta populated by less affluent people. Lyons knew this from personal experience. Well-heeled citizens demanded security, and they got it.

Able Team didn't want any problems with the local police. They planned to keep it simple. Go in, get Collins and get out. However, they saw no lights inside the house. The guy might not be at home or may have gone to bed early. He might not be alone.

Schwarz remained in the van to watch for the police, neighborhood security patrols or visitors who didn't represent any form of law enforcement. Lyons and Blancanales approached the house. They remained in radio contact with each other and their teammate by pocket-size receiver units with earphones and throat-mike transceivers. If they needed backup, Schwarz would come to their aid.

Lyons and Blancanales marched under the streetlight to the sidewalk. They didn't attempt to be stealthy. To do so would only make them more suspicious to any neighbors peering out windows at the strangers. The familiar weight of the Kevlar vest under his shirt gave Lyons some confidence, but the .357 Colt Python holstered under his arm offered greater security. The closer they moved to the house, the darker and gloomier it appeared.

"Let's not act like we've found a terrorist stronghold," he reminded Blancanales. "Collins may seem a little suspicious, but we don't have solid proof he's an enemy."

"Do you want the front door or the back?" the Hispanic commando asked.

"I'll take the front. I make a more convincing cop."

They separated. Blancanales strode across the lawn, into the shadows of a tree and to the rear of the house. Lyons slowly mounted the steps to the front porch. He wanted to give his partner ample time to get into position.

"Ready," Blancanales's voice whispered from the earphone.

"Roger," Lyons replied softly into his throat mike. "Gadgets?"

"Read you both loud and clear," Schwarz replied.

Lyons raised a fist to knock on the door, but froze in place when he saw it was already slightly ajar. The ex-cop instinctively reached inside his jacket for the grips of the Colt revolver. He stepped to the side of the doorway to present as little visible target as was possible. Slight pressure from the toe of his boot pushed the door open.

His trained eye spotted deep gouges in wood at the lock. It had been jimmied. He drew the Python. Blancanales's voice spoke from the earphone.

"Got an open-door policy. Forced entry."

"Same here," Lyons whispered in reply. "Stay put for now."

The big ex-cop inhaled a tense breath and crossed the threshold, crouching low. He quickly moved inside and dropped to one knee, his Magnum revolver clenched in both hands. His eyes had adjusted to darkness, and he scanned the room, recognizing shapes of furniture without evidence of human opponents lurking among the dim images.

Lyons stayed alert as he padded across the room. He kept his back to a wall and watched for danger. No one appeared to be in the house, but he knew better than to assume the place was safe.

The Able Team warrior glanced through an archway and saw a kitchen. It seemed probable the back door was located there. He whispered for Blancanales to enter and added, "I'll cover," letting his partner know he was inside and close to the rear entrance.

Blancanales appeared in the kitchen, and Lyons signaled with a hand gesture to identify himself. The other man nodded in confirmation. Lyons crouched low and snapped on a wall switch. Light flooded into the living room. Blancanales stayed in the dark kitchen and addressed his teammate by radio link.

"Sure that's a good idea?"

"If anyone's hiding here, they've been in the house longer than us and had time to get fully adjusted to the dark and familiar with surroundings. Playing hide-and-seek without the lights on would be more in their favor than ours."

"Well, there doesn't seem to be anyone here."

"Not so far," Lyons agreed. "But I don't think Collins forgot his keys and decided to jimmy both doors to his own house."

Lyons glanced at the wide-screen television, VCR, stereo system with CD player—a lot of merchandise to be overlooked by a burglar. He checked a coat closet with care, but found no one hidden there. Blancanales emerged from the kitchen. He shrugged.

"I don't think whoever was here is in the house, Carl."

"Maybe not. Let's check the other rooms. Gadgets? You hear us okay?"

"Roger. You need me in there, or do I stay on the street?"

"Stay with the van and keep an eye peeled. I don't think we need another guy in here, but we'll give a shout if that changes."

"Affirmative," Schwarz replied.

The two men continued to search the house. They saw no evidence that anything of value had been taken or any sign of a struggle. However, they made a grisly discovery in a downstairs room adjacent to the hall. They detected the stench at the doorway and knew what they would find.

The corpse lay on the carpeted floor in front of a wooden desk. Blood and bits of brain matter formed a brown-and-gray stain around the smashed skull. The body wore jogging shorts and a T-shirt. It had been a white male, probably in his midthirties before his life was snuffed out. Although part of the face had been shattered, they recognized Josh Collins from the dot-matrix image faxed to them by Stony Man.

"Dammit!" Lyons growled in frustration.

"You guys okay?" Schwarz's voice inquired.

"We found Collins," Blancanales explained. "He's dead. Definitely murder. Looks like he was shot in the back of the head execution style."

"Are you guys sure that whoever did it left the place?"

"Yeah," Lyons replied. "Collins has been dead for a few hours from the looks of it. We're going to look around just in case there are any other surprises. Better tell the Farm the bad news."

"Right," Schwarz said. "What about the police?"

"Yeah. I think we should contact them. Give us a chance to examine the place before we call."

"Roger. Looks like this milk run has gone sour."

Blancanales stepped to the desk and glanced at the home computer, fax and printer system. Collins had spent a fair amount of money on his personal-use equipment. The drawers stood open. Apparently the killer or killers had rummaged through them. Blancanales noticed a bare spot on a shelf, ringed by a film of neglected dust.

"Something was removed here. Judging from the size of the blank space and the fact it's here by the computer, my guess is it was probably a case of floppy disks."

"Sounds likely. Whoever did this probably lifted Collins's records for any research he was working on, or maybe he had some information on somebody. We're sort of spinning our wheels right now. Don't know enough to draw any conclusions."

"Somebody had a reason to take out Collins," Blancanales remarked. "I'd be real surprised if that reason isn't connected with the man's ACR work."

"Well, he sure as hell can't answer any questions for us. His murder just adds another one to the collection."

Stony Man Farm, Virginia

AARON KURTZMAN drummed his fingers on the armrest of his wheelchair as he studied the data on the monitor. The printer clattered to produce sheets that folded into a wire basket. Barbara Price entered the computer room, a clipboard in one hand and a pocket calculator in the other. Kurtzman's expression revealed his curiosity.

"I'm figuring out the time zones for Istanbul and Moscow compared to our time," Price explained. "Striker is on his way to Turkey. Phoenix is still scattered, but they'll assemble when they arrive in Russia."

"Able Team called in," the Bear stated. "Somebody got to Collins. He's dead."

Price raised her eyebrows. This was an unexpected event, yet her position with Stony Man forced her to evaluate news in a dispassionate and analytical manner. She considered the death of Joshua Collins in the framework of the mission.

"Sounds like we're on the right track," she said. "I think you're right about ACR technology being involved in this crisis."

"Yeah," Kurtzman said, "but the top U.S. expert in the field is history. There aren't many people knowledgeable on the subject. We needed somebody who could help us understand how ACR works, who might be doing this and how we can find them."

"If the top man in the field is dead," Price said, "it makes sense to use who is available . . . and alive."

"That helps," the Bear agreed. "Actually I'm trying to find the experts in the field. Not just here in America, but anywhere in the world. That still doesn't leave a hell of a lot to pick from."

"The Russians have been involved in ACR technology."

"That's right. They might have been ahead of us in the field until the cold war ended and the Soviet Union came crashing down."

Kurtzman wheeled to the basket and pulled out a data sheet. He glanced over the Intel until he found what he wanted.

"Okay, the leading Russian authority on ACR was a guy named Anatoly Bukovsky. He was a real big shot for a while. Lived the exclusive good life during the Communist regime, which rewarded the chosen few."

"Maybe Phoenix Force can enlist his help. The Russians have as much at stake as we do. They've agreed to cooperate with us."

"The problem is Bukovsky can't be any help to us. The guy died in a boating accident in the Caspian Sea last year."

"I wonder if it really was an accident or if somebody killed him, too."

"That's a possibility we can't dismiss at this time. A little professional paranoia can be a healthy thing in this business."

"If somebody wants to hold a monopoly on a type of technology," Price commented, "one way to do it is to kill off everybody else who is an expert in the field. Sounds like there aren't that many to remove."

"Not many," Kurtzman agreed as he consulted the data sheet once more. "Another top Russian expert is a fellow named Nikolai Volkov. He studied under Bukovsky and worked with him back in the 1980s. Volkov defected a few years ago and moved to the United States. He worked for the military for a while, but he wasn't too enthusiastic about it. Seems he wanted to retire from the cold war."

"Since it's officially over, he should have gotten his chance."

"He did. According to this, Volkov went into private business and started a small electronics outfit in the state of Ohio. Strange guy to pick a part of the Midwest with more than its share of economic depression."

"I'll tell Able Team to find him. Got the info on him?"

"Most of it," Kurtzman answered. "Haven't been able to get a fax of a recent photo. I'll have a dot-matrix copy of his driver's license by tomorrow. DMV computers will be easier to access then. Is Hal awake?"

"I think he crashed out on the sofa in his office. Think we should wake him?"

"The man has enough to deal with as our go-between with the White House and boss of this circus. The news we have for him can wait. We're doing everything that has to be done. Let him get some rest while he can. I got a feeling none of us will be getting much sleep until this is over."

CHAPTER SIX

Istanbul, Turkey
Monday, 1427 hours

"Who exactly are you working for, Belasko?" Wesley Rollins demanded.

His back was stiff, his arms folded defiantly on his chest as he glared at Mack Bolan through a pair of wire-rim glasses. Rollins was CIA, but a paper-pushing, office-bound operative, more bureaucrat than field agent. The big warrior, clad in black trousers, jacket and turtleneck, wasn't the sort of person Rollins was accustomed to dealing with. The Company man worked within a base at the U.S. Embassy and spent as much of his time meeting diplomats as evaluating Intelligence reports.

"You brought the pouch so you must have received notice about my status on this mission," Bolan replied. "That should be enough, Rollins."

Stan Fell also sat in the rear of the limousine bus with the Executioner and Rollins. The NSA operative noticed the angry flush across Rollins's round face, and figured the Company man had better back off. Whoever "Belasko" was, whatever outfit he worked for, the guy wasn't a man easily intimidated. Certainly a desk jockey like Rollins couldn't do it. The stranger looked as if he could go boar hunting with a bowie knife.

Rollins glared at Bolan, but wisely thought twice before he spoke. The man had authority straight from the White House, which made him in charge of the mission. At least for now. Rollins would naturally file complaints and demands to the deputy director. It was disgraceful to be reduced to the level of errand boy for this mystery hot shot, regardless of his Oval Office connections.

Orders from on high had told the CIA bureaucrat to have a driver and vehicle ready to take Fell and a diplomatic pouch, addressed to Belasko, to meet the stranger at the airport. The only explanation offered was that the new arrival had come to handle the Blind Eagle incident. CIA and NSA had been ordered to cooperate on this matter. The two Intelligence agencies regarded each other with distrust, contempt and a rivalry that frequently got in the way of constructive activity. Maybe that was the reason the President figured Belasko would be a neutral party to keep the others in line.

But the stranger wasn't a typical Company manager. The diplomatic pouch didn't contain file folders, pressed suits and a favorite brand of Scotch whiskey. The bulky rubber-coated package had arrived with diplomatic immunity and remained unopened until Belasko broke the seal. Rollins had wondered what was in it, because the large pouch had required the aid of his driver to carry to the van.

Neither Rollins nor Fell expected to see what was extracted from the pouch, but they did. It was packed with weapons, ammunition and other combat gear. The Executioner donned a special shoulder holster. Clearly he wasn't comfortable being unarmed, and quickly slid a fully loaded magazine into a Beretta 93-R. He jacked a round into the chamber, switched on the safety and holstered the sleek, powerful pistol.

Bolan continued to inspect the gear as the van rolled along Milet Caddesi. He barely glanced out the tinted windows at the colorful and exotic surroundings. Istanbul resembled many other large, international cities, yet retained a unique quality. Different cultures and religions had influenced the makeup of the city. Ancient churches and mosques stood among more recent architecture. Billboards dotted the landscape, while street vendors peddled a variety of goods and food on every corner.

Istanbul was a fascinating city, but the Executioner was more concerned with his mission than the local sites. He examined a .44 Magnum Desert Eagle pistol, oblivious to the startled expressions of the two Intelligence officers as he made sure the tools of his trade were in top working order.

"I would like to know who I'm working with," Rollins commented. "You might be in charge, Belasko, but we've been stationed here for some time. This is our turf, so to speak."

"This country belongs to the Turks," Bolan replied. "That's beside the point. I understand what you're saying, but we're all here for the same reason, and whatever organization we work for doesn't matter much right now. Has CIA come up with anything new about this Blind Eagle business?"

"We don't know what caused the satellites to wink out," Rollins admitted. "We've been watching the borders pretty closely, and there's plenty of unrest among the Iranians, Armenians and Azerbaijans.

However, there hasn't been any overt violence since the skirmish yesterday morning."

Bolan nodded. He slipped a coiled garrote in a jacket pocket as calmly as most men would some loose change. The warrior turned to Fell.

"You're directly involved with SIGINT recon. I understand you said there was no evidence of mechanical error."

"Nothing that can be explained," the NSA man replied. "The satellites went out, and our whole station was virtually deaf and blind. Couldn't pick up anything except some ham radio operators chitchatting on shortwave. We even analyzed the tapes of that conversation out of sheer desperation. Drew another blank."

"We have a theory that someone might have used aggressive concentrated radar to jam the satellites. You've heard of it?"

Rollins shook his head, but Fell nodded.

"I recall there was some research in the field a few years ago," the NSA man stated. "I don't know much else about it. Don't know how it works, and from what I understand, it didn't work too well. We were involved in it and so were the Soviets, but I don't think anyone made any important breakthroughs on the technology."

"Not officially," Bolan said. "Somebody might have taken it to a higher level on their own."

"Who?" Rollins asked. "The Iranians? I doubt they'd be capable of something like that. They're too damn backward."

Bolan glanced over his shoulder out the rear window. He noticed an unwashed Volkswagen Bug trailed behind the limo. The Executioner had first observed the car as they left the airport. It might simply be headed in the same direction, but he was suspicious because the VW seemed to lag behind one or two other vehicles while following the government rig.

"I wouldn't assume the Iranians or anyone else is 'too backward' to have some degree of advanced technology," Bolan replied. "A fundamental rule is not to underestimate a potential opponent. That's not to say the Iranians are responsible. We don't know who we're dealing with."

"Maybe the Russians," Rollins suggested. "I've never been totally convinced the Communist Party really fell from power or the Soviet Union changed as much as they want us to believe."

Bolan didn't comment. He had clashed with the KGB enough times in the past to appreciate the mindset Rollins expressed. It was hard to regard someone as an enemy for decades and alter one's opinion overnight.

"Like I said," the warrior stated, "we just don't know. Is either CIA or NSA providing an escort for this car?"

"We didn't think that would be necessary," Rollins replied. "Why do you ask?"

"I think we're being followed. This vehicle isn't very subtle. You should have used something that would attract less attention."

"Oh, for God's sake," the CIA man muttered. "I think you're taking this commando business a bit too far, Belasko. Loading up your guns and looking for enemies lurking in the shadows—"

"I'm not here because I've got nothing better to do."

The limo turned onto Ataturk Bulvari and headed north. The ancient buildings they passed were magnificent, but Bolan was more concerned about the dirty Volkswagen that continued to shadow the government vehicle. It started to gain on the limo, and the Executioner glimpsed the faces behind the windshield. Both were young, bearded men, wearing caps and dark glasses. Bolan's battle instincts were screaming a warning. He knew they were heading into an ambush.

"Stop the car," he ordered.

The driver obeyed, responding to the hard authority of the warrior's voice. Rollins groaned in exasperation. Fell leaned forward to look out the rear window and saw the VW pull to the curb and come to a halt.

"Doesn't look like they're trying to attack us," he commented.

"Out!" Bolan snapped. "A single grenade can turn this limo into a communal coffin!"

Rollins began to protest, but the Executioner opened the door and jumped outside, fisting the Beretta. Passersby on the street screamed in alarm when they saw the big man in black with the large black pistol.

Turkey had seen more than its share of terrorism during the 1980s, and a lot of people recalled those days vividly. They responded as if drilled for the occasion. Men ducked into coffee shops and alleys for cover. Women grabbed children and headed for shelter. A teacher herded a group of youngsters into a shop. Shoeshine boys scurried for cover like combat veterans.

Mack Bolan was glad the civilians reacted to danger. He wanted them out of the way, out of the line of fire. The warrior darted for a newsstand, abandoned

by the owner, and caught a glimpse of the men in the
VW. One opened a door and slipped outside, using the
vehicle for cover. Bolan saw the barrel of the guy's
machine pistol. The second man wasn't as bold and
ducked behind the steering wheel. He obviously didn't
intend to emerge from the driver's side, which would
present a clear target for Bolan.

The Executioner whirled around the stand, dropped
to a kneeling stance and scanned the street for the second team of gunmen. Only fools would attempt to use
only two men to ambush a large, well-made vehicle like
the limo bus. A hit like this one would logically require another team to cut off the limo so they could
catch the rig in a cross fire.

Bolan didn't have long to wait for them. Two figures jogged from a truck parked at the mouth of an
alley. Another hardman remained by the vehicle, stationed by the cab with a rifle. Apparently the hit men
had been prepared to use the rig to block the limo as a
preamble to the attack. The unexpected turn of events
forced them to improvise.

The pair that advanced toward him seemed apprehensive. One man fumbled with the bolt to his British-
made Sterling submachine gun as if he weren't sure
where it was located on the weapon. His companion
carried a revolver in one fist and a grenade in the other.
Both wore coveralls, caps and dark glasses as the uniform of the day.

The guy with the grenade posed the more serious
threat. Bolan snap-aimed and triggered the Beretta to
place two shots into the upper torso of the attacker.
The 9 mm parabellum rounds drilled the man in the
chest, and he collapsed to the ground in a lifeless heap.

A burst of automatic fire erupted from the VW, and bullets slashed into the flimsy wood-and-cardboard frame of the newsstand. Splinters rained on Bolan's crouched form.

A stray slug ricocheted against the sidewalk and sparked inches from his right knee. Bolan's muscles tensed, and his stomach knotted. Yet he was the veteran of a thousand firefights, and his hands remained steady, his breathing under control. He stayed low and waited for the wave of autofire to cease. The enemy intended to flush him out or pin him down. He didn't move or return fire. Since there were two opponents by the Volkswagen, he guessed one would probably try to reach his position to see if he had been hit or take him out, while the subgunner kept him busy.

The gunman jogged into view. He didn't even attempt to use the newsstand for cover, as he was probably afraid of being hit by his partner's wild spray of bullets. He held a blue-black pistol in both gloved hands, but didn't get a chance to use it. Bolan canted the barrel of his Beretta and squeezed off a single shot.

Glass shattered in a lens of the attacker's dark glasses. The 9 mm slug punched through the eye socket and burrowed into the man's brain. Literally dead on his feet, the man simply fell on his back, gun still clenched in lifeless fists. Bolan didn't waste time congratulating himself on scoring a lethal shot. He turned his attention to his remaining opponents.

Gunfire ceased from the VW. The killer had probably exhausted the ammunition in his magazine and was either reloading or getting another weapon. However, the gunman in the street now lay prone, startled by the death of his companion. He braced the Sterling chopper and opened fire on the limo bus instead of Bolan's position. Bullets crashed into the windshield. The Executioner saw the driver convulse behind the steering wheel when one or more slugs pierced the barrier to claim a living target.

Bolan switched the fire selector on the 93-R to 3-round-burst mode and returned fire. A trio of rounds hit the subgunner in the face and forehead. The man's skull exploded, and his weapon fired useless rounds into the air as his fingers convulsively squeezed the trigger.

A slug smashed into a support post to the newsstand just above the Executioner's head. The angle of the projectile told him it came from the rifleman stationed at the truck. Bolan hadn't presented the gunner with a decent target, but the man must have seen the muzzle-flash of the Beretta and estimated the best place to put his round. He came close enough to force Bolan to roll backward to the corpse of the hardman he'd shot through the eye.

The triggerman by the Volkswagen saw Bolan and slung the barrel of his subgun across the curved hood. The Executioner opened fire before his adversary could unleash another salvo of full-auto fury. A trio of parabellum rounds struck metal, sparks appearing along the frame of the car and the weapon. The impact ripped the scattergun from the gunman's grasp.

Stan Fell leaned from the open door of the limo. He held the Desert Eagle in both hands, fists at his chin and elbows jammed into his chest. The NSA man obviously knew little about the weapon and didn't realize the mistakes he made until he squeezed the trigger.

The shot rocketed for the truck, but didn't come close to hitting the rifleman.

However, the mighty recoil of the big .44 Magnum whipped the Desert Eagle back into the face of the inept shooter. The steel frame slammed into Fell's forehead, the front sight biting into the bridge of his nose. The Intelligence agent tumbled back into the vehicle, which probably saved his life as the rifleman returned fire and a bullet shattered the glass in the window of the car door.

Bolan switched to semiauto and braced his left elbow on a knee to reinforce the Weaver stance as he trained the sights of the Beretta on the figure by the cab of the truck. The target was more than one hundred fifty yards distant, a fair distance for a handgun, but Bolan had made more difficult shots at greater ranges in the past. He breathed in and squeezed the trigger as he exhaled.

The 93-R cracked another parabellum messenger. The rifleman's head snapped sideways when the 9 mm round connected. He dropped from view behind the truck, and Bolan knew the man wouldn't get up again.

"My God!" Rollins shouted. "They're dead!"

Bolan couldn't investigate the CIA man's claim at the moment. The surviving member of the hit team had crawled back inside the VW. After the subgun had been shot out of his hands, the man either decided to flee the area or seek another weapon in the car. The warrior quickly fired three rounds into the vehicle.

The unlucky ambusher retreated out the passenger side and landed gracelessly on the pavement. Bolan broke cover and jogged to the car, intending to capture the man for interrogation. He swung around the nose of the VW to find the guy on his back, his eyes wide with terror and a hand thrust inside his coveralls.

It emerged with a compact automatic. Bolan kicked out and sent the weapon hurtling from his opponent's grasp. The gunman lashed out with a kick of his own, but the Executioner dodged the attack and shot the man in the leg. Then the warrior stepped into a better position to slam a kick behind the wounded man's ear, rendering him unconscious.

Stan Fell staggered from the limo, a hand draped across his face. Rollins stood beside the stunned NSA agent, pale and trembling.

"What happened?" Rollins asked in the dazed manner of a person unable to accept what had occurred.

"Five men just tried to kill us," Bolan replied. "I saw the driver get hit. How bad is it?"

"I think he's dead," Rollins replied.

"You thought I was dead at first, too," Fell growled. "So did I for a minute or two. Still not sure what happened."

He moved his hand. Blood trickled from the gash at the bridge of his nose. Fell shook his head to try to clear it. Bolan gestured toward the unconscious man by his feet.

"You two stay with this guy," he ordered. "If he starts to come to, restrain him. Don't get careless. He might have another holdout weapon tucked away."

"What are you going to do?" Rollins asked.

"I'm going to check the driver," Bolan explained. "If he isn't dead, I'll do what I can for him. I'm also going to use the radio to call for an ambulance."

"Why do you think they attacked us?"

"We don't want that man on the ground to bleed to death, because he can answer that question," the Executioner replied. "If they hit us because they knew I was coming, it means you have a major security leak somewhere."

CHAPTER SEVEN

"When did this happen?" Hal Brognola asked as he removed another antacid tablet from the roll and placed it in his mouth.

"More than four hours ago," Mack Bolan replied. "Took me a while to get past the Istanbul police and to a secure line. I'm letting the contact from the embassy handle the local authorities. If nothing else, that'll keep him out of my way for a while."

Brognola held the handset to his face and used his free hand to punch in an access code on his desktop terminal. Data on Rollins, Wesley Albert of the Central Intelligence Agency appeared on the screen. The big Fed needed only a glance to see Rollins wasn't Bolan's kind of guy.

"You still there?"

"I'm here. Just getting an idea why you're pissed with the embassy man. How about Mr. Recon?"

"He ought to stick to satellites and stay away from Magnums. Our driver was killed during the shootout. One of the attackers survived, but he's recovering from surgery and still sedated."

"What did you do to him?"

"Shot him in the leg. I had to take out the other four. None of them got away, unless there were noncombatants who observed the ambush attempt from a distance. The attackers were apparently bottom-of-the-barrel thugs. Turkish CID identified them from their prints. All have criminal records, but no known affiliation with any terrorist groups or political extremists for either East or West."

"That probably means someone hired them for the job. That guy you caught might not have many answers."

"He might be able to tell us if he and his pals were tailing one of the Intel officers or if they knew I was coming. If I'm burned, Phoenix might be in the fire, as well."

"They've already reached their destination, and I haven't received a negative report from Yakov."

"They'd better watch their backs," Bolan warned. "Just in case."

"They generally do. Aaron tells me you already got a call on what Able found."

"Coded message in flight. Collins's murder isn't exactly good news, but it does suggest the Bear's theory about ACR is bang on."

"Yeah," Brognola agreed, "but we still don't know who's responsible."

"I'll let you know if anything else happens at this end."

"Right. Watch your tail, Striker."

"I always do."

Brognola hung up the handset, then glanced at his watch. The President was expecting a report in two hours, and there wasn't much to tell him. Certainly nothing terribly encouraging. The big Fed never lied to the Commander in Chief or sugarcoated news to give the impression things were going better than they really were. Brognola would tell him the truth, although that might not make the Man in the Oval Office very happy.

"Join the club," the big Fed muttered.

He left his office and opened the steel door to the War Room by punching in the proper access code. Barbara Price was inside, examining two maps. The world chart bore several multicolored pins that labeled the Turkish mountain range, Iran-Armenian border, Istanbul and Moscow. The U.S. chart had pins in Atlanta, Georgia, and Cincinnati, Ohio.

"This is sort of old-fashioned," Brognola remarked. "You can track this more accurately and in better detail with the computers."

"This helps me focus," Price explained. "Volkov, the Russian ACR expert who defected to the U.S., is living in Cincinnati. He has a wife and two kids. I think we ought to get to him pronto, before someone else does."

"Able Team will head north as soon as they finish in Atlanta."

"We might not have that much time. Collins was separated from his wife, and he didn't have any children. Volkov and his family are at risk."

"Okay. We'll send Leo. Jack can fly him to Ohio," Brognola suggested.

"Leo is in California. He left with some of our security people to find one of Collins's associates on the ACR project."

"When did this happen?"

"I authorized it after we heard about Collins's murder. You were asleep at the time, and I didn't think we should wait."

"You were right," Brognola agreed. "We'll protect Volkov and his family. I'd still prefer to have Able bring him in."

The pager on Brognola's belt suddenly beeped as one of several phones in the War Room buzzed. The big Fed crossed the room and picked up the handset to the phone with a flashing light. Carl Lyons's voice responded to Brognola's gruff greeting of "Yeah?"

"Got some interesting results on the investigation of Josh Collins's murder."

"Barb's here, too. You can tell us both."

The big Fed switched the phone onto a speaker and told Lyons to go ahead.

"The Atlanta police seemed a little suspicious of us even with our bogus federal ID. It was lucky Collins had been dead for some time, or we might have been considered suspects. At first the cops thought this might be a crime of passion. Collins had a thing for the ladies, you know, and his wife left him over it. We pointed out that the murder looked like an execution-style hit. Probably two or more assassins came through both front and back doors, easily got the drop on Collins and marched him to his office."

"Any idea what was taken?" Brognola asked.

"Couldn't find a single floppy disk for his computer or any sort of written records of much of anything. They ripped him off of everything. Needless to say, that pretty much cancels out the crime-of-passion theory. By the way, the murder weapon was a .380-caliber pistol. They haven't come up with an exact model, but ballistics confirm it was a low-grain projectile.''

''Subsonic for better use with a silencer?''

''You got it. Extra marks on the slug also suggest it passed through a fairly smooth metal cylinder of some sort. That sounds like a genuine silencer, not some homemade device, was used by the killers.''

''Anything else?''

''Not much. The cops are dusting for fingerprints and running tests on footprints found on the carpet. But whoever did this is too professional to make stupid mistakes like forgetting to wear gloves or changing footgear to avoid leaving any telltale evidence as to their identity.''

''We need you guys to move on to Cincinnati. Can you move out immediately?''

''Yeah. We had a little pissing contest with the local law. They wondered why the hell federal officers were breaking into Collins's house. We explained that we had been sent to question Collins about his association with some military personnel from Saudi Arabia. A call to the Air Force gained us some support. Cops don't trust Feds, but they're more comfortable with military forces involved in law enforcement.''

''Carl?'' Price began. ''We finally tracked down that Saudi business. Aaron had to contact some friendly sources in Riyadh, but he found out what that meeting was about. Collins was interested in getting a job in Saudi Arabia as an expert in radar and communications. Hoped to be working for the Riyadh International Airport, as well as with the military.''

''So he was looking for a better-paying job with a higher status,'' Lyons remarked. ''One that didn't involve ACR technology. Nothing sinister about that. What's in Cincinnati?"

"We'll send you a fax with all the details," Brognola stated. "We're sending some security people ahead of you. If they can take care of the matter on their own, we'll contact you and tell you to come on home."

"Not much of a mission," Lyons complained. "Come to Atlanta and look at a dead guy. That might be all we do this time."

"I just hope we'll be that lucky, Carl," Brognola replied.

They signed off, and the big Fed hung up the handset. He glanced at his watch. "I'm going to see Aaron. Phoenix might have contacted him."

"You think they might have had problems in Moscow?" Price asked.

"Striker called. Somebody tried to hit him."

The alarm on her face was something he had hoped to avoid.

"He's okay," Brognola assured Price, "but not sure if he was the intended target or the guys with him. One was Fell, the NSA SIGINT officer who reported the Blind Eagle incident observed at Mountain Balloon. The other guy is a CIA controller from the U.S. Embassy. Either one of them could have been under surveillance for some time. We don't know Mack's been burned."

"Even if he isn't," she replied, "it's obvious the people he's with have been."

"Striker can take care of himself better than any man I know. If anybody can survive a situation, he's the one. Of course, nobody lives forever."

"I know there's every chance that one day he won't come back from a mission," Price said in a quiet voice.

Brognola realized Price had gotten involved with Bolan. He didn't pry into their personal lives, and he wasn't certain how close they were. But Brognola did realize there was little chance for them to live happily ever after.

"People have a potentially short life span in our line of work. The classic advice for people like us is not to get emotionally involved with one another. Of course, that's bullshit. For Stony Man to be successful, it has to be low profile and use a small core group of people. That means we get to know one another. Nobody could do this kind of work unless he or she cared. You've got to have a lot of heart to do this."

"You're not telling me anything I don't already know."

"But something you have to bear in mind. There are some tough realities we have to live with here. You can't help what you feel, but you can't let it get in the way of the job."

"I haven't," she said somewhat defensively. "And I won't, Hal."

"Sorry," the big Fed said. "Maybe I'm talking as much for myself as for you. Sometimes I wish somebody else was doing this job and we could all just retire to a dairy farm in Wisconsin or something."

Price couldn't repress a smile. "But it has to be done. And if we don't do it," she said, "who will? Right?"

"That's about the size of it, Barb."

CHAPTER EIGHT

Moscow, Russia
Monday, 2210 hours

Major Mikhail Fedeyev belonged to the Russian Oboroney Obslooaivani, the defense service, and explained that the agency had no connection with the notorious KGB. OO was a new Intelligence branch of the Russian Ministry of Defense. Fedeyev addressed his guests in fluent English and frequently smiled. The expression seemed forced, and he was self-conscious about two steel teeth, which he tried to hide with his lower lip.

Yakov Katzenelenbogen sympathized with the Russian officer's awkward situation. Fedeyev appeared to be in his early forties, and taught from childhood about the evils of the capitalist West. Most of his military career had been spent preparing for confrontation with the United States. Now the rules had changed, and Fedeyev was trying to be a gracious host to men who had formerly been labeled as the enemy.

Katz understood the awkward position the man tried to cope with. He had known numerous "enemies" in his long career as a soldier, espionage agent, antiterrorist and commander of Phoenix Force. Most of those enemies of the past were now allies or at least no longer regarded as openly hostile opponents. Katz learned not to consider foes by nationality.

Calvin James and Rafael Encizo sat next to Katz, chairs set in a modified horseshoe pattern in front of Fedeyev's desk. The appearances of the three Phoenix Force commandos were markedly different. Katz was the senior man, with short-cut hair iron gray, and a prosthesis with steel hooks attached to the stump of his right arm. A well-muscled Cuban with striking good looks and a pleasant manner, Encizo was more than a decade younger than Katz. James, a tall, lanky black man from the South Side of Chicago, was in his late thirties. Though physically different, the three men worked effectively within one of the best counterterrorist groups in the world.

"I do want to assure you that the OO is quite different from the KGB," Fedeyev stated. "We're part of the new Russian progressive government."

"We appreciate that, Major," Katz said, "and we look forward to working with you and your organization in a cooperative manner."

"We've already willingly shared information about our reconnaissance satellites," Fedeyev said. "Your two comrades...I mean, companions or co-workers—"

He cleared his throat to try to cover up embarrassment.

"It's okay," James said. "We know what you mean."

"Yes. They are with our photograph-enhancement personnel to study the most recent information we have observed along the Armenian and Iranian border."

"The incident along the border is a major concern for us all," Katz said. "However, our main concern is what happened to the recon satellites and why they failed to detect the confrontation until it was already in progress."

Katz didn't tell Fedeyev that any current data the Russians could offer was insignificant because they had already received faxed updates on SIGINT coverage of the area. They also had other Intel from the Farm that intrigued them far more than the increase of Iranian and Armenian forces along the border.

"Experts in our department think someone might have used aggressive concentrated radar to affect the satellites," Encizo said bluntly. "Both your country and the United States had people working on ACR technology a few years ago."

"At that time this country was still part of the Soviet Union," Fedeyev explained. "Now Russia is part of the Commonwealth of Independent States. We're not involved in many of those projects of the cold war."

Encizo sighed and glanced at his fellow Phoenix Force warriors. James shook his head slightly. Katz's expression didn't reveal any frustration, but Encizo knew the Israeli was also annoyed by Fedeyev acting like a public-relations representative instead of an Intelligence officer.

"We're not accusing anyone of anything," Katz replied. "The fact is, during the cold war both sides researched ACR. The leading expert for the Soviet Union was reported to be a man named Bukovsky. The American top man was Joshua Collins. Both men are dead. Bukovsky apparently died in an accident, but

Collins was murdered just yesterday. We think there's a strong possibility that whoever is using ACR against the satellites had Collins killed.''

"And Bukovsky's death might not have been an accident," James added.

"Who would do this?" Fedeyev asked. "Do you know who might be responsible?"

"Not yet," Katz replied, "but we're trying to locate the ACR experts in the United States. They might be targeted for assassination or they might be working for the enemy...whoever that is this time."

"So you believe this might involve Russian scientists," the major said. "But you don't think our government is responsible?"

The honest answer was that Katz didn't know if there were factions within the Russian government connected with the conspiracy or not. Die-hard party extremists might have seen an effort to plunge Armenia into war, or at least the threat of war, as a way to restore control over the former Soviet republics. Phoenix Force wasn't ready to trust anyone outside the Stony Man organization, including Major Fedeyev.

"Right now," Katz replied, "we need to find the ACR experts. I trust you'll help us, Major."

"That's why we're meeting here."

The office door opened abruptly, and David McCarter stepped into the room. The tall, fox-faced former British SAS commando was flushed with anger. The man's short temper made him less than ideal for assignments that required diplomacy.

Gary Manning followed the Briton into the room. The big, muscular Canadian appeared disgruntled, but Katz didn't know if this was because he had discovered something that distressed him or he was simply annoyed by McCarter's conduct. The Briton got out a pack of Player's cigarettes and fired one up while Manning closed the door.

"Knock, knock," Manning said with a shrug. "Hope it's okay for us to come in. One of us seems to have forgotten his manners, although the British are supposedly famous for theirs...."

"This isn't a bloody tea party, mate," McCarter stated, his Cockney accent revealing his origin from the tough East End of London. "I can see why this new Russian outfit calls itself the OO. If you have to work with them, 'Oh-oh,' you're in trouble."

Fedeyev bristled at the remark. Katz shot a hard glare at the Briton, but McCarter didn't notice as he began to pace the burgundy carpet. The Israeli turned to Manning.

"What happened?" he asked.

"The photo and videotape recon experts didn't have anything new to show us. When we asked about the blackout, the technician in charge claimed he didn't know what we were talking about. We argued about that for a while, and he finally said that he knew why the Russian satellites failed to transmit real-time images of the border conflict."

"That's nice," James remarked. "Did he share this information?"

"He said the two U.S. satellites in the area must have caused the Russian equipment to malfunction and vice versa," McCarter snorted. "They caused static for each other and canceled out their transmission. Can you believe he actually came up with such a feeble excuse? You'd think we were talking about a couple of transistor radios playing in the same room instead of high-tech spy satellites.''

"It sounds like your recon chief isn't being very co-operative," Katz told Fedeyev. "What he told my friends here is pretty lame. Has the OO conjured this as the official explanation for the failure of the spy satellites to detect the incident at the border before the fighting erupted?''

The major appeared embarrassed. He cleared his throat and attempted another false smile. "We need to have an explanation that will ease the concerns of the public. Fortunately the general public does not realize how advanced and sophisticated our observation satellites are these days. Not many have wondered about what happened because most are unaware of what our equipment can accomplish. However, when questions do begin, we need to have a reply that will satisfy the masses.''

"I see," James commented. "It's the official lie for the general public. I don't suppose we could find out what really happened so you could tell them the truth?''

"We may find these things distasteful," the major replied, "but sometimes we must keep secrets from our own people. Certainly Washington does not always tell the truth.''

"I hate to say it," Encizo remarked with a sigh, "but he has a point. So far, Washington hasn't had to answer to anybody outside the establishment as to why we didn't know more about the border clash. When that happens, they'll either refuse to answer the questions or make something up. Even if we prove what really happened, they still might not tell the general public the truth."

"Politicians use tactics I have never cared for," Katz began, "but there isn't much we can do about their habit of deceit. However, we're not politicians or bureaucrats. We need to be fairly up-front with one another or we're not going to accomplish anything by this meeting. If the OO won't cooperate with us, we might as well leave right now and handle our mission on our own."

"I apologize for what happened," Fedeyev assured him. "I'll talk with my associates."

"That's not a primary concern right now," Katz explained. "Our first line of business is to locate the ACR experts still living in the CIS. You have information about them in your personnel computer files?"

"Of course," Fedeyev replied. "We'll look into that, but I'm not sure these scientists will still be working for the government. Much has changed since the Soviet Union was dissolved. If they're private citizens, we can't just go down and arrest them. We're not the KGB, gentlemen."

"No," McCarter muttered. "KGB was more efficient."

Fedeyev once again stared at the Briton with anger. McCarter didn't flinch, meeting the glare with equal acrimony. Katz realized he needed to cut in before tempers flared out of control.

"Major, I appreciate the fact the OO does not want to be accused of resorting to tactics reminiscent of the KGB, but you can't allow that to keep you from taking necessary action. We have to find the ACR experts. We need to talk to them."

"Nobody would be arresting them," Manning added. "They'd simply be brought in for questioning about their recent activities and possibly how they can help us deal with the ACR technology."

"What do you think the KGB used to say as an excuse for breaking into people's homes and bringing them to headquarters without actually having charges against them?" Fedeyev asked. "Some terrible things happened in our recent history. I'm sure you're aware of that. Our people are not likely to forget the abuses of the Committee for State Security."

Katz tried to imagine the situation Fedeyev and other Russian Intelligence officers faced. They were obviously trying to avoid the stigma of the KGB. Even the initials of the new OO had probably been selected to avoid sounding similar to the KGB. Yet sensitivities and public relations couldn't be allowed to prevent them from carrying out their mission.

"Major," the Phoenix commander began, "we have to find those scientists. If they're not part of an enemy conspiracy, they might soon be victims of it. Don't forget Collins has already been murdered."

"If nothing else," Manning added, "they can help us determine if ACR technology is being used. We've been told there aren't many experts in the field. We need information from somebody who really knows this ACR business."

"I understand," Fedeyev said. "We'll see what we can do."

"Can you see about doing it quickly?" McCarter asked, his tone dripping acid. "We might not have much bloody time, Major."

"Our British friend tends to be sort of blunt and not very tactful," James remarked, "but he's right. We have to come up with some answers and soon."

Fedeyev nodded. He looked at the five commandos who had entered his office to suddenly take charge of his operation and wondered if he really wanted them as allies. Maybe the cold war hadn't been so bad after all.

Ural Mountains, Russia

PROFESSOR BUKOVSKY uncorked the bottle of clear liquid. The contents appeared to be water, but he gulped with urgency greater than thirst. Heinz Giessler didn't like the Russian scientist's weakness for vodka. Officially alcohol was forbidden at the covert stronghold, but Giessler realized Bukovsky, and probably some of the other personnel, had smuggled in a private stash. As long as it didn't affect a man's ability to do his job, the ex-SSD agent didn't care enough to insist on a room-by-room search to confiscate the liquor.

It wouldn't be good for morale. If spirits in a bottle helped uplift the spirits of the personnel in the isolated base, it was worth overlooking the violation. However, they had to keep their vice hidden from the Arabs at the base. Many weren't devout Muslims, but all at least gave lip service to Islamic values, including abstinence from alcohol as taught in the Koran.

Giessler approached Bukovsky. The scientist didn't notice the man until he stood by the desk, and the Russian nearly choked on vodka in his throat. Giessler shook his head, wondering how such a brilliant scientist could be such an incompetent when faced with a crisis not related to his own expertise.

Middle-aged, overweight and soft, the Russian wasn't cut out for the sort of operation he had been pulled into. His lower lip trembled, and the blurred eyes behind his glasses registered terror as he stared at Giessler's stern face.

"Hard at work, Anatoly?" the German asked in Russian, the inflection in his voice expressing disapproval.

"I'm just trying to ease some tension," the Russian replied as he mopped his mouth with the back of a hand. "It is frightening to realize the entire world might be hunting us. I've been thinking about what could go wrong."

"Don't. That will drive you insane. No one is hunting you. Officially you're already dead, remember?"

"Raya and little Yuri went to my funeral," Bukovsky replied. "They mourned my death. I couldn't even tell them I'm still alive."

"Why do you Russians always get sentimental when you drink?" Giessler asked with a sigh.

"It is easy for you to leave everything behind. You have no wife, no son, no friends...."

"Anatoly," the German began, "you never cared much for your family, and your friends were artificial sycophants whom you always regarded with contempt. I was with you on too many occasions when you were with other women, and I've heard you complain about what a worthless cow Raya was too many times to believe you really gave a damn about your wife."

"I didn't say our marriage was perfect," Bukovsky replied, "but she was still my wife, and little Yuri—"

"Is sixteen years old and almost two meters tall. You always complained that he was stupid and lazy and had no desire to join the Party. He's probably glad communism fell, you're gone and they have rock and roll disco clubs in Moscow these days."

"You have no right to say such things to me," Bukovsky declared. "What do you know about marriage and family?"

"I know it didn't mean that much to you or you wouldn't be here. Stop feeling sorry for yourself and sucking on that vodka bottle. You have to program the machine for the right coordinates. It's time for you to work your ACR magic again."

Bukovsky was obviously rattled by fear and looked away from Giessler. He nearly reached for the bottle, but realized the German wouldn't allow him to soothe his nerves with vodka.

"I still think this is too soon. What if they realize aggressive concentrated radar is being used? What if they found a way to detect it and track us here?"

"The former Soviet Union and the United States lost interest in this technology some time ago. You're the leading expert in the world. The best man the Americans had is already dead. Muller's team took care of Collins, and they'll find that damn traitor you used to work with."

"Volkov," Bukovsky said sadly. "I rather liked Nikolai. He was a very good scientist and a good chess player."

"Don't start moaning about the past again," Giessler warned. "Volkov is a potential problem, and we're going to remove him. We should have assassinated all your fellow technicians who know enough about ACR to cause us any worries before we launched the first assault."

"You shouldn't have listened to those Arabs."

"We need them," Giessler insisted. "In case the vodka has blurred your memory about recent events, as well as how you regard your so-called friends and family, I ran out of money. We need financing, and those three supplied it."

"I don't know why the troops here have to be paid every month. There's nothing to buy out here anyway."

"If you were more a student of military history, you would understand that soldiers like to get paid. Their morale suffers if they aren't. Sometimes they desert or even turn against their leaders. That's happened to enough armies in the past to serve as a lesson to us. Besides, the monthly payroll is only one expense. There are quite a few others, you know."

"I still don't see why the Arabs couldn't wait."

"Mostly Gahiz," Giessler remarked. "That Iraqi is convinced Saddam is as ripe as a bunch of grapes about to fall from the vine. He's afraid someone else will overthrow Hussein if we don't act quickly enough. Somehow Gahiz managed to convince Kadafadem to support him on the push to act quickly. Mahdi soon took their side. That Syrian bastard probably agreed simply to ensure he and his fellow Arabs could make some Europeans jump on command."

"I don't like working with them."

"They don't like us much, either. We all want the same thing—power. They need us and we need them. It's as simple as that. However, I already explained to you that Kadafadem and Mahdi are not convinced your ACR technology works. The commando force in Iran is in position, and they're waiting for the time to make their next move. You'd better have those satellites blind and deaf when they make the strike."

"I've already programmed the coordinates into the computer," Bukovsky stated. "Everything is ready."

"Except you. I want you ready and fully alert for this. That means you'd better start drinking tea instead of vodka. We can't afford to have this operation fall apart due to some sort of mechanical failure because you were too drunk to handle the equipment."

"I've done my part so far, Heinz," the Russian stated. "And my ACR beam worked well enough before. Even better than I thought it would. This next incident will surely convince the Arabs of that. Still, I can't help worrying about what might happen with the combined Intelligence forces of Russia and the United States investigating this matter."

"During my career in the SSD I worked with the KGB on numerous occasions and we often had to match wits with the American CIA and NSA. Trust me, Anatoly. Neither the Russians nor the Americans are as clever as you give them credit for."

"I can't believe they're all fools. Someone is certain to consider ACR as the possible method used against the satellites."

"Even if they do," Giessler replied with a shrug, "why would they suspect us? They think you're dead and I simply ran away from East Germany when the authorities allowed SSD headquarters to be raided by those barbarians. Stupid scum probably destroyed whatever files were left on me that I didn't manage to get rid of myself."

Giessler smiled as he added, "Besides, we're about to give the entire world something to keep them busy. Everyone, especially the Americans, will be too concerned about what will happen next to be very concerned about why they couldn't see it coming."

CHAPTER NINE

Persian Gulf, near Iranian coastline
Tuesday, 1204 hours

The smell of the ocean filled Sadek Nimeri's nostrils as he stood at the bow of the fishing vessel. He inhaled deeply, savoring the salty fresh scent. Nimeri's homeland of Iraq was nearly landlocked and mostly desert. The sea fascinated him. Water surrounded the boat, deep, blue-green water in every direction.

If they could sail east, through the Strait of Hormuz, past the Gulf of Oman and on to the Arabian Sea, Nimeri and his men would reach the open seas. Eventually there would be no sign of land in any direction. Nimeri thought he would like that. Perhaps when he retired he would get his own boat and cruise the oceans. Gahiz had claimed Nimeri would be very well paid for the mission. Paid enough to afford such a dream.

Yet Sadek Nimeri wasn't a dreamer. He realized his goal was unlikely to become reality. Nimeri had been a soldier all of his adult life. He had served in the Iraqi army and fought against the Iranians and the forces of Desert Storm. The latter conflict convinced him Saddam was an unfit leader and mentally unstable. No rational man would challenge the rest of the world and invite a war Iraq had no hope of winning.

Nimeri had rejected his country's armed forces after that disaster, yet he was still a soldier. It was the only trade he knew. With nearly a decade of combat experience, Nimeri was very good at his work. He'd become a mercenary, but he found the occupation had few opportunities that suited him. There always seemed to be some small wars in progress somewhere, mostly civil conflicts, neither side interested in or able to afford soldiers of fortune.

However, Gahiz had need for a man like Nimeri. He appreciated the skills and abilities of a veteran commando, trained in infiltration, sabotage and guerrilla tactics, a warrior who spoke fluent Farsi and knew the country, customs and people of Iran. The mission was extremely dangerous, the odds stacked against Nimeri or any of his team surviving to collect their handsome rewards. Dead men don't buy boats to sail the oceans.

Nimeri rapped his fist on the handrail, angered that he allowed his mind to wander or to contemplate defeatist notions. The first phase of the mission had been a success. Igniting the border clash between Iranians and Armenians had been easy. They had simply launched a few RPG rockets at both sides from their hiding place near the Iranian encampment. The troops had responded as predicted, opening fire on one another.

Yet Nimeri's commando team hadn't escaped the conflict without suffering losses. Two of his men had been struck by stray rounds and shrapnel. One was killed and the other seriously wounded. They couldn't allow the dead man to be found by the Iranians, so the corpse had been carried from the site when they retreated. The wounded man had been hurt too badly for treatment available to the team. Nimeri had had no choice—he shot the unfortunate trooper in the base of the skull with a silenced pistol. The dead had been buried with only a pile of rocks—to conceal the graves—as a marker.

Their target in the Persian Gulf was potentially far more dangerous. Nimeri saw the U.S. naval vessels on patrol in the distance—giants plated with armor and armed with fearsome weapons and the awesome technology of the West, the same sort of power that had allowed the Americans and their allies to make sport of Iraq during the brief Gulf War. Nimeri smiled with grim satisfaction as the thought of rendering part of that damnable technology useless while striking out at U.S. forces.

Success depended on the aggressive concentrated radar used by the European allies of Gahiz. Nimeri didn't like having to rely on some invisible force he didn't understand. It reminded him of those who prayed to God for protection. Some of his men did so aboard the fishing boat. They knelt on prayer rugs, facing Mecca, asking for divine consideration. Nimeri had lost his faith in such things long ago. He didn't argue with the men in his unit who still practiced Islam. Some were Syrians and Libyans. Nimeri didn't know them well, but they followed orders, and he couldn't deny they displayed courage and skill equal to his fellow Iraqis.

Unseen forces, whether from heaven or a covert base in the Ural mountains, didn't inspire Nimeri with confidence. He believed in what he could see, touch and hear. If the ACR failed to work its modern-day magic, Nimeri and his men would certainly be slaughtered.

The Iraqi commando glanced at his wristwatch. Only a few minutes remained before the time to carry out the attack arrived. He could only hope the ACR beams operated as promised.

Nimeri thought once more of the open seas beyond the gulf. He wondered if he would live to sail the world in peaceful retirement. Perhaps he would be bored after the first month of such a journey, but he still wished he could live to find out.

USS Grover Cleveland
Persian Gulf, international waters

COMMANDER DOUGLAS BAKER hated his frequent bouts of insomnia. It seemed that so much preyed on his mind that it drove away the ability to sleep. The burden of command was never easy, but things became more complicated and difficult for Baker. He had served in Vietnam as a young sailor and saw action in Operation Desert Storm. He planned to be a thirty-year man, but he was afraid the Navy would force him to retire ahead of schedule if he didn't make the next promotion.

Peacetime military, he thought bitterly as he sat at the small desk in his cabin, eyes fixed on images on the computer screen. Tiny spaceships darted about, firing light dots at one another. He absentmindedly punched the trigger key. Most of the shots missed the enemy craft, and Baker's little rocket ship soon stopped a round and exploded. He keyed for another game, although he had little interest in the contest.

A forty-three-year-old commander of a frigate, sitting at a desk past midnight, playing video games on his computer. Baker sighed. The civilians would probably have a tantrum if they knew what he was doing, as if a man became a machine when he wore the uniform. They loved the military during the war, but now they cried for defense cuts. That meant less money for the Navy, and lots of careers would be cut short, as well.

His current assignment would end in three months. Another frigate would replace the USS *Grover Cleveland*, and Baker would head for home. The assignment was rather dull. They simply patrolled the gulf to make sure oil tankers could pass through the Strait of Hormuz, and they would be on hand if Saddam or some other bad boy in the Middle East decided to cause another conflict. Still, Baker was in no hurry to leave. He feared a pink slip from Uncle Sam more than a potential battlefield or the drudgery of quiet monotony.

The Navy had been his life since Baker was eighteen. His wife had filed for divorce and was probably humping away with some damn civilian in San Diego. Baker's teenage son and daughter seldom wrote to their father except to ask for money and whine about problems that seemed absurd to the commander. Baker no longer loved their mother, and he was afraid he didn't really feel much for his kids anymore. He cared more for his fellow sailors. If Baker lost his home in the Navy, there would be little left to live for.

The sudden wail of a siren startled the man. He saw his rocket ship burst at the bottom of the screen as he bolted from his seat. Baker hastily pulled on a pair of white uniform trousers and donned his cap with its gold laurels of authority. It wouldn't do to rush out to the bridge in his skivvies. A pair of slippers completed his outfit before he left his cabin. Baker didn't notice the computer screen was flushed with static.

"WHAT THE HELL is going on?" Baker demanded.

Yablowski, a crew chief with communications, turned from a sonar screen and cast a short glance at the commander. Wavy lines bounced across the display like some cheap version of a laser show. Other crew members punched keyboard buttons and fiddled with dials in frustration. Radar and radio communications didn't seem to be doing any better than sonar.

"Danford!" Baker barked. "I want some answers PDQ!"

Danford, the communications officer, pulled off a headset to a transceiver. The expression on his face was so confused, Baker was annoyed with the officer before the man could say a word.

"We might be under attack, sir."

"Under attack?" Baker repeated with astonishment. "From where?"

"We're not sure," Danford said with an uncomfortable squirm. "All our equipment suddenly went haywire. Never saw anything like this before."

"What seems to be the cause?"

"No idea."

"Why do you think we may be under attack?"

"A swabbie on deck thought he saw something that might be a round fired at us," Danford replied. "Whatever it was—assuming it was anything—it fell short and hit the water. Probably dismiss it if this hadn't happened."

The roar of an explosion outside the metal cave of the bridge abruptly ended the discussion. Baker almost ordered his men to tell him what was on the closed-circuit TV, but saw that those monitors were also filled with static.

"Shit," Baker rasped. "I'm going topside. You men find some way to locate the enemy and establish contact with the fleet!"

"There's no radio!" Danford stated. "We can't get help or request information for our choice of action. Do we engage or retreat?"

"I'll make that decision!" Baker snapped. "We're fired upon. We shoot back. Can't retreat if we don't know where the enemy is. Could run right into them if we tried."

"Pretty hard to shoot back if we don't know where they are, sir," Yablowski pointed out. "Can't use torpedoes. Not without sonar."

"Our computers aren't functioning properly," Danford added. "They aren't completely useless, but certainly unreliable. Whatever is affecting our radar, sonar and radio seems to be causing some degree of interference on just about every other system."

"Our guns will still work," Baker insisted. "We can't just sit here and take it."

"But without computer tracking and reliable night vision . . ."

"Then we'll do it the old-fashioned way if we have to," Baker said, frustrated by Danford's attitude. "One thing we won't do is give up, damnit!"

He exchanged his officer's cap for a helmet and steel pot. Baker considered donning either a flak vest or a life jacket. One could stop bullets or shrapnel, and the other could keep him from drowning if the frigate went down. He couldn't guess which would be more valuable, and there wasn't enough time to contemplate the odds. He wore neither as he headed for the deck.

THE SOUNDS OF BATTLE rocked Baker as if he had been jarred from his sleep by a vivid nightmare. He felt a sudden rush of conflicting emotions. Fear, excitement, anger, disarray and curiosity rose within him. For a moment he wondered if he was actually asleep in his bunk and simply having a very detailed, complicated dream. Wishful thinking, he realized. The battle was genuine, and real human beings in the United States Navy were at risk.

Men darted about the deck of the frigate. Unlike the men on the bridge, these sailors hadn't been bogged down by confusion or astonished by the failure of high-tech equipment. The situation seemed clear to them, and they performed accordingly. Baker watched them with pride.

Projectiles streaked the night sky. A .50-caliber machine gun blasted rounds at other vessels. Baker couldn't identify the nationality of these craft, but they exchanged fire with his frigate. The sailors on the deck had no doubt who the enemy was or how to respond to the threat. Explosions bellowed. Most shells burst in midair, but flames along the stern of an enemy vessel marked the lethal accuracy of the Americans' marksmanship.

The rattle of metal striking metal sounded a warning along the ship. Bullets of shrapnel struck the *Cleveland* and presented a constant threat of deadly hail. Baker stayed low as he moved across the deck to a group of sailors positioned by portside cannons. An ensign recognized Baker and stepped forward. The commander didn't recognize the young officer and had to read the name tag on the man's shirt.

"I just got here, Ensign Arlan," he explained. "Status report. What's happened, who did it, and how are we holding up?"

"Rounds were fired at us," Arlan replied. "Not sure where they came from at first, but then those three Iranian battleships started shelling us. Lucky for us, they're not very accurate and they don't have much range."

"But we were hit?"

The ensign nodded. "Took a round starboard. Some men were hurt. Maybe dead. I've been too busy trying to organize our counterattack to check on our losses, sir."

"Hospital corpsmen looking after the wounded?"

"Yes, sir. They were here as soon as the battle started."

"I'm not surprised," Baker said, proud of the corpsmen, Arlan and the others that performed so well under fire.

"At least one other American ship is involved in the battle," Arlan explained. "We haven't been able to identify it or establish radio contact. I've got two translators on hand. They could talk to the Iranians in Farsi, but we can't get through to them. No computer sighting for the guns, either. What's happened to us, sir?"

"I don't know," Baker admitted. "Have to handle the guns manually. So far, we seem to have an advantage of better range. We'll keep some distance from the

Iranians and continue to return fire. The rest of the fleet will certainly see what's happened to us even if they're having the same technical problems. Reinforcements will be on the way."

"How bad are these technical problems, sir?" Arlan asked. "I thought we'd launch torpedoes by now, but if that's happened we didn't score any hits out there."

"No sonar," Baker said tensely. "If we used torpedoes, it would be like shooting blindfolded. Get anti-aircraft guns ready in case the Iranians have air support. Detail men to watch the skies."

"Watch the—" Arlan realized what this order meant. "We don't have radar, either? Jesus, sir! The Iranians have Silkworm missiles along the coast. They could launch those at us, and we wouldn't know until the damn things are right on top of us!"

"I know. Let's just hope the Iranians are having the same problems we are."

"That's a lot to hope for, sir."

"Maybe not," Baker said as he considered the situation. "They haven't launched any torpedoes at us, have they?"

"None that hit," Arlan replied. "What the hell could make sonar and radar blank out—"

An exploding shell suddenly showered them with flying shrapnel. A shard struck Baker's helmet and drove him to his knees, stunned by the impact. A black mist fell across his eyes as he began to lose consciousness. He was vaguely aware of pain in his left upper arm. The blow to his head dulled the pain, but he felt the discomfort of something lodged in the limb. It was similar to a large splinter stuck under his skin. Baker reached for the wound with his right hand. The fingers touched something warm and wet.

"The old man's been hit!" a voice seemed to call from a long, dark corridor. "Corpsman!"

The voice melted into the dark void.

COMMANDER BAKER OPENED his eyes. His vision was blurred, and he felt weak and disoriented. His mind had trouble recalling recent events. The sensation was similar to being slightly intoxicated. Yet Baker struggled against the artificial sense of well-being. The painkillers left him numb, but he realized he lay on his back, head on a soft surface. It was comfortable, and he resisted the urge to simply drift off to sleep.

Memories began to return and jolted him wake. The cobwebs fell from his mind, and his vision cleared. Baker discovered he was on a bunk, white sheets across his torso, his left arm heavily bandaged. He wasn't alone in the sick bay. Others lay in the surrounding bunks. Some appeared to be seriously injured, bound in bandages that covered chest wounds and damaged skulls. One man's arm ended at the elbow, the gauze-bound stump stained crimson.

"Commander?" Dr. McMahan said. "Are you awake? Can you hear me?"

"Hell, yes," Baker replied. His throat was dry, and the words croaked as he spoke. "Tell me what happened."

"Take it easy, sir," McMahan urged. "Some shrapnel went pretty deep in your arm. Cut the bracial artery, and there was a major problem with internal bleeding. It's under control now, but I don't want you moving around."

"I'm not talking about what happened to me. The ship and the crew. What happened?"

"Just relax, sir," Danford said as he approached the bunk. "The ship came through the battle fairly well. Suffered some damage, of course, but nothing that can't be repaired in port. That's where we're headed."

"How many men did we lose?"

Danford hesitated. "Eight dead and twice that number wounded. A couple might not make it."

"Damn," Baker rasped. "Tell me about the battle."

"The Iranians came out of the battle a lot worse than we did. Sunk two of their vessels and drove the others off. Even without our high-tech gear, they were no match for us."

"Did they launch missiles or torpedoes?" Baker asked. "How about air support?"

"No," Danford answered. "Our side didn't do much along that line, either. Some gunships finally flew over the scene at the tail end of the conflict. The damn aircraft carrier seemed to have technical problems, as well. They had trouble sending up fighters or choppers because they couldn't trust their computers."

"You established radio contact?"

"Oh, yeah. Whatever was wrong before seems to be over. Radio, radar, sonar are all back to normal. Damned if I know what happened, sir."

"Somebody better figure it out," Baker remarked. "Any idea why the Iranians attacked us? I thought it was just a crazy fringe group who figured America was involved in that border clash with Armenia."

"I don't know, sir," Danford replied. "We picked up some of their radio broadcasts. Bastards are claiming we started it. That figures. I guess that's what you can expect from a country full of fanatics."

"I don't know if it's that simple," Baker said. "Not many military engagements are caused because somebody went nuts and decided to take action without any reason. We've been in these waters for some time, and the Iranians never pulled anything like this before. Putting our high-tech gear out of order wasn't the work of an insane mind."

"You think the Iranians caused that?" Danford asked with a startled expression. "I don't think they're capable of anything like that. Hell, sir, I don't think our military has that ability. Sure kept it secret if they do."

"A hell of a coincidence that happened just when a battle erupted," Baker commented. "If the Iranians are responsible, it didn't seem to help them much. Must have rendered their sonar and radar useless, too."

"There must be some other explanation. Maybe some kind of weather condition or a natural magnetic effect... I don't know what it might be."

"I guess that's somebody else's job to figure it out," Baker said. "There was a young officer on deck who impressed me by how he handled the crisis. Ensign Arlan. I'd like you to send him in to see me later. I'm going to write him a commendation and tell the fleet commander about his performance. I also want him to tell me the names of the other sailors who deserve recognition for their valor, as well."

"I'm sorry, sir," Danford replied grimly. "Arlan was one of the men killed in the skirmish."

Baker clamped his lips together into a tight line. Anger, sorrow and a sense of loss hammered at his brain. The commander barely knew Ensign Arlan and hadn't really noticed or appreciated the officer until those few moments of terror aboard the deck.

"Son of a bitch," he growled, not knowing what else to say.

Stony Man Farm, Virginia

"OUR SITUATION has just gotten worse, Hal," the President stated.

"I know," the big Fed replied, one eye on the monitor of a lap-top computer. "We're still getting data on the incident. None of it looks good."

The President's image on the wall screen looked tense, jaw muscles knotted and eyes filled with anger. Brognola realized the Commander in Chief was looking at a middle-aged, weary figure in rumpled clothing who appeared overworked rather than upset. Too bad, the big Fed thought. He didn't have time to conjure up an act for the President.

Brognola didn't particularly want to hear from the President at that moment. He had his hands full trying to evaluate information Kurtzman collected and reports from the Stony Man personnel in the field.

"Believe it or not, Hal, we have sources of information, too," the President stated dryly. "They tell me the U.S. Navy vessels in the gulf suffered a total shutdown of radar, sonar, radio and partial loss of computer functions. A number of sailors were killed or seriously wounded in the sea battle with the Iranians."

"I realize that, sir," Brognola replied. "I also got data from NSA, ONI and CIA that suggests our spy satellites were blocked out again. No film footage, videotape, photos of the incident were possible for nearly half an hour.''

''That's correct,'' the President confirmed. ''You didn't mention that this aggressive radar could affect sonar, as well as radar and radio.''

''We didn't know it could,'' the big Fed admitted. ''We never claimed to be experts in this ACR technology. Never even heard of it before this happened. Kurtzman tells me we shouldn't be too surprised, since sonar works in much the same manner as radar. Of course, that's underwater, and liquid density makes sound reception more receivable than sound carried by air. From what we've been able to gather about ACR, not even the people involved in the American and Soviet research teams knew it would be powerful enough to blot out sonar, as well as radar and radio frequencies.''

''What about the computers? Why didn't anyone notice this before? There was no report of computer malfunction at Mountain Balloon.''

''Actually there was,'' Brognola corrected. ''We didn't realize it because those were computers hooked to the radar and radio systems. Not surprising that the effects on the communications and receivers would also cause problems for the computer system under those circumstances. Since most computer terminals to a big system use the same mainframe, an attack on one function can cause a domino effect.''

''My God,'' the President rasped. ''Do you know what this could do to us? They might be capable of jamming communications, computer operation and radar services on a national level!''

"The information we have so far doesn't allow us to make any estimates as to how great a range the ACR can cover. We don't even know the technology works. Jamming the satellites was obvious, but Aaron didn't come across any data on file that suggested it could affect systems on the ground or at sea, as well."

"Apparently it is capable of doing that and more."

"Yeah," Brognola said with a sigh. "We've already considered the possibilities of widespread sabotage using ACR. It doesn't take much imagination to guess what could happen if they targeted any international airport. Half an hour without radar or radio communications could cause enormous destruction and loss of life. At night or in poor weather conditions, planes could easily crash into each other or hit towers in airports while attempting to land. Some really terrible possibilities."

"Not to mention what this could do to our space program," the President remarked. "We've had enough problems with the shuttle in recent years. Now they could be rendered blind and deaf, as well. There's no point in launching another space shot until this is over. Who's responsible for what's been going on, the Iranians?"

"We don't know yet," Brognola admitted. "Unless the Iranians decided they wanted to start fighting half the world, it doesn't make much sense."

"Iran has been involved in state-sponsored terrorism in the past," the President reminded him.

"Sure, but there haven't been too many recent accusations that link the current government with terrorism. Besides, there's no evidence Iran has done any work on ACR technology."

"The Soviets did. Some of their experts could have been hired by Tehran."

"That's true," Brognola admitted. "We have people trying to round up everybody who has expertise in the subject. The ones that are still alive."

"Nothing suggests any of them might have gone over to Iran?"

"No," the big Fed replied. "And I'm not convinced Iran is behind this. If they wanted to carry out terrorism or sabotage, there are a hundred ways they could do it without drawing attention to themselves. Why would they use the ACR force to blot out satellites, radar, sonar and radio only to launch inept attacks that don't work in their favor? The border conflict with Armenia was probably a draw, and they apparently lost the sea battle with the U.S. Navy."

"Maybe they didn't realize the ACR would affect their radar, sonar and communications, as well. The Iranians didn't use torpedoes or radio for air support, so they must have been having the same problems our people experienced."

"Hell, I think they would have tested under noncombat conditions before pulling any stunts like that sea engagement or the border clash. Only idiots would decide to use it to start a fight without knowing what it would do to their own equipment. There might be some fanatics in the Tehran government, but they're not idiots. Certainly no mental dwarf is responsible for carrying out an ACR assault campaign on this level."

"So you think someone is trying to get us to go to war against Iran? Why?"

"Once again we don't know. Iran does make a good fall guy. A lot of people remember the takeover of the

U.S. Embassy in Tehran after the Ayatollah took power and how Americans were held hostage for more than a year. You already mentioned state-sponsored terrorism. Iran hasn't been a candidate for the 'good neighbor' award from any country in the region. The Soviet Union wasn't exactly thrilled with them in the past, either. Iran gave protection, if not military support, to the mujahedeen who were fighting the Soviet occupation of Afghanistan."

"That's all changed," the President replied. "The world is different. There's no more Soviet Union, and Iraq was considered to be a greater threat to world peace than Iran... at least until now."

"Well, Iran has oil," Brognola remarked. "Lots of oil. We all know how valuable the oil trade is."

"That's why Saddam invaded Kuwait."

Brognola nodded, but didn't mention that the oil trade was also the reason for Operation Desert Storm. The U.S. and allies hadn't sent troops to Afghanistan when the Soviets invaded that country, and the Syrians still occupied Lebanon—and they had been there during the Gulf War. However, Afghanistan and Lebanon don't have oil. Brognola wasn't diplomatic by nature, but he had learned there were times to hold his peace.

"Maybe the Iraqis are behind this," the President mused. "They had an eight-year war with Iran. Saddam more or less won, but I doubt he got everything he wanted. Maybe this time he figures he can get us to do the dirty work for him and move after the smoke clears to claim territory and oil reserves."

"If that's the case," Brognola began, "Saddam didn't learn anything from the invasion of Kuwait.

Uncle Sam and whoever we could get to throw in with us would head right back to the gulf to kick his ass out of Iran.''

"He didn't always act in a rational manner during the invasion of Kuwait or the war," the President stated. "Who knows what goes on in that man's head?"

"I just don't like pointing fingers at anybody until we know they did something," Brognola said. "We don't have any proof Iraq is involved in this mess."

"Part of your job is to find out," the President said. "If this is the sort of mission your people can take care of, frankly that's fine with me. I'd rather not have to carry out a major military campaign. But you'd better come up with something fast. There's no way we can keep a lid on the sea battle in the gulf. People are going to demand to know what happened, and they'll want us to do something about it."

"Believe me when I say everybody at the Farm and all my people in the field are working overtime on this," the big Fed assured him. "I'm sure we're on the right track, but I can't give you any real sign of progress."

"I'm sorry, but that's not good enough. We can't stall on this very long. It's obvious the Iranians have suddenly become aggressive for no reason and have begun attacking both Armenia and our patrols in the gulf. The American people and the world in general will expect us to take action."

"But how things appear is not the whole story."

"Hal," the man in the Oval Office said with a weary sigh, "you know as well as I do that we can't let the public know what we're faced with. Can you imagine

the panic if we admitted that we are presently power-
less against a threat to our national security that could
leave this country open to attack? That we could have
a repeat of Pearl Harbor on a far larger scale? That our
military and commercial aircraft are vulnerable to attack due to the very technology we worked so hard to
achieve?''

Brognola didn't comment, but he didn't like keeping the American people in the dark. Panic or not, it
seemed to him the public had a right to know that if
they tried to fly to Miami to visit Grandma, they would
face a greater risk of crashing into a jumbo jet headed
for New York. He understood the President's concern, but he still didn't like it.

"We'd also have to admit that we can't confirm the
locations of missile bases, military installations and
nuclear weapons,'' the President continued. "Any
hope of arms reduction will go down the drain. Worse,
we can't even be sure of using our own high-tech
weapons systems if we are under attack. How can we
locate targets without recon satellites or even radar?''

"Yeah,'' Brognola said. "It's a hell of a mess, sir.''

"That's an understatement,'' the President replied.
"Of course, we've got other organizations working on
this, but you've made more headway than anyone else
so far. You're our best hope, Hal.''

"Nice to be needed, sir,'' the big Fed replied dryly.

CHAPTER TEN

Ankara, Turkey
Tuesday, 0640 hours

Mack Bolan awoke to the sound of a muezzin calling the faithful of Islam to prayer. He instinctively reached for the pistol under his pillow. Strange sounds in a strange environment. He glanced about the room—a small desk, chest of drawers with mirror and a window wide enough to spill sunshine into his quarters. The Executioner relaxed and sat up in the bed.

The warrior padded barefoot to the window and gazed out at Ankara in the morning. The traffic below was light. The capital of Turkey seemed pleasant and intriguing from the window of the hotel room. Although modern buildings dominated the scene, Bolan saw the ancient ruins of the Baths of Caracella and the Column of Julian. The former had crumbled to little more than brick foundation, but the column stood sixteen meters high, its fluted structure carved in stone centuries earlier.

Ankara had a very long, fascinating history. Numerous cultures had influenced its development. The muezzin crier stood by an archway of a pavilion to a minaret in front of a mosque. The man in the tower was only a couple of blocks from the hotel, and Bolan had a clear view of the great white dome and cupola of the mosque. In the distance he saw a church steeple. Although most Turks were Muslim, Christians and Jews freely practiced their faiths, as well.

The Executioner couldn't spare much time admiring the local color of Ankara. He needed to know what progress had been made while he grabbed some much-needed sleep. Bolan headed for the desk and opened the lid to a lap-top computer. He punched in the access code. The system demanded identification. Bolan keyed "Striker," and a menu appeared on the screen.

He selected "Stony Farm," and data rolled in from the Farm. There wasn't much good news. Under the category of "Gen Info," Bolan learned about the mysterious encounter in the Persian Gulf. The failure of the recon satellites to detect the sea battle was distressing enough, but the effects on the equipment aboard the naval vessels revealed the threat was even greater than they thought.

The cryptic comments that followed explained the update on Able Team and Phoenix Force. "Home Team" referred to efforts by Stony Man within the United States. This included operations in the field conducted by Leo Turrin and Stony Man security personnel, as well as Able Team. Unfortunately the statement "Still Seeking lost sheep" suggested no major breakthroughs had occurred thus far.

Phoenix Force didn't appear to be doing any better. Their declaration "Spotchecks neutral" revealed the five commandos had neither met with major obstacles nor made any worthy progress in Russia. Bolan was already aware of this due to the NSA and CIA connections in Turkey. Stan Fell and Wesley Rollins ranked high enough in their Intel outfits to have access to information from their fellow operatives in Russia. Apparently the new OO Intelligence branch was more benevolent than the KGB, but it was also reluctant to take action and lacked the professionalism of its predecessor.

Bolan hadn't been terribly impressed by the NSA or CIA since he'd arrived in Turkey. Rollins handled the authorities better than he had performed during the gun battle in Istanbul. He had managed to keep Bolan's cover intact and arranged for the room at the hotel. The Company man was well connected in Ankara because he was based at the U.S. Embassy in the capital city. Fell hadn't done much better during the ambush attempt, but he seemed to know his business when it came to SIGINT spy satellites and high-tech recon.

They weren't soldiers. The Executioner felt most at home in the company of fellow warriors. These weren't necessarily soldiers who carried weapons into battlefields to kill or be killed. Bolan considered Brognola, Price and Kurtzman to be warriors. Although occasionally they had to place their lives in physical danger, they generally fought the battles from behind the lines. They put their hearts and souls into each mission and worked with as much determination and dedication as any commando in the field.

Fell and Rollins didn't seem to have these qualities of courage. The former was a technician who had done his job well enough, but felt no real passion or personal involvement. The latter was a bureaucrat and probably remained in the CIA because he had managed to land a comfortable position and had his eye on a fat government pension when he retired.

Bolan wondered if the Russian agents of the OO were similar to their American counterparts. He hoped not, for the sake of Phoenix Force. The warrior decided to call downstairs to see if room service could send up some coffee before he continued the computer probes.

"Good morning, Mr. Belasko," a voice from the telephone said in a slightly guttural English. "You wake early, sir?"

"Depends on how you look at those things," Bolan replied. "Is your kitchen open?"

"Of course. All day and all night. Many of our guests are international visitors like yourself. Before I forget, there is a message for you here."

"What is it?" the warrior asked.

"A man called Stan left a phone number and asks that you call when you wake up."

Bolan copied the number, gave the clerk his order for breakfast and thanked the guy. He called the number Fell left for him. The NSA man picked up on the second ring.

"Hello, Belasko?" he asked.

"Yeah. I'm calling from the hotel."

He said this to make certain Fell realized it wasn't a secure line. Anybody could be listening at the switchboard downstairs.

"I thought you might like to see the Museum of Anatolian Civilization today."

"Sure," Bolan answered.

"Okay. I'll pick you up in an hour and a half."

Bolan assured him that would be fine and hung up. He returned to the computer, less than hopeful it would spawn any encouraging data.

STAN FELL PULLED UP to the hotel in a blue Honda. Bolan was relieved that Fell wasn't using another vehicle that had "government issue" written all over it. He entered the Honda, and Fell headed into traffic flow to the northeast. Bolan noticed the NSA officer had bags under his eyes and still wore the same clothes he had the day before.

"Long night?" Bolan asked.

"Very. You won't believe what happened in the Persian Gulf."

"U.S. and Iranian naval vessels clashed in combat," Bolan answered. "Our satellites didn't work again."

"That's right," Fell said with surprise. "Your people are really on top of this."

"Not yet. We're still working on it. Have they interrogated the surviving gunman from the bush yet?"

"Glad I can tell you *something* you don't already know," Fell replied dryly. "The son of a bitch spilled his guts, apparently hoping to cut some kind of deal. He said he and his hoodlum cronies had been hired to keep tabs on our friend Rollins at the embassy, and a couple of them were also watching me shuffle to and from Mountain Balloon."

"How long have they been tailing you guys?"

"For about two months," Fell replied, obviously embarrassed by this revelation. The fact he still wore a bandage across the bridge of his broken nose didn't make the story any easier to tell. "I know. I know. We should have noticed we were being followed, and this is more evidence we're dullards—"

"Too late to change what's already happened," Bolan cut him off. "Who hired them?"

"Supposedly two men who claimed to be Arabs," Fell answered, "but he said they conversed with each other in Farsi. That's the language spoken in Iran."

"Uh-huh," Bolan said. "Does this guy know Arabic or Farsi?"

"He says he and a couple of the other scum have done some illegal trade with Iranians along the border. Iranians smuggle hand-woven rugs and carpets across the border to sell or trade. Persian rugs have an international reputation, and these traders can make a much larger profit outside Iran than in their own country. Hell, even during the Iran-Iraq war in the 1980s, Iranians were traveling to Kuwait and the United Arab Emirates to sell carpets."

"So this man supposedly knows enough Farsi to recognize it when he hears it spoken," the warrior remarked. "If he's telling the truth, why did they attack us in Istanbul?"

"Because they were keeping track of both Rollins and me, and this led them to the airport. They figured something big must have happened when the two of us picked you up. The ringleader of the little band of hoods decided they ought to jump us. Planned to take us prisoner if possible. Of course, that didn't work out."

"It's possible he's telling the truth. Pretty complex lie for a small-time criminal to conjure up on short notice. Did he tell us where we can find the ringleader?"

"In the morgue," Fell replied. "He was one of the men you killed in the gunfight."

"At least he won't try anything like that again. Did he say where we can find the two so-called Iranians?"

"Apparently they used to contact the now-deceased ringleader," Fell answered with a sigh. "Sorry."

Bolan considered the information. He glanced out the window at the traffic. It seemed as heavy as in Istanbul, yet the drivers were more relaxed and the pace wasn't as frantic in Ankara. No one appeared to be following them this time.

"The evidence we're getting seems to point at Iran," Bolan said. "It seems almost too obvious."

"Iran doesn't exactly deserve any great praise for its behavior in the past," Fell commented. "According to the last reports I read by Amnesty International, Iran still didn't have a very favorable record of human rights. They still have political prisoners, lots of cases of people being tortured and other violations."

"Yeah," Bolan agreed, "but I seem to recall there were more than ninety other countries on that list by Amnesty International, governments that carry out torture, throw people in prison for political reasons and pretty much dump on their rights. Wasn't Turkey included on that list?"

Fell squirmed behind the steering wheel. "So what's your point, Belasko?"

"My point is, we can't start jumping to conclusions, because that might be what somebody wants us to do. Whoever is using this ACR technology must be pretty clever."

"Don't you think Iranians are capable of being clever?"

"Sure I do," the warrior replied. "That's one of the reasons this seems suspicious to me. Blocking the spy satellites didn't give the Iranians any sort of advantage in combat. A clever opponent wouldn't develop advanced technology and not make the most of it."

"Governments don't always make sense," Fell stated. "That's an observation based on working for our government and spying on the activities of other governments for quite a few years now."

"Yeah," the Executioner replied, "but I'm not sure we're dealing with a government in this case."

"Talk about jumping to conclusions! How'd you come to that theory? Figure some renegade Martians are behind this? How about a cult of Satanists?"

The hardness in Bolan's eyes made Fell regret his remarks.

"I don't know who we're after," the warrior replied. "It might not be a government, because they hired a gang of hoods instead of using veteran Intelligence personnel or cutouts with genuine experience."

"I know our rundown on those guys stated they had no history with espionage, but the bastards managed to track Rollins and me."

"Neither one of you have survival sense," Bolan told him. "I spotted the tail immediately. You and Rollins never saw them following you before because you didn't look for anyone shadowing you."

"I guess I deserved that," Fell admitted.

Bolan ignored his remark. "But whoever hired them," he went on, "must have known about their trade with Iranians in the past. I doubt they would have conversed in Farsi in front of those goons if they really intended to masquerade as Arabs."

"So they wanted the crooks-for-hire to get caught?"

"They probably figured the thugs would be caught eventually and tell everything they knew," Bolan answered. "The big questions are still who is doing this and why. If we assume, for a moment, Iran is being set up, that tells us part of what they want."

"They want Iran to go to war."

"They certainly want attention focused on Iran," Bolan said. "It could be a distraction. Like a magician performing a trick or a boxer feinting with his right to throw a punch with his left."

"A hell of a distraction," Fell said with a soft whistle. "What would be the real goal? It would have to be something really big."

"I'm sure they're after something very big," the Executioner agreed. "This whole scheme is on a huge scale. Blacking out satellites, assassinating scientists in America and possibly Russia, surveillance on you and other Intelligence agents. Nobody would go to this much effort unless they had something enormous as their objective, something to make it worth the time and effort."

"I still don't see why you think this is a free-lance venture instead of a government scheme," Fell remarked. "Iraq could be behind this. Saddam is certainly ambitious enough and ruthless."

"He's also been under close scrutiny ever since the Gulf War. Saddam Hussein got a lot of assistance from the West in the past. We looked the other way and allowed him to do a lot of terrible things without doing or saying much about it."

"You mean the chemical-warfare attacks on the Kurds and against the Iranians during the war?"

Bolan nodded. "Among other things. That was a violation of the Geneva Convention, not to mention a glaring violation of human rights. Yet when the incidents occurred in the late 1980s, nobody complained much. The UN, the U.S. government and the nations of Western Europe and the Soviet Union barely acknowledged this or condemned it. Not until Desert Storm.''

"Yeah," Fell agreed. "Then the outrage came in all directions. Except not much was said about how American, British, French and West German sources had helped supply Saddam when he was still at war with Iran. They even sold him the chemicals for poison gas.''

"But that was before Desert Storm," the Executioner stated. "He'd have a hard time trying to develop and use ACR technology without anyone knowing about it. The other aggressive regimes in the area of the Middle East would also have problems trying to carry out something like this unobserved.''

"Unlikely but not impossible.''

"Not impossible," Bolan agreed. "We still have to consider every possibility. How much information do you have on the naval battle?''

"We're still gathering data on it," Fell answered. "I don't know how much good it will do us. You already have a general idea what happened.''

"That's not enough," the warrior insisted. "I know the radar, communications, sonar and even the video cameras aboard the ships failed to function during the encounter. So let's check out some old-fashioned sources.''

"Such as?''

"Eyewitness accounts," Bolan replied. "Might help us get an idea where the first shot came from.''

"Apparently the battle started when rounds were fired at the USS *Grover Cleveland*," Fell said.

"We also need points of view from Iran."

Fell rolled his eyes. "Hell, you know they'll say we started it. We can pick up their official radio and television broadcasts, but that's run by the government. All we'll get is propaganda."

"That's not what I have in mind," the soldier replied. "I want to talk to someone in a position of authority in Iran who would know about the incident."

"That's not going to do any good, either, Belasko. Even if we can find somebody willing to talk to us, he'll just parrot what the guys in charge tell him to say."

"Maybe not. That depends on who we talk to and how we arrange the meeting."

"Meeting?" Fell asked with surprise.

"That's right. This requires more than a phone call. Whoever we can contact will take us more seriously if we meet him face-to-face to discuss this business."

"Hell, Belasko," the NSA agent stated, shaking his head in astonishment, "you figure some high-ranking Iranian official is going to fly to Turkey to have a chat with us?"

"No," Bolan replied. "I figure we'll have to go to Iran so he'll know we're serious."

"Go to Iran?" Fell was certain the other man had lost his mind. "After what happened in the gulf? You're talking suicide, man!"

"So you won't have to go with me," the Executioner assured him. "Help find the right man, establish contact and arrange the meeting. I'll handle the suicide part myself."

CHAPTER ELEVEN

Ustinov, Russia
Tuesday, 1020 hours

The bus rolled through the poorly paved streets of Ustinov. The town had never received much from the national government under communism, and it had been largely ignored by the new regime, as well. Local residents watched the bus, aware it was a vehicle from a major city. Their faces expressed distrust and resentment at the presence of intruders from Moscow or Minsk or wherever the bus had come from.

Rafael Encizo glanced out a window at the people on the street. They wore shabby, patched clothing, and their eyes had the hollow quality of despair and disappointment. The Cuban had seen such faces dozens of times in the past, in numerous countries throughout the world. The people of Ustinov had been through the wringer, and it had taken its toll.

The sight was especially disheartening for Encizo. He had been a freedom fighter against Castro's regime, participated in the Bay of Pigs and suffered in a political prison. He hated all forms of tyranny, but communism was his least favorite due to personal experience. The Russian people had endured the yoke of communism so long it seemed unfair they should still have to suffer poverty, disillusion and despondence.

Of course, the Cuban realized the fall of communism would not bring Utopia. Yet he had hoped to see the lives of the Russian people improve. They had witnessed little evidence of this. Perhaps Russians and other members of the CIS had more freedoms, but the standard of living still seemed on Third World level for most.

"You see something?" Calvin James asked.

Encizo turned from the window to face the t̲al̲l̲ warrior seated beside him. "The same as you̲,̲" he̲ explained. "It doesn't make me happy."

James nodded. A product of a ghetto in th̲e̲ South̲ Side of Chicago, he also appreciated the struggle̲ faced by the majority of the Russian people. He also̲ understood why the residents watched the bus with resentment. In James's old neighborhood, they used to view the police cars in the same manner. Authority had not brought them much protection, but plenty of accusations and hassle.

Their guide was a young OO officer who insisted they call him by his first name Sergei. He was cheerful to the point of annoyance under the circumstances, and chatted away in fluent English, occasionally tossing in a slang term to display his expertise.

"Well, it's sort of hard to imagine an accomplished scientist would be living in a place like this," McCarter said. "Are you people sure Kurrimov is here?"

"Khurumov," Sergei corrected. "Aleskandr Khurumov. Certainly Major Fedeyev explained that Dr. Khurumov worked with Professor Bukovsky on the special radar project for the military."

"Yeah," James said. "Khurumov replaced Volkov after he defected to the West."

"Correct," Sergei confirmed. "That was before the reforms started here. Back during the old regime. Volkov can come back now if he wishes to do so. Maybe he's got a hot gig in America and wants to stay there."

Sergei smiled, certain his comment would amuse the passengers. It didn't. The three Phoenix Force commandos knew that Stony Man was desperately searching for Volkov because he was either a potential enemy or a potential target of the assassins who murdered Collins.

"I guess when they decided the ACR project wasn't so promising and the Soviet Union began to fold," James began, "they also figured this Khurumov dude didn't rank any special privileges anymore."

"Like choice housing in Moscow or Minsk," Encizo added.

Sergei nodded. "Unfortunately this is true. Khurumov had to move here in Ustinov and live with his wife and her parents. A big step down on the social ladder."

"The sort of thing that could make a bloke pretty bitter," McCarter commented. "Maybe bitter enough to take part in a crazy scheme involving ACR sabotage."

"Maybe," Encizo agreed, "but let's not assume Khurumov is an enemy. That means don't lose your temper or get nasty with the man."

"Don't look at me when you say that," McCarter replied, eyes open wide in mock surprise.

THEY SOON LOCATED the address and parked near the home of Khurumov's in-laws. The building was neither a house nor an apartment complex. It vaguely resembled a brownstone, but the central portion of the structure appeared considerably older than the sections that flanked it. Additional construction had been added to the original to house more people. The alterations had been made long ago, during the Communist rule that made the property state owned and controlled. It remained a dwelling for group housing because the economic conditions in Russia still prevented most from owning homes or renting larger apartments.

The three Phoenix warriors and Sergei approached the building on foot. James and McCarter headed for the rear of the structure to cover the back doors and windows. They recalled what Able Team had discovered at Collins's house in Atlanta. Evidence of a jimmied door or window would probably mean Khurumov had already been dispatched by the mysterious "other side."

Encizo and Sergei mounted the steps in front of the building. The Cuban wore a throat mike to stay in contact with his partners. He also carried a Walther P-88 in shoulder leather, and a Cold Steel Tanto fighting knife was in a belt sheath. Encizo suddenly wished they had taken a few extra seconds to don Kevlar vests and possibly station one or more members by the bus to watch the backs of the others. Something worried him the moment he saw the door to the Khurumov flat.

The door was slightly ajar. Ragged splinters along the jamb, at lock level, confirmed his concerns. The door had been forced. The intruder had probably done it simply with a hard shoulder ram. A casual observer would have assumed the door had simply been stuck, not locked. Whoever was inside would certainly know better, but would already be in a potentially lethal situation.

The Cuban opened his mouth to speak into the throat mike and report to his two teammates. A curtain moved at a window near the door, and Encizo reacted. There was no time to consider possible actions or that he might have mistaken the evidence of a break-in. If the assassins had struck, at least one of them was still inside. A split second of indecision could cost him his life.

Encizo threw himself at the door. Sergei uttered a startled gasp, unprepared for the Cuban's bold action. The commando hit the door low. It slammed into something solid, and a grunt announced contact with a person hidden behind it. Encizo tumbled inside and rolled across the carpet, drawing the P-88 on the move.

He landed in a kneeling stance, pistol in hand as he glanced about the room. Two men stood before him. One reached inside a jacket while the other swung the silencer-equipped barrel of a pistol toward the Cuban. Encizo quickly pointed his weapon and squeezed the double-action trigger twice. The Walther barked out two 9 mm rounds, both striking the gunman in the upper torso. The guy toppled backward into his comrade as the second man tried to draw his piece.

A blur of movement at the corner of his eye warned Encizo of new danger. A figure charged from the door, no doubt the man struck by it when Encizo had burst across the threshold. The Cuban glanced up at the tall shape clad in dark pinstripe. An angry Slavic face with a broad nose, snarling mouth and burning Eurasian eyes glared down at him. Encizo started to move the P-88 when the attacker launched a kick.

The boot struck Encizo's gun hand and sent the Walther flying from numb fingers. Once again he responded by instinct and training. The Phoenix commando dropped to his side and lashed out with both feet. He hooked an instep at his opponent's ankle and stamped the other foot into the man's knee. The tactic sent the assassin to the floor with a cry of surprise and pain. The crunch of cartilage in the assaulted kneecap was lost amid the other sounds.

Gunfire erupted toward the rear of the quarters. The killer who had drawn a silenced Makarov pistol to deal with Encizo turned to face the new threat. The Cuban barely noticed the metallic rattle of a full-auto weapon. Neither James nor McCarter carried such a firearm, so a fourth opponent must have confronted the pair. The Cuban couldn't contemplate their plight. He had enough to cope with just staying alive.

The hardman on the floor grimaced from a dislocated kneecap, but the pain didn't prevent him from reaching for a pistol in his belt. Encizo pushed away from the floor with a foot and a palm to propel himself to the enemy. The Phoenix fighter pounced on the gunman, snared the wrist above the Makarov pistol with one hand and balled the other into a fist.

He punched the man's face, knuckles striking hard between the eyes. The Cuban twisted his opponent's captive wrist, trying to force the weapon from the other man's grasp or redirect the barrel to press against the gunman's body. An explosion erupted, and searing pain knifed along Encizo's rib cage. His body jerked, yet he held on to the opponent's wrist.

Encizo hissed, but he realized he hadn't been shot. The Cuban had stopped more than one bullet in the past and knew the awful sensation of a hot metal projectile in flesh from firsthand experience. The bullet hadn't hit him. The pain was simply powder burns. He slugged the other man again with a fist to the side of the jaw.

The gunman grunted from the blow. Pinned on his back, unable to free his gun hand from Encizo's strong grip, the assassin reached up with his free hand and grabbed the Cuban's hair. He pulled hard and pumped a knee into the powder burn at Encizo's side. The Phoenix warrior gasped and reached for the combat knife on his belt.

His fingers found the rubber-grip handle, and he drew the knife in an "ice pick" hold, 14.24 centimeters of sharp steel extended from the bottom of his fist. He quickly raised the knife and struck before his astonished opponent could react. The blade struck the assassin in the chest, left of the sternum. It pierced flesh and muscle, splintered a rib to stab deep into the chest cavity. The slanted point found the man's heart.

The gunman thrashed about the floor, Encizo still on top of him. The Phoenix commando concentrated on pushing the pistol away from himself, aware the guy would pull the trigger due to the spasms even if he didn't attempt a desperate final effort to take the Cuban with him as he died. He managed to shove the muzzle into his opponent's abdomen an instant before the pistol went off. The report was muffled by the man's body. Encizo felt the recoil ride through the other man's wrist, and the figure beneath him bucked with the impact of the bullet. The gun fired three times before the assassin's body was still.

Encizo took the pistol from the dead man. Breathing hard, muscles tight with tension, he glanced about the room. Gunfire raged beyond his view, but there was no immediate threat. The Cuban's gaze found Sergei at the front door. The OO agent held a gun in both hands as he leaned along the doorway, his eyes wide with confusion.

"Thanks for covering my back," Encizo muttered.

Sergei failed to detect the sarcasm and replied, "Oh, you are welcome."

THE MOMENT THE FIRST SHOT had been fired, David McCarter and Calvin James realized the Khurumov house would be tougher than it looked. The British commando drew his Browning Hi-Power in a rapid, smooth reflex action. James produced his Walther P-88 as he jogged for the rear entrance.

Glass shattered and the snout of a gun barrel appeared. James and McCarter jumped for cover as a salvo of full-auto fire headed their way. The ex-navy SEAL hit the ground and rolled to a telephone pole for shelter. McCarter ducked by a row of garbage cans. Bullets pounded their positions of cover, the controlled 3-round bursts letting them know their enemy had been well-trained to handle an automatic weapon.

Slugs splintered the frame of the pole above James's head, and a projectile tore a clump of dirt from the ground a few inches from his right elbow. The enemy fire shifted to McCarter, and rounds hammered the trash bins with a violent rattle. James returned fire, triggering the Walther twice. He barely aimed, interested in drawing his opponent's attention for the moment. James realized McCarter was a better pistol marksman, and he would be more likely to take out the enemy gunman if he could get a chance to aim and fire.

The hardman's weapon snarled in response to James's pistol. McCarter took advantage of the situation. He held the Browning in a two-handed Weaver grip and peered across the sights. The Briton had been a member of his country's Olympic pistol team. Although the other Phoenix members packed the P-88, he still carried a Browning because the Hi-Power was a weapon he handled with uncanny skill and accuracy.

McCarter raised the Browning. The front sight found a half-moon silhouette at the windowpane above the enemy gun barrel. The curve of an eyebrow and the tip of a nose confirmed this was the foe's head. The British ace squeezed the trigger. He saw the shape jerk from the 9 mm punch of the Browning. The figure dropped from view. McCarter was confident he wouldn't get up again.

"Clear!" the Briton announced, and scanned the area for more of the enemy.

James believed him and bolted for the door. The black warrior mounted the stairs in two leaping strides, Walther in hand. He knew he could rely on McCarter to cover him. He noticed the door was ajar before he reached it, and slapped his back flat against the wall by the hinges. He lashed out a long leg to kick the door at the bottom panel. It swung inward.

Two pistol shots rang out. James stayed clear of the door until certain a third shot wasn't on the way. He thrust the barrel of the Walther around the corner and triggered the double-action autoloader without exposing himself or taking aim. He didn't hope to hit the enemy with blind fire, but intended to force the unseen opponent to duck for a moment.

James dived inside. He used the same method Encizo had employed at the front entrance and came in low to shoulder roll across the floor. He crashed into something solid, which gave way from the force of his hurtling form and landed on the floor with a cry of alarm.

The commando had unintentionally rammed the enemy and clipped the guy's legs out from under him.

James pivoted on a knee and swung his pistol at the figure. A large man, dressed in dark gray clothing and black gloves, had fallen next to a small table with four chairs. His Makarov pistol lay more than a yard from his grasp. The gun had been jarred from his grasp when he hit the floor. Good, James thought. He wanted to take the guy alive if possible.

"Okay, pal," James said, "get on your knees and keep your hands raised."

The man glared at him with cold blue eyes in an angular face, his mouth contorted with anger. He started to raise his hands in surrender. Suddenly he swatted a big palm into a chair and caught it under the seat. The chair seemed to hop forward and leap at James's face. He dodged the unconventional projectile, but a chair leg struck his wrist to knock the Walther from his grasp.

"Aw, shit," James growled.

The hardman attacked, his gloved hands launched at James's throat. He sidestepped the lunge and hooked a kick to his opponent's abdomen. The man staggered, but didn't double up from the blow. James karate chopped the guy across a forearm to lower the limb and present a clear target for a left jab to the chin. The man's head rocked from the punch, and James followed with a right cross.

He missed.

The assassin ducked under the attacking fist and charged into James. His shoulder rammed the commando in the stomach as the momentum carried both men into a wall. James's back connected with the surface hard, but he responded with a karate chop to his foe's collarbone. The man's body jerked from the blow. The side of James's hand struck the same target again.

The enemy folded at the waist, and James whipped a knee kick to the man's face. The blow straightened the guy's spine, and James caught him in the side of the jaw with a solid left hook. The punch spun the guy around. James swung a roundhouse kick, his boot landing at the small of the other man's back. The killer hurtled across the room to slam into a kitchen sink.

"You doing all right, mate?" McCarter inquired.

James glimpsed the Briton in the doorway. He nodded and turned his attention to the dazed hardman. The assassin slumped across the sink, apparently semiconscious. James reached for a pair of handcuffs at the small of his back as he advanced.

A figure appeared from the next room. McCarter swung the Browning toward the shape, recognized Encizo and quickly pointed the gun muzzle toward the ceiling. The Cuban shoved his own Walther pistol into shoulder leather as he entered the small kitchen. He glanced at the man being cuffed by James.

"Wondered where he got to," Encizo remarked. "He was in the front room when I first entered. Sounded like there was another one with a full-auto."

"Not anymore," McCarter assured him.

"I had to take out two more in the other room," Encizo said. "At least we can question one of them. Any signs of Khurumov or his family?"

"Haven't noticed them," James replied, "but we haven't really had time to look for them, either."

"Well, I just got here," McCarter said as an explanation. "Don't look at me."

Sergei staggered into the kitchen, his face pale and eyes wide with revulsion. He clutched his stomach with one hand and covered his mouth with the other. The Phoenix Force commandos had seen that sort of reaction before. They guessed what Sergei had found.

"Where?" Encizo asked.

"Bedroom," the Russian replied, voice muffled by his hand. A gurgle in his throat announced he was about to be ill.

McCarter grabbed the distraught Sergei by the back of his collar and hauled him to the back door. The OO agent stumbled outside and nearly fell down the stairs.

"Stay out there if you're going to throw up," the Briton harshly instructed. "There might be important evidence in here, and you shouldn't puke on it."

Encizo and James headed for the front room. They soon located the adjacent bedroom and the reason Sergei had become sick to his stomach. Four bodies lay on the carpet, two male and two female. Judging from apparent age and physical characteristics, the lifeless forms had been Khurumov, his wife and mother and father-in-law. Brains still leaked from bullet-riddled skulls. The blood surrounding the corpses was fresh, bright scarlet. They had probably been murdered only a minute or two before Pheonix Force arrived.

James and Encizo had seen far more appalling sights on battlefields across the world, but they weren't immune to the effects of such a grisly discovery. Yet what truly sickened them was the knowledge they might have prevented the murders had they arrived a few minutes earlier.

"Those bastards didn't have to do this," James said with disgust. "I can almost understand taking out Khurumov, but they could have done that without killing the other three."

"Probably wanted to search the place for papers and records of Khurumov's work like the killers did at Collins's home," Encizo remarked. "That's probably why they were still here."

"At least they didn't get away with this," James commented. "But we still don't know who is behind it."

"We'll find out," Encizo assured him. "This situation could have worked out better, but it's still the first major loss for the other side."

CHAPTER TWELVE

Ural Mountains, Russia
Tuesday, 1405 hours

"Good news, Comrade," Ivan Suslev announced. "Nimeri radioed a report. He and his men have made their way inland, toward the center of Iran. They've reached Kerman with no sign anyone has followed them or suspects them of being anything more threatening than a band of traveling merchants."

Heinz Giessler nodded, but he was less pleased with the news than Suslev. The former SSD agent hadn't been as concerned about Nimeri as other teams in the field. Iran was a large, heavily populated country, but it was deficient in technology and advanced communications systems. It also suffered from a state of general confusion due to the efforts by the late Ayatollah to turn back the clock under a strict Islamic rule and the present government's attempts to reestablish more-favorable relations with the West.

Nimeri was well trained for operations within Iran, and he commanded a very good team of men. Giessler also appreciated the ability of the teams stationed in Russia and the United States, but he realized they faced a far more difficult challenge than the commandos in Iran. Giessler had yet to hear from the team in Russia, and the unit in America hadn't reported a successful termination of ACR scientists since Collins was dispatched. Volkov was the most important target on the hit list, and he had yet to be accounted for.

Giessler wasn't certain how useful Volkov could be to the Americans or even if they realized ACR technology had been employed against their spy satellites. The Americans, like the Russians, had underestimated ACR in the past and might not suspect it could have been developed to such efficiency. Still, Volkov was a potential threat to their mission. They couldn't afford any mistakes.

"Comrade?" Suslev asked. His tone revealed he had noticed the disturbed expression of Giessler's face.

"There isn't much point in calling one another 'comrade' anymore," the German told him. "Communism isn't going to rule the world. That should be clear by now. The empire we'll be part of in the future will not be a Marxist-Leninist system. Our three Arab friends aren't Communists, but the countries they wish to control are basically socialist with strong emphasis on military controls and some recognition of Islamic law. I don't think Gahiz and Kadafadem plan any major changes aside from putting themselves in charge of Iraq and Libya. Mahdi might have other plans in mind for Syria."

"But that isn't what worries you," Suslev remarked.

"This operation is a tremendous gamble. We knew the risks when we started, and now we've gone too far to go back."

"But you do believe we'll succeed," the Russian asked, "don't you?" Suslev looked at Giessler's cool features, trying to read the other man's stern expression. Giessler would have been a good poker player. His face and voice revealed little of the concerns that preyed on his mind.

"Of course I believe we'll succeed. However, many things can go wrong in a plan as bold and ambitious as this one. I will probably worry about every one of them until this business is over."

"Bukovsky is once again in good humor," Suslev said. "He's thrilled with the fact the ACR waves not only blotted out the satellite reception but also transmitted to the ships in the Persian Gulf to affect their equipment, as well. Even he didn't anticipate how well it would work."

"I know," Giessler said. "We knew from experiments the ACR would neutralize the ship radar and probably sonar, as well. The apparent malfunction of computer operation and perhaps even electronic gear in general was unexpected."

"Naturally that pleased Bukovsky because it proves his pet project was a far more effective form of technology than anyone gave it credit for. Right now he seems confident this makes us invincible."

"He's wrong," Giessler said grimly. "Eventually Bukovsky will realize this is a long way from being over. He'll start to fret and brood again. I have to keep him away from that damn vodka. Fortunately it shouldn't be necessary to use the ACR device for a while."

"Have you talked to the Arabs?"

Giessler rolled his eyes toward the plastic ceiling. Once again he wished they hadn't built such a bland and antiseptic base in the mountains. Giessler himself had seen no need for aesthetic concerns when the place was under construction, but after spending many months at the base he realized some details to making the structures visually pleasing would have made it more agreeable.

"I spoke with Gahiz and Madhi," Giessler stated. "Gahiz is delighted that Iran appears on the brink of war with the United States and possibly Russia or at least Armenia. Mahdi isn't convinced it will work. He's afraid both sides will decide the whole incident was some sort of technical mistake that got out of hand. Kadafadem didn't comment, but I suspect his attitude will be 'wait and see.'"

"How long do you think it will take for the West to start sending troops as they did during Operation Desert Storm?"

"That will depend on how the governments involved respond to the sea battle," the German answered with a shrug. "If they fail to take action as we wish, then we'll simply encourage them with another incident."

Suslev frowned. "You said we shouldn't use the ACR again too quickly after the last encounter."

"That will increase the risk to us," Giessler admitted. "If they're trying to track us, the more often we use the ACR device, the more likely they might be able to locate our base. Still, we might not have a choice. We need the backing of the Arabs, and they are impatient. A war with Iran offers a perfect distraction from other activities within the Middle East. It would allow them to carry out their revolutions and place themselves in control of Iraq, Syria and Libya."

"In theory," the Russian remarked.

"Let's hope that theory works. All our plans for regained power and influence depend on it. The plan does have a good chance of success because it requires the removal of three Arab leaders the United States and its Western allies would like to see out of power. Saddam Hussein isn't very popular even with most of the other Arab nations, let alone the West. Assad might have joined forces against Saddam during Operation Desert Storm, but the United States and Western Europe aren't likely to forget Syria's state-sponsored terrorism in the past."

"And Khaddafi?" Suslev asked.

"He's probably a more popular leader within his own country of Libya than either Assad or Saddam," Giessler replied. "But the West has tended to regard him as a villain for more than a decade. They won't mind seeing Khaddafi go, either. The fools will probably cheer when the revolutions occur and claim it to be more evidence of democracy sweeping the world. They might even receive increased foreign aid from the Americans before they realize the new regimes aren't democracies."

"I doubt the Americans are that foolish."

"Really?" the German asked with a smile. "Did you know the United States covertly supported Khaddafi's coup in 1969 when he overthrew King Idris and took control? The Americans and their Western allies supplied military and technical support to Saddam during the Iran-Iraq War . . . only to have this same weaponry used against them during the Operation Desert Storm conflict. Never underestimate the absurdity of foreign policies."

"This operation can be an incredible success if the momentum continues in our favor," Suslev said. His tone implied he might have spoken to reassure himself.

Giessler didn't comment. He was still concerned about the hit teams in the U.S. and Russia. The former was composed of a special unit of Giessler's old comrades, fellow ex-SSD agents led by Warner Muller. The other was a team of former KGB agents, commanded by a man named Markin who was a veteran of the former Soviet wet-work assassination section.

They were the best men Giessler could get for the job. Yet the other side would respond with their best people if they realized what was going on. The German schemer couldn't shake a nagging concern—would their best people be better than his?

Cincinnati, Ohio
Tuesday, 1958 hours

TWILIGHT FELL across the downtown business center. Shadows draped the tall, monolith-style Carew Tower and the pointed dome of the Central Trust tower. Carl Lyons thought the two buildings looked as if the Empire State Building had been transplanted to Ohio, broken in half and reconstructed as a pair of buildings.

Cincinnati had once been a thriving center of business, banking and industry. It had suffered along with the rest of the Midwest in general and Ohio in particular during the economic hardships of a long recession. All things considered, the city seemed to be holding up fairly well. Many of the older buildings revealed the influence of old-world European architecture. Some even boasted Greco-Roman style pillars, seldom found in American structures less than a hundred years old. Indeed, "the Queen City" had been founded in 1819 and largely built by the swarms of European immigrants drawn to Cincinnati at the time.

Lyons and his fellow Able Team members paid little attention to the historical surroundings. They had parked their van near the old market and met Leo Turrin at Fountain Square. The little Fed nodded as the trio approached. They were surprised to see Jack Grimaldi, Stony Man's ace pilot, with Turrin.

"Hi, guys," Turrin greeted. "Have a nice drive?"

"Delightful," Rosario Blancanales replied. "I take it they told you what we found in Atlanta?"

"Yeah," Turrin said with a nod. "Tough break. Collins was the top American pro on this ACR stuff. We've been rounding up some of the lesser lights in the field."

"Collins was taken out in a classic execution style," Blancanales stated. "We're still not sure what the killers might have taken, but they definitely ripped off his private records."

"Hal told us," Turrin replied. "Well, we located two of the scientists who worked with Collins and on a separate ACR project the Navy was working on in the late eighties. We found them with little trouble and explained enough to get them to pack up their families and move to a safehouse. Some of our security people are protecting them."

"Stony Man personnel?" Schwarz asked. "Not agents pulled in from Justice or the FBI?"

"No," Grimaldi replied. "We're using our own people from the Farm for this one. Right now we can't be a hundred percent sure we can trust anybody outside Stony Man, since we don't know who's responsible. Could be renegades within the U.S. Intel outfits. Happened before."

"Yeah," Lyons agreed, "I know. So far, no trouble with the guys you rounded up?"

"It's all gone smoothly," Turrin replied. "Either we got to them before the killers could, they don't know about the ACR dudes or they're not worried about these scientists. Hate to say it, but none of these technicians were really on the cutting edge of ACR research."

"Do they know enough to help us?" Blancanales asked.

"Hey, I don't understand this ACR jazz enough to even have an opinion on that. The Bear and his magic machines back at the Farm can better answer that question. As far as we can figure, the Russian defector Volkov is probably the leading expert in the U.S."

"That's why we're here," Lyons said. "Didn't know you'd fly out ahead of us."

"They've had me flying around quite a bit over the past twenty-four hours," Grimaldi explained. "These ACR techs are scattered all over the country. Still some more out there, too."

"What about Volkov?" Schwarz asked.

"He's not home," Turrin answered. "Neighbors say they saw him and his family climb into their station wagon and take off a couple of days ago. Haven't been back since."

"That's sort of inconvenient," Lyons muttered. "Any idea where they went?"

"The neighbors say the Volkovs sometimes take camping trips. They noticed some fishing poles in the rear of the wagon, sticking out a partially opened window."

"That suggests the back of the car was probably packed pretty full," Blancanales remarked. "They might plan to be gone for a few days."

"That's what we figure," Turrin confirmed. "Supposedly they like to go to Kentucky, but the neighbors aren't sure exactly where. Said the Volkovs have a cabin there."

THE FIVE MEN were crowded in the rear of the Able Team van. The confined quarters annoyed Lyons, and he decided to move up front. A variety of equipment lined the walls of the vehicle. High-tech surveillance gear, such as laser-lock rifle microphones and Starlite scopes, was stored in the van. So were M-16 assault rifles, H&K MP-5 submachine guns and other weaponry.

Yet the most sophisticated item was a computer terminal mounted to a folding desk. Although small, it was a direct link to Stony Man Farm and Aaron Kurtzman's massive artificial intelligence complex. A fax machine and word processor were also hooked to the terminal.

Gadgets Schwarz sat at the keyboard. He was right at home with electronic devices of any sort, and computers were old friends. Schwarz punched in the access code and password. A counterpassword was required from the Stony Man HQ before he continued. These were changed frequently and revealed subtle details to the operators. He smiled when he saw the counterpassword appear on his screen.

"Chairman," he read aloud for the others. "That means the Bear keyed the response. I'm in touch with him directly, not just talking to his machines."

Schwarz could have gathered Intel from the Stony Man computers without going through Kurtzman. He wasn't intimidated by the mighty teraflops system in the Bear's lair or the fact it stored trillions of items of information, could draw in even more and summon up data faster than the "old" megaflops that handled the same functions with mere millions of items. Still, contact with Kurtzman added a personal touch.

"How's Ohio?"

The question on the screen wasn't idle chitchat. Schwarz keyed in a response.

"Didn't find what we came for. Believe Volkov is in Kentucky. Camping and fishing. May have a cabin. Owns or rents."

"Hold. I'll search."

Schwarz adjusted his eyeglasses and glanced up at the faces of Blancanales, Turrin and Grimaldi.

"How long do you figure it'll take?" Turrin asked.

The answer appeared on the screen almost as soon as Turrin asked the question.

"Volkov rented cabin 23 at Pleasant View Resort Area, along Ohio River. See maps. Good luck. Chairman."

The fax machine hummed as photocopies of two maps rolled out. One presented a road map and instructions to find the resort area. The other was a map of Pleasant View with cabin 23 circled.

"I guess that's that," Turrin remarked. "The state border isn't far from here. You guys figure you can handle this on your own?"

"Sure," Blancanales replied. "You have another job?"

"Got another ACR expert in Pennsylvania to bring in," Grimaldi said. "Probably not as important as Voklov, but the guy did work closely with Collins for more than a year. He's pretty high on the list."

"You go get your guy, and we'll find Volkov," Schwarz said. "We came this far. Might as well wrap it up."

"I just hope we get to these guys before the assassins do," Turrin commented. "That's assuming neither one of them are on the enemy side. Both scientists have wives and kids."

"That means we don't have any time to spare," Blancanales stated.

CHAPTER THIRTEEN

Stony Man Farm, Virginia
Tuesday, 2116 hours

"Well," Hal Brognola said in a weary voice, "everybody seems to be following up some sort of lead out there."

Barbara Price had just met him in his office at the basement level of Stony Man Farm. She had just spoken with Kurtzman and learned about the message from Able Team. Hopefully they would find Volkov at the cabin in Kentucky.

The stress of the assignment had taken its toll on Brognola. Price saw the lines etched into the corners of his mouth, and bags hung under eyes that had seen little sleep since the job began. She understood the incredible pressures of their occupation. They all had to make decisions and plan strategy that could possibly have global implications. Mistakes could cost not only the lives of the courageous Stony Man operatives in the field, but also possibly those of hundreds or even thousands of innocent people.

Price knew firsthand how great a burden this kind of stress could be. She also realized Brognola had to carry more than anyone else at the Farm.

"Any word from Striker?" Brognola asked.

"Not since he contacted us for evaluations of Iranian field-grade officers," Price answered. "He wants synopsis formats on the records of Iranian officers who are well educated, political moderates and not fanatics toward the West or militant Muslims opposed to everybody who isn't a Shiite. If the guy speaks fluent English it would be a nice plus, but Mack can get a translator from NSA if necessary."

"Sounds like he wants to meet with the officer," Brognola said. "I don't know how the hell he plans to manage that. The U.S. State Department hasn't had much luck trying to establish diplomatic contact with the Iranians at this point."

"They're probably not willing to take the risks Striker will accept in order to meet with the guy," Price said. "Assuming we can find someone who fits the profile he's looking for. The problem isn't that Iran is filled with fanatics. The general public might have the mistaken concept that's true, but of course that's because they've been bombarded by a lot of negative images of Iran since 1979."

"Yeah," Brognola added. "It didn't help that the Ayatollah wanted to present the impression that every single Iranian was a frothing-at-the-mouth fanatic, eager to kill or be killed in a holy war against 'the Great Satan' of the United States."

"Iranians are actually pretty much like people anywhere else, and the majority aren't extremists," Price continued. "Trouble is, a lot of the higher-ranking military personnel *are* extremists or at least pretend they are in order to remain in good standing."

"Aaron's computers are the top-of-the-line, state-of-the-art, high-tech...gizmos," Brognola muttered.

"With trillions of details in those data banks and more coming in all the time, I would have thought he could come up with an answer by now."

"No computer can look inside somebody's head to know what that person really thinks or believes."

"Yeah," the big Fed agreed. "I know. You're right. Guess I'm just getting a little frustrated. I also realize the Bear is working on other matters, as well as searching for Striker's request for Mr. Perfect from Iran."

"Probably the most encouraging news we've got so far is from Phoenix Force," Price reminded him. "They did manage to take one of the assassins alive. With a little luck, he'll be able to tell them where the enemy headquarters is, and we'll be able to end this whole nightmare by going directly to the source and shutting it down."

"I sure hope you're right. One thing is certain. Nobody is better qualified to interrogate that dude than Phoenix Force."

The red phone rang and the wall screen suddenly flickered to life. The President appeared. Dressed in baggy work jeans and a short-sleeve blue denim shirt, open at the neck, the Man looked more like an Iowa farmer. He had used that "just-folks" image from time to time during his campaign. Brognola found it annoying because it obviously wasn't true. Nobody became President of the United States by being just like everybody else, and it had been an insult to the intelligence of the American people to present that impression.

Brognola dismissed these notions. The President wasn't running for office and dressed in a casual manner to try to be more comfortable. He wasn't trying to impress Brognola with a phony image. By now the man in the Oval Office knew that would be a waste of time. In fact, the President spoke quite bluntly and to the point.

"I've heard from CIA in both Turkey and Russia," he stated without any preamble of polite greeting. "They're not very happy with your people. Aren't they supposed to be working with your men in the field?"

"Actually they're working for my people. My guys are in charge, and the Company can just lump it if they don't like it. Stony Man personnel have White House authority. That means we got it from you, sir."

"Is there a reason CIA is being kept in the dark?"

"If that's what my guys are doing, there must be a reason for it. What's the Company's problem? Don't tell me a Phoenix Force member with a British accent lost his temper and punched a CIA case officer in the mouth again."

He recalled the previous occasion when McCarter had knocked out a Company man. Brognola thought he would never hear the end of it.

"No," the President replied, "not yet at least. By the way, I heard about that incident. You are sure that Briton is reliable?"

"He just doesn't handle bull very well. Put him in a high-stress or combat situation and he's solid gold. Still, he's no diplomat and doesn't suffer fools gladly. That's sort of a problem because apparently this new Russian Intel outfit known as the OO is full of fools and amateurs."

"We're not responsible for what the Russians do. Your people will simply have to try their best to work with the OO, and your friend from England had better keep his temper in check.''

"As far as I know, he has so far," Brognola replied. "Does CIA have any other beef besides the fact we don't share enough?''

"A gun battle occurred in the town of Ustinov. A scientist and some family members are dead, along with three or four unidentified persons.''

The President reached for some notes on his desk. Brognola saved him the trouble of checking information.

"I know about it, sir. You're right if you think Phoenix Force was involved. They arrived too late to save the scientist, Khurumov, but they did prevent the killers from getting away.''

"The scientist is still dead.''

"He probably wouldn't be if OO was less reluctant to do anything other than fret about looking like the KGB.''

"Or if Phoenix Force cooperated with CIA.''

"The Company wouldn't have sent anybody to Ustinov under those circumstances, and we both know it. They'd still be debating which form to fill out and who they could blame it on if things didn't work out.''

"Your people didn't report to them.''

"They reported to me. That's what matters. If CIA needed to know or could have helped, they would have been contacted.''

"Don't they trust the CIA?''

"Does anyone?''

The President didn't appear to appreciate the remark, but he didn't argue. "What about this business in Turkey?'' he asked. "Why is your man there trying to contact a high-ranking member of the Iranian military?''

''Trying to determine what's going on with that sea battle in the gulf,'' Brognola answered. ''And that CIA case officer in Ankara would do better if he spent more time helping Striker than lodging these official complaints. This is just wasting time, sir.''

''I have to rely on the CIA, NSA and other Intelligence networks for information because you aren't keeping me posted as often as I need to be.''

''If we had any real progress, I'd let you know,'' Brognola assured him. ''There's not much point contacting you with every minor setback or to tell you about a situation that looks promising but might not pan out.''

''You admit there have been setbacks?''

''Of course. There usually are. My people are the best in the business. Look at our track record, including some previous missions we handled under the previous administration that I know you're now aware of, and you know we're the best.''

''I appreciate that, Hal.'' The President seemed sincere. ''That's why I hoped for more results by now.''

''We're doing better than anybody else so far,'' the big Fed replied, ''including those crybabies in the CIA. We're dealing with opponents who are still virtually invisible. Now, we might have some breakthroughs fairly soon.''

''How soon?''

''Could be a matter of hours,'' Brognola answered. ''Could be a couple of days.''

''We could be at war with Iran in a matter of days.''

"That might be a very tragic mistake, Mr. President. We think it's possible, in fact probable, Iran isn't responsible."

"Iranian ships attacked our Navy in the gulf. Do you know I have advisers who want us to retaliate with bombs and missiles?"

"I'd suggest you get rid of those advisers. Sounds to me like they're too trigger-happy for the job."

"The Iranian government is blaming us for the attack. They're also claiming Armenia, and thus the CIS and Russia, have joined forces against them. There's a good chance Iran might declare war even if we don't."

"The Ayatollah did that a couple times, and Ronald Reagan just shrugged it off. Iran isn't capable of waging war against the United States or the Commonwealth of Independent States, let alone trying to fight us both at the same time."

"They might be able to if they've perfected ACR technology to the level suggested by the sea battle. We discussed how crippling this could be to our defenses."

"Yes, sir," Brognola replied. "But I don't think they've got it. We're trying to bring in the top expert on ACR who isn't listed as deceased. We already have some others tucked away in safe places and guarded around the clock. If Justice and FBI complain, tough luck because we're doing this with our own people to avoid possible leaks in security."

"What about in Russia and Turkey?"

"That business in Russia might have a positive side, and they're checking out a possible lead now. CIA and NSA in Turkey might be bent out of shape, but Striker knows what he's doing. With the ACR assaults on spy satellites, our high-tech sources are unreliable, and there aren't enough human Intelligence sources working for the U.S. inside Iran to give us needed data. Striker is just taking a direct approach. He usually does."

"If he manages to establish contact and arrange a meeting," the President said, "he could be walking into a trap."

"I'm sure he's considered that, sir."

"If he's killed or captured, we won't be able to do anything to help him."

"If he's killed, there won't be much to do," the Fed replied. "And he knows the risks if he gets captured. He wouldn't expect any help if that happens."

"Your people wouldn't try to rescue him?" the President asked.

Stony Man wasn't supposed to take on independent operations. Brognola knew what he should say to reassure the man in the Oval office that the outfit would function as designed. Yet the big Fed knew his face might betray the truth. Stony Man wouldn't allow Mack Bolan to be a prisoner if there was a chance he could be saved.

"That's not likely to happen. Striker wouldn't be taken easily. He wouldn't surrender. More likely they'd have to kill him. A hell of a lot of people have tried to kill that man in the past. Most paid for their failure with their lives."

"A clandestine meeting with an Iranian official could be an embarrassment if the effort became public knowledge."

"Your administration would be embarrassed by an effort to find out whether war might be justified?"

Brognola asked. "That doesn't make much sense to me. Doesn't matter. You know how tight security is with Stony Man. It has to be for a small group like ours to be successful."

"Even the possibility of war isn't as serious a threat as that posed to our national security by the ACR device in the hands of whatever hostile force currently has it."

"We've discussed the possible threats before, Mr. President."

"And they're even more serious than we imagined. My experts on the Strategic Defense Initiative tell me that not only does the possibility of ACR beam assaults render future plans to set up SDI as unfeasible, but it could also supply the enemy with a weapon. Since the ACR seems to actually reflect off other radar cones, the massive radar dishes on the proposed SDI spacecraft could magnify the ACR waves and redirect them at whatever earthbound target the enemy might select."

Brognola didn't see fretting about possible effects on SDI. The system didn't even exist beyond theory. Yet there was enormous danger to systems that already were in full operation, systems vital to the protection of the United States and most of the world, as well.

SDI might be a pet project for the future to the administration and the Pentagon, but Brognola was more concerned about what they faced in the present.

"We appreciate the importance of the mission, Mr. President," the big Fed assured him. "They're all important. As for CIA, I'll be concerned with their opinion when they can show they get better results than we do."

"They haven't so far," the President admitted. "We'll try to keep the hawks from pushing us into war with Iran as long as possible. But we need results, Hal. We need some answers, and we need them soon."

AARON KURTZMAN STARED at his computer screen. An animated satellite hung above a mass of simulated terrain, blue-green water and cartoon ships. The Bear's fingers danced across a keyboard as he watched white dotted lights descend from the satellite to the vessels.

Brognola and Price were stunned by the display. The computer graphics were such high quality, at first glance the images appeared to be three-dimensional. They marveled at the precise detail of the animation. The computer had produced the images on the screen according to exhaustive data programmed by the Bear. Everything was according to scale except selected features Kurtzman had magnified to observe at closer angles.

The satellite slowly revolved like a metallic basketball. Brognola noticed the camera mounts, radio antennae, radar cups and laser scopes on the animated sphere. Kurtzman barely glanced at the pair, but smiled with satisfaction at the expressions they wore.

"You like it?" he inquired.

"Yeah," Brognola replied, "but I'm not sure what it is."

"Computer graphic simulation of the sea battle that occurred between the U.S. and Iranian vessels. It's based on the information we've been able to gather about the incident, right down to the air temperature and the direction the waves were flowing when the conflict took place."

"I'm impressed," Price admitted. "But how does this help us?"

"I was wondering the same thing," Brognola added. "This might be a nifty video game you could market if Stony Man goes out of business, but I don't see how this will tell us how the sea battle got started."

"If that's what you're looking for," Kurtzman replied, "I guess you'll be disappointed. But I also programmed in everything we've been able to gather about aggressive concentrated radar. The computers analyzed the information and the details about the positions of the satellites and ships during the conflict. Now, watch this."

He punched some keys, and a pale yellow wave of light descended from the satellite to the simulated area of the Persian Gulf. Thin strands of broken white light extended like blinking tentacles to link the space sphere with the ships below.

"Okay," the Bear began, "this is the area covered by the reflected beam of the ACR wave. The white lights reveal targets affected by it. Radar, sonar and so forth aboard the ships. I included the Iranian vessels because all evidence suggests they suffered the same effects as the American ships. You can see that a large area was covered. This is based not only on reports by the crews of the ships, but also tracking stations, radio reception and other communications affected during the incident."

Brognola stepped closer, still impressed by the display. Yet it didn't seem to add to what they already knew. He was confident Kurtzman wouldn't go to this much trouble unless there was a good reason.

"Let's see the rest," he declared.

"You bet," the Bear replied. "Based on what we know about ACR, it has a great range for effective use but it isn't infinite. Now, using the data, we extrapolate to determine the area from which the ACR beams came from."

The screen changed once more as the pale light expanded. A graph blinked on in the lower right-hand corner. It explained that the area of possible origin extended from eastern Turkey, much of Russia and the former Soviet Union to include virtually all of the Middle East and part of the northeast tip of Africa. Brognola uttered a deep sigh.

"Doesn't really cut it down to a tiny area," Price commented. "That's still an awful lot of territory."

"Well," Brognola said, "I guess it does exclude the rest of the world. At least we don't have to look for the enemy base in Central America or mainland China. Australia is pretty well ruled out, too."

"Cuts it down a little more than that," Kurtzman insisted. "Don't forget, ACR is basically a variation of standard radar. Now, radar works best from an elevated position. That suggests they're probably based at a mountain range."

The screen transformed to a detailed map of the area selected by the computer. Bright orange lights illuminated mountain regions. These included large strips of Russia and CIS territory, parts of northern Iraq, Turkey, western Saudi Arabia, portions of Iran and some clusters in Lebanon, Syria and Jordan.

"Congratulations, Aaron," Brognola said. "You've managed to whittle it down a bit more. I don't suppose we can reduce the selection any further?"

"Well, that depends. If we're right and Iran isn't responsible, it's unlikely these guys have their base in that country. Apparently they want to push Iran into war with the U.S. and maybe the CIS, as well. That means they'd have to be suicidal to hang around in a country that could get the hell shot out of it. The same would probably be true about the smaller Arab countries along the gulf. Bahrain, Qatar, the UAE and Kuwait could get shelled just due to geography. Besides, you don't see too many lights on those countries. Not much mountain range on any of those places except Oman. Right offhand, just based on what seems logical from what we know, I'd say the areas at the outer perimeter of the possible origin section are unlikely. Areas like northeast Africa, the outer east portions of the CIS countries and probably Yemen and Turkey."

"Yeah," Brognola agreed. "You wouldn't get out to the limits of the range of the ACR beams if you wanted to use it with precise accuracy."

"That still leaves sections of Russia, other former Soviet states in the CIS, Iraq, Syria, Jordan, Saudi Arabia and Lebanon," Price commented, studying the map. "Searching that much terrain won't be easy. That's also assuming they can't just close down shop, carry the ACR gear downhill, load it on a truck and head for another location."

"Aw, geez," Brognola muttered. "Did you have to say that?"

"Well, she has a point," Kurtzman said. "Whoever is doing this has obviously taken ACR beyond anything that was previously accomplished with this technology. Unfortunately neither I nor the computers have been able to determine exactly what that would require. Does it need a bigger dish? Lots of bulky amplifiers that would have to remain stationary, or could more compact items work just as well? Does it need a constant source of energy and how great? An advanced model might require a hydroelectrical generator powerful enough to run a small town, or maybe it could run on a couple of dozen car batteries. We just don't know."

"And the computers can't make any intelligent guesses based on what we have?" Brognola asked.

"There isn't much on file because everybody pretty much gave up on ACR," the Bear explained. "Somebody seems to have taken it further by using imagination. Computers aren't so great when it comes to imagination. You need human minds for that."

"So what's wrong with your imagination, Aaron?" Price asked.

"Not a thing," Kurtzman assured her. "I can imagine them making lap-top ACR devices that will fit inside suitcases or needing radar dishes as big as Yankee Stadium. I can conjure up sci-fi theories that have them bouncing ACR off the face of the moon. Trouble is, none of that helps. What we need is the imagination of somebody who has actually worked on this stuff and has an educated, logical idea based on real experience to know what's most likely to be the advanced form of ACR we're dealing with."

"We need Volkov," Brognola said. "Assuming he's not working for the enemy."

"I talked with Able Team recently," the Bear announced. "They're on their way to Kentucky to find Volkov. Hopefully he'll be there. Leo and Jack are off to the Keystone State to look up another scientist. I think the guy's name is Mead, but I'm not sure. The stuff we've been able to get from the technicians at the safehouses hasn't been much help so far. They just don't seem to know anything we haven't already found out from the limited sources on ACR that were available to us."

"I'll contact Striker and Phoenix to let them know what we've got so far," Brognola said. "They're already in the general area where the enemy base is probably located. Maybe that will help them find the base if they have an idea where it might be."

"That's still close to a hundred mountain ranges scattered over a very large area," Price said as she glanced at the map. "If they're based in the mountains in Syria or Iraq, it's going to be tough."

"Everything's tough these days," Brognola commented. "Have you come up with an Iranian field grade for Mack yet?"

"Actually Fell selected a guy based on NSA data," Kurtzman answered. "I patched through to the computers in Mountain Balloon to cross-check the officer based on what we have in the banks. To be honest, it isn't easy to evaluate military personnel in a place like Iran. The guy seems to be about as good as we can hope for."

Kurtzman rolled his chair to a wire basket and glanced through a printout sheet. "Yeah," he said. "The man's name is Lieutenant-Colonel Mohammed Sabzeh. Partially educated in England and attended some military schools and training in the United States back in the late sixties when America was still on good terms with Iran."

"Back when the Shah ran the country," Price added. "And the United States supported him, regardless of how he treated his people."

"Uncle Sam has made some mistakes in the past," Brognola remarked. "Too late to change them now. Any idea if this lieutenant colonel is a genuine moderate or if this is some wishful thinking?"

"I couldn't come up with anybody who sounds better, and neither could the NSA," Kurtzman replied. "I just hope we've got a good choice here and NSA can manage a meeting. You know Striker said he'd be willing to meet the guy in the Persian Gulf, even on Iranian turf."

"I know," Brognola confirmed. "I guess he wants them to know he's serious. I sure hope he doesn't wind up seriously dead."

CHAPTER FOURTEEN

Persian Gulf, Iranian waters
Wednesday, 0403 hours

The helicopter hovered through the dark, predawn sky. Stan Fell was a nervous passenger, seated next to Mack Bolan as the Executioner piloted the chopper. The NSA case officer didn't talk much, aware that the mysterious warrior needed to concentrate on the controls.

Although he had logged fewer hours in a helicopter than Jack Grimaldi or David McCarter, Bolan was more than competent as a pilot. He operated the cyclic and collective controls, working the rudders simultaneously with his feet. Bolan glanced at the windscreen, but saw the oil derricks along the coast.

"The flat platform is the improvised helipad," Fell explained. "This is where we're supposed to meet Colonel Sabzeh."

Bolan could barely hear him above the bellow of the great rotor blades. He guessed what the NSA man said, already recognizing the rendezvous site based on previous description. The warrior probably could have found it on his own, but Fell had insisted on coming because he knew the area from years of recon operations.

The NSA and CIA had worked together with uncharacteristic cooperation to help set up the meeting.

Through informants within Iran, they knew where to contact Sabzeh. They had first established radio contact. The colonel had spoken with Bolan, clearly suspicious of the reasons for the conversation. He was surprised the American had insisted on a face-to-face meeting. When the warrior had explained this wasn't something he could discuss on radio, the site was agreed on and Sabzeh gave him the time.

Although the helicopter was an American-made Bell, it had been purchased by the Turkish military and bore the colors of that country. Sabzeh had managed to get clearance for the craft to safely pass through Iranian airspace to the derricks by the coast. Bolan appreciated the risk, but also realized the Iranians had little reason to blast him out of the sky. It was clear he had come for diplomatic reasons, not to launch an attack.

The greatest risk was the possibility they might try to take him hostage. The Executioner was armed for that reason. He carried the Beretta 93-R in shoulder leather and the big .44 Magnum Desert Eagle on his hips. He also packed some grenades and spare magazines for the pistols. If they tried to take him prisoner, the warrior wouldn't surrender. He would attempt to shoot his way out of the trap and flee by any means possible—in the helicopter, diving to the sea of running for cover inland. None of which offered much hope, and Bolan would almost certainly be killed if they ambushed him under circumstances that stacked the odds in the favor of the Iranians.

He applied gradual downward pressure on the collective control as the chopper hovered about the platform, and it began to descend. Fell sat tensely, eyes wide as he stared out at the figures that appeared along a bridge to the platform.

"Somebody's coming," he said, his voice barely a whisper.

Bolan didn't hear him, but had also noticed the reception committee. The aircraft touched down, and he pushed the collective to complete the landing. The soldier unbuckled his safety harness, opened the door and climbed from the chopper. The powerful air current of the still-whirling rotor blades assaulted Bolan's ears and tugged at hair and clothing. He didn't bother to duck his head or bend low, aware that the rotor churned more than a yard above his head and offered no threat of decapitation.

He marched toward the three figures at the bridge.

LIEUTENANT COLONEL Mohammed Sabzeh watched the tall stranger approach. A veteran military man, he noticed Bolan's fine-tuned balance in his stride. This was a fighting man, Sabzeh realized, not a diplomat. One of the colonel's aides saw that the Executioner was armed and unslung an assault rifle from his shoulder. The colonel barked an order in curt Farsi, and the trooper slid the strap back on his shoulder.

"Welcome," the Iranian officer said. "You're Belasko?"

"That's right, Colonel. I recognize you from the photos in your file."

Yet those pictures hadn't revealed the commanding presence of the man. Although a head shorter than Bolan, the Iranian seemed taller due to his ramrod posture. His fatigue uniform was clean and recently pressed, the boots polished but not highly shined.

Sabzeh hadn't come to stand review. He wore black rank emblems, not flashy metal. The officer's lean face was stern, but not hardened into a stony mask. The dark eyes were alert, intelligent. Nothing about him suggested the man was a fanatic of any sort. Bolan knew a fellow soldier when he saw one.

"You have an advantage there, Mr. Belasko," Sabzeh replied, his English an odd combination of Cambridge British and American Midwest with a slight guttural accent. "My men are a little concerned because you came armed."

"So did you," Bolan observed, glancing at the colonel's gun belt and side arm. "So did they."

Sabzeh smiled and nodded. He understood a warrior never went anywhere unarmed if possible. As a military man, he understood pistols were regarded as defensive weapons and didn't see Bolan's actions as aggressive. The grenades were a different matter, but Sabzeh realized they might have been brought as an emergency weapon.

"You've come in peace?" Sabzeh asked.

"If I hadn't, you'd know it by now," the Executioner replied. "And you realize I could have mounted a machine gun or rocket launcher on the helicopter. This platform could have been reduced to a heap of splinters with your three corpses splattered all over the wreckage before we got close to landing here."

Sabzeh nodded again. "Why did your Navy attack our ships?" he asked. "Are you going to explain that? Why has your government decided on these acts of aggression?"

"My country didn't start the sea battle," Bolan replied.

"Of course that's what you'd say. Most probably what you believe. I understand that, Mr. Belasko. Did you think you could convince me my country is responsible because I've spent some time in the West? Your American military schools didn't make me less Iranian. I am still a Shiite Muslim and still loyal to my country."

"That's fine with me, Colonel," Bolan replied. "If you care about your country, you won't want it to go to war because an ambitious and ruthless syndicate is trying to force Iran into such a conflict."

"A syndicate?" Sabzeh raised his eyebrows. "You mean like the Mafia? I remember those movies and TV shows where the 'boys from the syndicate' were trying to 'rub each other out.' I'm disappointed. I would expect a more logical, believable story from a man who went to such trouble, accepted such danger, for this meeting."

"The fact it seems unlikely is one of reasons they could succeed," the warrior explained. "They aren't the mafia or any kind of criminal organization in the usual sense of organized crime. We're not certain who they are yet, but we know they're well-organized, large enough to operate in more than one country simultaneously and they have advanced technology. Radar, sonar and some electronic functions on our ships failed to perform properly during that sea battle. Did the same happen to the Iranian vessels?"

Sabzeh glanced down at the boardwalk. "I am astonished that you would tell me this happened to your Navy," he remarked. "Isn't this betraying a confidence of American national security? Perhaps you just told me these lies to try to lure me into revealing

Iranian strengths and weaknesses for your military to exploit in the future."

"I'm telling you the truth. One soldier to another. Face-to-face and without the bull politicians, diplomats and bureaucrats always use. That's why I wanted to meet you in person. We've both been in wars. We know what war really is. The parades and the slogans try to hide the face of war. They can pretend war is glorious, patriotic or the will of God, but we know it's hell on earth. We've seen our closest comrades killed in front of us, and bloodied, butchered remains on the battlefield. We've seen war slaughter civilians who were just in the wrong place at the wrong time."

"Yet war is the duty of a soldier," the colonel stated.

"Sometimes war can't be avoided, but I think we can stop this one before it starts. Look, Colonel. We're talking bluntly here, so I won't pull punches. The United States can take Iran, and we both know it. Your country fought Iraq for eight years and couldn't beat them. You know how long it took the U.S. and her allies to defeat Saddam Hussein's military."

"So my country would have more to lose than yours," Sabzeh said in a quiet voice. "I know that's true, and I don't want Iran to go to war. Not against the United States, Armenia, Russia or any other country. We have suffered enough."

"I know," Bolan replied. "Iran suffered under the rule of a dictator who called himself the Shah. His SAVAK secret police used tactics similar to those of Hitler's Gestapo."

"I'm surprised you admit this," Sabzeh said. "Your country supported the Shah because he was anti-Communist. America helped build the Shah's army, supply his forces with weapons and remain in power for decades."

"I don't make foreign policy and I don't always agree with what Washington does," Bolan replied. "How about you, Colonel? Did you approve of taking those Americans from the U.S. Embassy in Tehran and holding them hostage for more than a year? Did you think it was any better when the Ayatollah's goons dragged Iranian civilians into political prisons to be locked up, tortured or executed? Or did that only bother you when SAVAK did those things?"

"No," the Iranian officer admitted, "I didn't approve of any of those things. Like you, I didn't make those decisions or have any part in such atrocities."

"We wouldn't be talking if you had," Bolan assured him. "I don't do business with butchers, regardless of what nationality they might be. All I want from you is a little information, Colonel."

"I can't jeopardize Iran's national security by telling you whether the equipment aboard our ships malfunctioned."

"You don't have to," the warrior replied. "The fact you won't answer the question tells me the same thing happened to your ships as happened to ours. It also tells me you don't want to lie to me, Colonel."

"We soldiers aren't much for bull," Sabzeh said with a smile. "What do you want to know, Mr. Belasko?"

"Some of the sailors aboard the USS *Grover Cleveland* reported sighting a fishing boat in the immediate area shortly before the battle occurred," Bolan began. "It might be a long shot, but I think the enemy—the real enemy—could have been on the boat."

"You think a small fishing boat could attack battleships?"

"An unexpected attack by a vessel hardly anyone paid attention to. All they'd have to do is launch a couple of rounds at both U.S. and Iranian ships. They could do that with a hand-held rocket launcher like an RPG. Then they could just let the battleships start firing at each other."

"How could they be certain such a tactic would work?" the colonel asked.

"If they knew the radar, sonar and other high-tech gear wouldn't function," Bolan replied, "they could be certain our ships would start shooting at each other. There's still so much distrust and resentment between Americans and Iranians it was guaranteed nobody would hesitate. Both sides would react just as our enemies wanted them to."

Sabzeh nodded. "You're right. I can see how that could happen. How do we change these attitudes?"

"A little bit at a time," Bolan answered. "It's too much to expect everybody to just admit both sides have been wrong in the past and simply forgive and forget overnight. Let's take care of one problem at a time, Colonel. That fishing boat must have headed for the Iranian coast. They probably abandoned it and headed inland on foot."

"So you want us to find it." Sabzeh wasn't asking a question. "It might contain evidence to support this theory. They would have certainly taken their weapons or thrown them in the sea, but in their haste they might have overlooked something. Correct?"

"We can hope," Bolan replied. "If we're real lucky, they might even leave a trail. Don't count on it. Whoever these people are, they don't make many mistakes."

"Everyone makes mistakes."

"Yeah. They've made a couple already, and we're trying to make the most of that. We still can use all the help we can get."

"I'll see what I can do, Mr. Belasko," Sabzeh assured him. "A pity our leaders don't talk like this. Maybe it would be a better world if nations were run by men with the hearts of warriors rather than politicians who make their trade by lies and manipulation."

"One problem at a time, Colonel," the Executioner replied.

They exchanged curt farewells. Bolan returned to the helicopter. Fell remained inside, his face pale with tension. The meeting was over, and the NSA man uttered a long sigh of relief. Bolan slid into the pilot's seat. The chopper faced the wind so the takeoff would be easy. The warrior reached between his knees for the cyclic control.

"How did it go?" Fell asked.

"Promising."

Bolan raised the collective control, and the rotor blades increased speed. As the chopper rose, Bolan glanced at the platform. Colonel Sabzeh and his companions were gone.

Moscow, Russia
Wednesday, 0510 hours

CALVIN JAMES SLUMPED into a leather armchair. He was clearly exhausted and frustrated. Major Fedeyev offered him a cup of tea. The Afro-American commando hated the drink, but reluctantly accepted because there was no coffee in the office of the case officer.

Yakov Katzenelenbogen shook a Camel cigarette from a soft-sided pack. He caught it between the hooks of his prosthesis, holding it to his lips as he fired up a lighter. Fedeyev was impressed by the dexterity exhibited by the Israeli with the artificial limb, unaware Katz had lost his right arm decades ago and had fully adjusted to his disability.

The Phoenix Force commander felt as tired as James. Both men had spent most of the night interrogating the surviving member of the hit team that had murdered Khurumov and his family at Ustinov. James had administered scopolamine, and Katz questioned the man in Russian. The results had been unsuccessful. Katz had spoken to him in French and German, but the subject didn't seem to understand either language.

They had subjected the prisoner to a second dose of truth serum. Katz was convinced the man understood Russian and probably spoke it as his native language, yet he answered only a few questions. The subject babbled some slurred sentences in a language Katz didn't understand. James checked the prisoner's heart and blood pressure. He decided the drug might place too great a strain on the subject if they used it a third time.

"Scopolamine is supposed to be the most effective form of truth serum," Fedeyev remarked, "and you said you'd used it many times in the past."

"And it usually works," James replied. "This guy has been programmed to resist it. That's not easy to do.

I'd say he's undergone extensive sessions to create a condition in his subconscious that would throw him into a trance so he'd do nothing but spit out useless information in whatever language he was speaking.''

"Our linguists studied the tapes,'' the major stated. "They tell me the man is speaking an obscure Altaic dialect, probably a tongue spoken in some remote areas of Turkmen.''

"Turkmen?'' James asked. "Where's that? Part of Turkey?''

"It's a CIS nation,'' the major replied, "another former state of the Soviet Union. It isn't part of Turkey, but many people there speak Turkish or similar Altaic tongues.''

"But this isn't the prisoner's native language?'' Katz inquired.

"Our linguistic personnel don't think so,'' Fedeyev answered. "In fact, they say his accent suggests Russian is his first language. Although they haven't been able to translate or even identify the Altaic dialect, they did notice he's repeating the same sentences over and over.''

"Cute,'' James commented. "They drummed this stuff into the guy's subconscious by hypnosis. Probably doesn't even know what those words mean. Then they conditioned him to go into a posthypnotic trance if scopolamine or any other truth serum was used.''

"Why?'' Fedeyev asked. "And who could have done this posthypnotic conditioning?''

"I think you know the answer to those questions even if you don't want to admit it,'' Katz replied with a sigh. "The reason he was conditioned in this manner was to prevent him from telling any secret information if truth serum was used. The obscure peasant language is supposed to give the impression the man isn't Russian, and the difficulty of breaking the language barrier would discourage anyone from continuing interrogation with drugs because it would appear to be hopeless. Scopolamine and other truth serums work best when you interrogate a subject in his native tongue."

"And you also think you know who did it?" the OO officer asked with a frown.

"Of course I do," Katz stated. "The KGB did it. This sort of conditioning is very sophisticated. Only a few experts in chemical-questioning procedures and advanced hypnosis could accomplish this. KGB was able to do this sort of thing. We've seen it in the past."

"Yeah," James added. "The guy was probably programmed years ago, during the nasty old days of the cold war. The dude was almost certainly a field operative for the KGB. Probably got some pretty hairy assignments, too. They wouldn't have gone to so much effort unless they figured he might be captured and given truth serum. That means he must have had a high-risk MOS, man."

"MOS?" Fedeyev asked, unfamiliar with the term.

"Military Occupational Speciality," James explained. "KGB might not have been regular military, but you catch my meaning."

"Since he and his chums had been sent to murder Khurumov and the others in the apartment in Ustinov," Katz said, "I'd say there's a good possibility our prisoner used to be with a wet-work team."

Major Fedeyev appeared uncomfortable with this subject. Although his organization had not been responsible for the infamous assassination units, the fact these things had occurred under a Soviet Intelligence agency was an embarrassing legacy for the OO.

"How do we find out if you're correct?" he asked. "Perhaps we should give him a third injection of truth serum."

"No way," James insisted. "Scopolamine is a dangerous drug if it isn't used in precise doses. Another injection could kill him. I won't take that chance and I won't let anyone else take it, either."

"You seem oddly concerned about the life of a murderer," Fedeyev remarked.

"That's because I'm not a murderer," James replied. "You can wait for a trial and carry out whatever justice you use here, but not while the man is under my care. He's sort of my patient right now. Nobody kills one of my patients."

"He's quite serious, Major," Katz added. "I'm afraid we aren't going to get much information out of the prisoner at this time."

A knock at the door interrupted the conversation. Fedeyev unlocked it to find Gary Manning in the hall. He let the big Canadian enter and locked the door.

Although Manning hadn't slept and he had been almost as busy as James and Katz, he didn't appear tired. The Canadian commando had vast reserves of energy that allowed him remarkable stamina. He seemed able to pace himself for any long-term task. Manning carried a folder in one hand and a coffee mug in the other.

"Hey," James began when he saw the cup, "you got coffee in there?"

"What else?" the Canadian replied with a shrug. He turned to Katz. "I have results of the medical examiner—or whatever they call him here—on those dead assassins from Ustinov."

"We know how they died," Fedeyev remarked. "Your friends killed them in self-defense. The bullet holes should make that obvious."

"Two were shot and one was killed with a knife," Manning corrected. "That's not what we wanted to find out. They hoped to get information that might help identify the killers."

"Excuse me," James said. "Coffee?"

"The fingerprints had been surgically altered," Manning continued. "The scar tissue prevents definite ID. Of course, that suggests they were either intelligence operatives in high-risk positions or members of an unusually sophisticated criminal organization."

"Or both," Katz said. "What about dental records?"

"Nothing definite so far," Manning replied. "All three had steel fillings. That's pretty uncommon dental work outside of Russia and other CIS nations. However, it's done here quite often."

"More evidence these men were KGB," Katz remarked.

"That's what I figured, too," the Canadian agreed. "Now, one of the men also had two silver fillings. The examiner thinks this might have been done in another country. Maybe Europe. They'd also had some plastic surgery done. Alterations at the nose and mouth. A chin clipped slightly or ears trimmed. Minor changes done to alter appearance. One guy had gray hair at his temples that turned out to be dyed to give him an older appearance, as well."

"I sure would like a cup of coffee," James stated.

"So go get some," Manning told him. "Of course, even with the cosmetic changes, we still had information to work with. We figured these guys were KGB or something like that. We could also determine approximately how old they were, body build, height and weight would be about the same, and there were also old scars. One had a bullet wound. I mean an old bullet wound that appeared to be from a small-caliber handgun. Another had a fair amount of scar tissue on his right leg that probably occurred from a fire when he was young."

"So you had enough to identify them?" Fedeyev asked.

"We ran a computer scan on the information available," Manning answered. "We figured we'd start with KGB and GRU, since that seemed most likely. I also figured we might be looking for former Soviet Intel personnel who might have vanished over the past few years, agents who left the country when communism fell or before it happened when the handwriting of *glasnost* was on the wall. Anyway, we came up with some candidates."

"Uh," James prompted, "the coffee?"

"We got positive ID on the three dead men based on their physical descriptions, scars and what have you," the Canadian stated. "The plastic surgery wasn't enough to alter their appearance beyond recognition. The computer records confirmed all three had disappeared in 1991. Two guys were KGB, and the third was GRU."

"Where did you get it?" James asked.

"At the data bank center here in OO headquarters," Manning replied. "You just look for the sign on the door with data written in Russian. Now, it has that Russian *D,* like a Roman numeral for two with little hooks at the bottom. The *A* is the same as in English, but it's followed by two *H*'s, which are pronounced like the letter *N* in English...."

"I mean where did you get the coffee?" James insisted.

"That's what I'm telling you," Manning said. "They have a coffee maker in the data bank center."

"Oh," James replied. "Thanks. See you later, guys."

"I don't think the *D* in Russian resembles a Roman numeral," Fedeyev commented.

"He'll find the data center, Major," Katz said, annoyed by the interruptions.

James left the office in quest of hot coffee. Manning handed Katz the file folder, which included general information on the missing Soviet agents who were now found and identified in the morgue.

Katz glanced over the Cyrillic writing in the printout sheets. His mind had shifted to Russian, and he had to shift back to English before he spoke.

"I don't see much connection between these men," he said, "except they all spent some time working operations for the Second Chief Directororate of the KGB, handling missions out of Soviet embassies for the East European Department when those countries were still Soviet satellites. And they worked on highly classified duties in East Germany."

"You think the Germans are responsible?" Fedeyev asked.

"That seems very unlikely," Katz replied, "but there's some sort of connection here. Let's see what else it can lead to."

CHAPTER FIFTEEN

Ohio River, near Erlinger, Kentucky
Wednesday, 0210 hours

Pleasant View Resort lived up to its name. The area was peaceful and attractive. Even in the subdued light cast by the moon and stars, the setting appeared very green. Lush grass and tall evergreens surrounded the river. Able Team scanned the area in search of cabin 23.

"We should be there soon," Blancanales declared as he checked the map supplied by Kurtzman via the fax machine.

"I hope this one is up-to-date," Lyons commented. "That road map of Kentucky didn't include some of the changes in construction that meant we'd have to reroute to find this place. Should have been here two hours ago."

Blancanales knew Lyons was complaining because he was worried. The Able Team commander feared they might arrive too late to find the killers had beaten them to the site. The murder of Joshua Collins in Georgia had been bad enough, but Volkov had a wife and children. The latest update from Stony Man told them about the hit in Ustinov, Russia. The enemy didn't have any qualms about murdering innocent women or elderly men. They probably wouldn't hesitate to kill children, as well.

"We're almost there," Blancanales assured Lyons.

The Able Team captain nodded. He knew his partner was right. They could do only their best, get there as soon as possible and pray that would be good enough.

Gadgets Schwarz rode in the back of the van. He had already donned a Kevlar vest and had the protective garments ready for his companions. Schwarz loaded spare magazines for two MP-5 submachine guns and an M-16 assault rifle with a Starlite night-scope mount. Hopefully they wouldn't need the arsenal, but Schwarz was a man who believed in being prepared.

"There it is," Blancanales announced when he spotted number 23 on a door under a porch light.

"Okay," Lyons said, and turned the steering wheel to roll to the side of the road. "About time. We got enough room back there to give these folks taxi service, Gadgets?"

"Yeah. I put everything away except what I figured we might need in the immediate future."

"Hope you didn't lock up the scanner," Lyons remarked.

"I said I kept out what I figured we might need."

"Okay. Take a look and see if there's anyone suspicious hiding out in the woods."

Schwarz peered through a periscope mount. The lens at the roof of the van was equipped with special night-vision optics similar to the old NOD system, but more compact and practical. Ghostly images appeared in green and yellow, the two-tone quality of reflected light in the special lens. The scope revolved slowly to scan the surrounding area.

Lyons and Blancanales quickly donned their bullet-resistant vests. Neither man had to check his weapons. They knew their gear was ready. They attached throat mikes to stay in contact with Schwarz. Blancanales stuffed an MP-5 into a black AWOL bag. Lyons decided not to take a subgun, even concealed from view. Volkov would be rattled badly enough when they came calling at such an unexpected hour. They didn't want to scare him too much so that he refused to open the door.

If the Russian scientist and his family were still alive...

"Clear," Schwarz announced. "No sign of any big bad wolves out there."

"Let's go," Lyons announced.

He and Blancanales left the van and approached on foot. They used the same procedure as in Atlanta. The Able Team leader walked to the front of the cabin while the Hispanic tough guy headed for the back. Schwarz would remain in the rig, alert for danger and ready to back them up if needed.

"Everybody hear everybody else okay?" Lyons whispered into the mike.

The other two commandos responded in the affirmative.

Carl Lyons glanced at the station wagon parked by the cabin. It fit the description of the Volkov family car. Good, he thought. They would hate to pound on the door at 2:00 a.m. to wake up the wrong family because Volkov had changed his vacation site and the cabin was rented to someone else. Of course, a lot of people owned station wagons. . . .

He stepped onto the porch and rapped a fist on the door. Lyons moved to one side, hand near his open jacket to reach for the Colt Python in shoulder leather. He knew what Phoenix Force had encountered in Ustinov and couldn't dismiss the possibility assassins might already be inside the cabin. Unlikely but not impossible. There was no other vehicle parked close by, and the lock to the door hadn't been forced. Still, he wasn't taking any unnecessary chances.

Besides, Lyons still didn't know if Volkov was a target or an enemy. Able Team and the rest of Stony Man were concerned about the guy's wife and kids, but the fact he was a husband and father didn't mean he was innocent. It would be nice if all villains were bachelors and only associated with vermin like themselves. Unfortunately that wasn't reality.

Lyons knocked on the door harder.

"Mr. Volkov!" He called out. "Justice Department. We have to talk to you!"

He heard a child begin to cry inside the cabin and felt a twinge of guilt. The poor kid was probably terrified to be awakened by a stranger banging on the door, making demands on Daddy. Volkov and his wife were no doubt as upset as their children. Better a little rattled than dead, Lyons reminded himself.

"No sign of forced entry at back door," Blancanales's voice spoke from the earplug to Lyons's receiver unit.

"Same here," he said into the throat mike. "Stand by. I'm at the door now."

"Yeah," the Hispanic warrior replied. "I hear you."

"Still looks okay out here," Schwarz stated, letting them know there was no evidence the enemy had arrived.

Voices within the cabin were muted and whispered. Lyons heard movement, but couldn't determine if this indicated a threat or simply the family moving about. If Lyons was in Volkov's position, he'd probably try to get his wife and kids to some sort of cover, arm himself and demand the federal officer slip his identification under the door or hold it to a window. If that didn't satisfy him, Lyons figured he'd want the Fed to give the name of someone he knew who could confirm the stranger was who he claimed to be. Otherwise, the alleged federal officer at the door would have to either talk to him through the door or wait until Lyons could call friends or the police to arrive in case this was a trick. If the stranger decided to force the door, Lyons would probably blow his head off... and hope the guy didn't turn out to be an impatient Fed.

However, Volkov wasn't Carl Lyons. The door opened and Lyons peered into the round, soft face of Nikolai Volkov. The Able Team leader recognized it from a faxed photo, but the Russian was slightly paunchier, and gray streaked his black hair. The man seemed shorter than the height listed in his file. His head didn't reach Lyons's chin.

Volkov wore a bathrobe, but neither hand was in a pocket. In fact, both hands remained in clear view as the Russian looked at the stranger through red-rimmed eyes. He looked tired, and not just from lack of sleep. Volkov had the appearance of someone who wanted to be left alone and couldn't find peace regardless of how he tried to achieve it.

"I'm sorry to bother you, Mr. Volkov," Lyons said. "I know this is a very bad hour to pay a visit, but this isn't a social call."

"I am not involved in government research," Volkov stated, his English clear and precise, yet with a thick Slavic accent. "I am not working for the government in any way. Your government, the Russian government or any other. I wish you people would realize that and respect my privacy."

"Right now we're more concerned with protecting your life and the lives of your family. That's why we're bothering you at this house. You and your family are in danger."

"I can look after myself and my family."

"Sorry," Lyons replied. "I don't think so. You didn't even ask to see my ID to know if I'm really a federal agent. You opened this door like an old friend came knocking. You're lucky I'm not an assassin. You're lucky we got here before they did."

"We and they." The Russian chuckled, the bitterness in his tone revealing he wasn't amused. "I had hoped that attitude would end when the cold war was over. Have they conditioned you people so much you can't think any other way?"

"This is about ACR," Lyons explained. "You can come out here and talk to us or we can come in. You might not want your family to hear all the details."

Volkov suddenly became suspicious. He was reluctant to meet with these strangers. Although he saw only the big blond man, Lyons had referred to "we" and "us," so there were more than one of them. The Russian was uncertain what to do.

"If we intended to harm you," Lyons said softly, "you'd already be dead, Mr. Volkov."

"Kidnap perhaps," the scientist said.

"We have to move you and your family," Lyons admitted, "but we won't separate you from them. Not yet at least. Then it would only be temporary until the danger was over and the crisis passed."

Volkov hesitated a moment, turned and spoke briefly with his wife in Russian. Then he stepped outside and closed the door.

"What crisis?" he asked.

"You heard about the incident along the Iran-Armenia border and the sea battle between U.S. and Iranian ships?" Lyons asked. "Aggressive concentrated radar was apparently involved both times."

Volkov raised his thin gray eyebrows.

"Successfully?" he asked. "Against spy satellites?"

"Blanked out recon of every kind," Lyons replied. "Even put out the radar and sonar aboard ships."

"Somebody finally made it work," Volkov said, almost pleased by the news. "They thought we were wasting our time, but it really works far better than they imagined."

"Works too well," the Able Team commando admitted. "That's why we have a problem. We need your help. Most of the other experts on ACR are either dead or don't know enough to help us deal with the problem."

"Dead?" Volkov asked. "You mean in the United States or in Russia?"

"Both. At least two were assassinated. One in Atlanta, Georgia, and the other in Ustinov, Russia. Did you happen to know either Josh Collins or a guy named Khurumov? He replaced you on the Soviet ACR project after you defected.''

''I knew them both. Not very well. Khurumov assisted us on the work before I left the USSR, and your government put me with Collins for a short time. But they decided ACR was not practical because it would not function in their Stealth bomber.''

''They were both murdered. No doubt about it. Some colleagues of mine operating in Russia even caught the killers in Ustinov before the bastards could get away.''

''Who is doing this?''

''We don't know, but we figure you're on the hit list. They wasted, uh, killed, family members at Khurumov's place without hesitation, and they'll do the same if they catch up with you. We've got to get you, your wife and kids to someplace safe.''

''Is any place safe?''

''Yes,'' Lyons assured him. ''We'll protect you. Only a handful of people are involved, and we can maintain airtight security. You'll all be safe.''

''I had hoped this was all behind me,'' Volkov said sadly.

''Sorry to drag you into this, but whoever is responsible has already done that. They won't go away because we back off. It's not fair, but...''

''That's the way of the world,'' Volkov finished with a nod. ''I know that all too well. You say you have contacts in Russia. What about Bukovsky? He was the leading authority in the field.''

"He's listed as dead. Supposedly from an accident, but it could have been murder. Right now we just don't know."

"All right," Volkov began. "We'll get dressed and packed. I don't really have a choice in this matter anyway, do I?"

"Afraid not," Lyons admitted. "Between the killers stalking you and the fact we're on the brink of war with Iran that might be prevented if you help us, I'd say none of us has much of a choice."

"I suppose you're right," Volkov agreed.

He headed back into the cabin. Lyons consulted his wristwatch. It was past two-thirty in the morning. So far, everything was going fairly smoothly. He hoped it continued that way.

"You handled that very well, Carl," Blancanales's voice stated.

"I appreciate your approval. You guys ready to roll as soon as Volkov gets his family out here?"

"Heads up, guys," Schwarz warned. "We might not be able to go right away. Just spotted two cars coming down the road."

"Okay," Lyons said. "It's pretty late for folks driving around, but that doesn't mean they're a threat."

"They aren't using their headlights, and they're coming this way, slow and easy...like maybe they're looking for something."

"Doesn't sound good," Blancanales commented.

"Yeah," Lyons agreed. "Better assume the worst. Get ready just in case."

"I'll stay here," Blancanales declared. "I can cover the back and use the cabin for cover while I back you guys."

"Shit!" Schwarz hissed. "I just spotted reinforcements coming in on foot. No doubts now, fellas. These suckers are heavily armed and serious."

Lyons glanced about the shadows beyond the cabin. He didn't see any movement, but didn't doubt his partner's claim. Schwarz had the advantage of the special night scope in the van.

"How many?" Lyons asked.

"Counted ten so far," Gadgets replied, "not including however many might be in the cars. They're about five hundred yards and closing."

"From what direction?"

"Take your pick. We're surrounded."

WARNER MULLER PEERED through a pair of infrared binoculars. He watched his assault unit approach the cabin. The former SSD agent frowned. The men he had hired for the hit didn't move well in the forest terrain. They were men of the night, but familiar with sidewalks and alleys. The fools behaved as if they had never seen trees before. Muller's regular teammates had to keep coaxing the idiot Americans to use the trees for cover as they advanced.

Locating Volkov had been more difficult than Muller expected. The information supplied by Giessler was outdated, and it took Muller and his team some time to track down the Russian. They finally learned about the cabin in Kentucky. At last they had found their most important target.

Taking out Joshua Collins in Atlanta had been easy. The man had been alone, unawares and unarmed. However, there had been nothing in the dead man's records that suggested he had been involved in ACR research recently or that he knew any more about the technology than was already available to the U.S. government agencies. It probably hadn't been necessary to kill Collins, but Giessler said the man was a loose end so he had to be terminated with extreme prejudice.

However, Muller had learned the hit team in Russia had been killed or captured after taking out a target in Ustinov. He didn't know if the American authorities might present a threat, but Muller didn't intend to take any chances. Volkov had to be removed, and anyone who got in their way also had to die.

So Muller recruited some help. The SSD agent had formerly worked in the United States, had trained to pass as an American and spoke fluent English with a proper Midwest accent. That was before the party buckled under to the demands for democratic reform. East and West Germany hadn't been united, in Muller's opinion—it had been turned into a pale copy of the corrupt system in the United States.

Yet he knew the criminal elements of America and how to contact greedy, amoral men willing to do anything for a price. They had no convictions and were loyal only to money. Such men couldn't be trusted, and after the mission Muller would see to it they never talked to the authorities.

These street thugs would serve as cannon fodder if Volkov was protected. Muller didn't care how many of the Americans died during the hit. In fact, it would make his job easier when the time came to remove the survivors if there were as few of them as possible. His fellow East German agents were another matter. They were his countrymen, his comrades in dangerous operations past and present. He cared about his men and didn't want to lose any of them that night.

Of course, the SSD veterans had to supervise the hired hoodlums. The lowlife lacked training or experience. Left on their own, they would have simply charged the cabin like berserk beasts, yelling and firing their weapons in mindless frenzy. Muller hadn't given the thugs automatic weapons, which required training and practice to use properly. The stupid brutes carried handguns and shotguns instead. Only the ex-SSD personnel packed full-auto hardware, wore bullet-resistant vests and carried two-way radio units to stay in contact with Muller.

One of them relayed a message when he saw the van parked near the driveway to cabin 23. This wasn't good news. Someone had arrived ahead of Muller's unit. Lights were on inside the cabin. It was extremely unlikely a man with two young children would be up at that hour unless roused from sleep by visitors. Muller had to assume they were government agents of some sort, which meant his people had to expect trouble. Lots of it.

"Stop the car," the German told his driver. "Don't advance until I tell you to do so."

The driver obeyed. The second car, behind Muller's vehicle, also came to a halt. The German assassination leader opened a briefcase and removed a KG-99 machine pistol. He slid a fully loaded magazine into the well and jacked the first 9 mm cartridge into the chamber. A semiautomatic civilian model of an AK-47 assault rifle lay on the back seat beside Muller.

"Attention," the German said into the radio to his troops. "Those on foot, close in for detailed recon.

Remove the silencers from your weapons. We won't be able to do this quietly, and those things reduce accuracy and slow the velocity of bullets. If you see anyone outside the house, kill them. Shoot anyone at a window. No one inside or within the immediate area of the cabin can be permitted to live.''

"Must we even kill the children?" a man named Schroder inquired.

"Those are our orders," Muller insisted. "Every person there must die. No exceptions. Don't go soft. We can't afford it.''

"Why not use the grenade launcher?" another voice asked.

Muller didn't recognize the speaker, but suspected it belonged to Dieter, the agent who put together the launcher. It was an improvised device. Dieter had altered a rifle, some cartridges and powder loads to power a long, thin stick through the barrel with a pipe bomb attached to the end.

The man was eager to try his contraption, but Muller was reluctant to do so. He wasn't sure the thing would work and feared it might blow up in the hands of whoever fired it. Muller had locked the thing in the car trunk, but didn't intend to risk using it except as a last resort.

"We might need it if more federal officers arrive," he said, an explanation that ought to appease Dieter. "You can take them out with the weapons you have. They couldn't get more than six or seven men in that van. Probably less. We outnumber them and we have enough firepower to slaughter a brigade.''

The hardmen moved forward, intent on surrounding the cabin.

CHAPTER SIXTEEN

"Everybody get down and stay away from the windows!" Lyons ordered as he entered the cabin.

Volkov stared at the Able Team leader, his eyes wide and mouth open. His wife clasped a hand over her mouth, clutched her stomach with the other arm and turned away. The short, stocky woman seemed about to be ill. Their children appeared to handle the crisis more calmly, perhaps because they didn't realize how serious it was.

The kids looked at the big Colt Python in Lyons's fist. Their expressions seemed confused, as if they weren't sure if this was real or some sort of playacting like on television. Their mother gestured for the children to go to her. Daughter and son clung to Mrs. Volkov as she herded them to the bedroom.

"What happened?" the Russian asked, a tremble in his voice.

"Trouble," Lyons replied. "The assassins are here."

"My God. What do we do?"

"Are you any good with a gun?"

Volkov shook his head. "I served two years in the Soviet army. It was mandatory. Aside from some training with a rifle and such, I have no experience with firearms. My job in the military concerned electronics and radar."

"Figures," Lyons muttered, but he couldn't fault the guy for not being a soldier. At least Volkov was honest enough to admit the truth.

"I'm sorry," the Russian said sheepishly.

"It's okay. Just look after your family. We'll take care of the bad guys."

Volkov nodded and headed into the bedroom to join his wife and children. Blancanales appeared at the front entrance. He carried an M-16 tucked under one arm and a Heckler & Koch MP-5 subgun in the other hand.

"Company is getting closer," the Puerto Rican commando announced. "Better get ready."

He tossed the H&K to Lyons, who deftly caught it and holstered the Python. He joined Blancanales by the doorway as his partner handed him some extra magazines for the chopper. Lyons didn't ask about the M-16. Obviously his compadre got it from the van.

"Gadgets says there are about twenty of them out there," the Hispanic warrior declared. "The good news is a lot of them appear to be stumblebums. They look like amateurs who never had any real training or combat experience."

"Yeah?" Lyons asked with raised eyebrows. "As good news goes, that's not so great. Even an amateur can pull a trigger, and his bullets are as deadly as anybody else's. Besides, the bad news is there are about twenty of them and three of us."

"So much for trying to cheer you up," Blancanales commented.

Lyons stuffed the spare magazines in his jacket pockets. The safety catch was on, so he knew there was already a round up the spout. The Able Team warrior trusted his partners and knew Blancanales wouldn't have done this unless the weapon was ready to fire.

The Puerto Rican tough guy pulled back the charging lever to the M-16 and chambered a round. He also fished a 40 mm cartridge grenade from a ditty bag attached to his combat harness. He fed the shell into the breech of an M-203 launcher attached to the underside of the rifle barrel.

"Gadgets?" Lyons said into the throat mike.

"I've been listening. No more spot reports, guys. I got outside because these suckers are getting close enough to start lobbing stuff."

Lyons knew what he meant. The van was reinforced with armor plating in the frame and bullet-resistant glass. A projectile with adequate velocity, force, construction and accuracy can pierce any glass or vest. Repeated pounding by lesser rounds can weaken and penetrate such a barrier, as well. The van might have held up under volleys of gunfire, but the windows would eventually give way if the hailstorm continued long enough or the enemy used armor-piercing ammo.

Schwarz's comment about "lobbing stuff" voiced Lyons's greatest concern, as well. If the enemy used grenades or rocket launchers, the cabin, as well as the van, could be blown to pieces. Gadgets had left the van for that reason, aware his odds would be better outside the vehicle, still using the sturdy rig for cover. Yet the Volkov family had to remain inside the cabin. They wouldn't be able to react swiftly to a firefight, which depended on instincts developed by training and experience. The Russian and his wife and kids would simply be in the way if they were outside.

So Able Team would have to protect the cabin from heavy fire and try to prevent it becoming an oversize coffin. But there was no guarantee this could be done. The Stony Man warriors hadn't expected the enemy to consist of numbers larger than half a dozen. Schwarz had described the majority of opponents as "stumble-bums," a term that had a different meaning to the commandos than used by most people. Apparently the professional hit men had picked up some hired hands to reinforce their assault, probably street muscle willing to do dirty, violent jobs for the right price.

Fortunately most of the breed tended to be unreliable and often cowardly. They were probably drug addicts with gorilla-sized monkeys on their backs or freelance leg-breakers who usually busted up welshers for loan sharks. For a couple of thousand bucks, they'd cut their own grandmothers' throats. However, they might run like rabbits in a real gun battle. They were probably more familiar with baseball bats and switchblades than firearms.

The Able Team commander realized he was spinning his mental wheels. There was no way to predict what would happen in a firefight. They would just have to do what they had been trained to do and handle whatever the other side threw at them when it came.

GADGETS SCHWARZ CROUCHED by the rear of the van, holding his M-16 in both hands. He wore a pair of night-scope goggles with the same special optics as the periscope lens. The increased night vision allowed him to see the figure behind the cover of some shrubbery and the shadows of a tree. The hardman held a long-barreled revolver in both hands and started to aim it at

Schwarz. He apparently thought he could take his time to sight in because he believed he hadn't been detected in the dark.

Schwarz quickly braced the M-16 against his hip, pointed the rifle and triggered a 3-round burst. Flame spit from the muzzle, and the man fell backward, his chest ripped and bloodied by the trio of 5.56 mm slugs. The gun spun from the hardman's fingers as the body dropped from view. Although the Able Team warrior barely glimpsed his target, he was certain at least one M-16 round had pierced the guy's heart.

A shotgun roared from the bushes. Buckshot struck the ground more than a yard from Schwarz's position. Clumps of dirt and pebbles sprayed from the earth, but none of the pellets reached Gadgets. The inexperienced triggerman had opened fire out of effective range—a fatal mistake because the muzzle-flash of the big-bore weapon lit up his position like a flare in the darkness.

Schwarz immediately exploited the error. He snap-aimed and fired the M-16. The shape of the shotgunner was visible to the commando, thanks to the night goggles. The attacker dropped his cut-down pump-action 12-gauge and collapsed to the ground. Schwarz wasn't certain where he hit his opponent, but the hardman didn't look as if he'd get up again.

Aware that his own muzzle-flash presented a target for the enemy, Schwarz moved to one side of the van. A short burst of automatic fire revealed his decision was wise. Bullets sparked along the metal frame of the vehicle. The volley revealed that the assault force wasn't armed only with shotguns and handguns.

Although Schwarz didn't notice the origin of the subgun fire, Blancanales did. The Able Team warrior knelt outside the cabin, near the front door. He raised his M-16 and returned fire, aiming at the glare of the enemy's subgun. Bullets slashed the tree trunk and low branches used as cover by the gunner. Blancanales saw the vague outline of the man rush for shelter by some bushes.

Brush closer to Blancanales moved. He swung the M-16 toward the new threat and squeezed off six rounds. The 5.56 mm projectiles sliced a Z-shape in the bushes. A scream rewarded his efforts, and Blancanales saw a body tumble into view. He sprinted toward Volkov's station wagon for cover, followed by pistol fire.

A volley of full-auto rounds peppered the car. Glass burst from a side window as Blancanales ducked low. A shotgun-wielding figure stepped closer to point his weapon at the Able Team commando. Blancanales dropped to his side, pointed the M-16 in an unorthodox sideways angle and triggered a short salvo. The attacker stopped his charge and doubled over, blood dripping from under his ribs.

The injured man fired his shotgun, but the muzzle was pointed at the ground near his feet. The blast pulverized the toes and instep of one of his feet. The recoil shoved back into the hardman with enough force to drive him off balance. He collapsed to the ground, curled in a ball of screaming agony. The shotgun lay nearby, forgotten. The man soon passed out from shock.

Another spray of automatic fire spewed from the surrounding foliage. Cracks appeared in the station wagon windshield, and a bullet ricocheted along the metal rim to whirl past Blancanales's face. It missed the tip of his nose by scant inches. The Hispanic commando flattened his back against the frame of the car to try to stay clear of the sizzling projectiles.

Schwarz saw the muzzle-flash of the enemy chopper, glimpsed the outline of the weapon and recognized the distinctive flared front sights and cocking knob. An Uzi. Whoever these guys were, they knew their hardware. The Able Team pro also detected the shape of the gunman's head and shoulders above the submachine gun.

He pointed the M-16, instinctively aiming for the upper torso, but quickly raised the barrel slightly. The few opponents armed with full-auto weapons seemed to be commanding the others who packed only shotguns and pistols. Schwarz figured there was a good chance these squad leaders might also wear bullet-resistant vests.

Gadgets opened fire. The hardman's head snapped back from the impact of three 5.56 mm slugs. The Uzi slipped from lifeless fingers, and the gunman fell into the shadows. Another figure swung around the trunk of a tree, arms extended and both hands fisted around a pistol that resembled a Colt .45 from that distance. He pointed the handgun at Schwarz.

Blancanales saw the threat to his partner and swiftly triggered the M-16. One bullet chipped bark from the tree trunk, but at least one round struck the pistol man's exposed right arm. The handgun spun from his grasp as the man retreated. Blancanales readied the M-16 to fire at the fleeing form, but he didn't squeeze the trigger. The guy was unarmed and appeared to be interested in only one thing—getting the hell out of the area.

Some of the other hired thugs also decided the job wasn't worth dying for. The Able Team fighters saw part of the assault team flee the battlefield. Automatic-rifle fire snarled from the two enemy cars on the road. Apparently the hardmen by the vehicle had prepared for this possibility, and they weren't as merciful as the Stony Man commando trio. Bullets cut down the escaping men or force them to duck for cover among the trees.

"THAT'S WHAT I LIKE to see," Carl Lyons muttered. "The bastards are killing each other."

Yet he knew better than to get overconfident. There were still plenty of hardmen left to deal with, and they hadn't unleashed the full fury of their arsenal. The ruthless gunfire from the enemy by the cars was proof of that.

Lyons couldn't worry about what the men by the vehicles might have up their figurative sleeves. They would have to deal with that later. At the moment the Able Team commander had other problems as he exchanged fire with a group of assailants who had launched an attack at the rear of the cabin.

The first two attackers were clumsy, careless and soon dead. They tried to rush the cabin, so preoccupied with the mindless charge they failed to see Lyons until it was too late. He opened up with the Heckler & Koch and hit them both with a stream of 9 mm slugs at chest level.

The hardmen went down, but others soon took their place. A full-auto weapon spit a wild volley of rounds from Lyons's left, and a shotgun barrel appeared among some bushes to his right. Bullets raked the cabin near the Able Team leader's position, biting into the log wall about a foot from his head. He hit the door and dived inside an instant before the shotgun boomed. Splinters showered him when buckshot chewed off parts of the door frame.

Lyons triggered a short burst with the H&K, not taking time to aim. He intended only to discourage the attackers from advancing to a better position to try to take him out. He kicked the door shut and rolled to a small table and chairs. The sleeve of a plaid jacket brushed his face. He pushed it aside, annoyed until he realized the jacket hung across the backrest of a chair. The padded shoulders at the crest of the back rail presented a vaguely human shape.

He buttoned his jacket loosely, bringing the garment together around the chair to create an improvised dummy. He moved the chair to a window, slipped the submachine gun under a sleeve and shoved hard. The barrel shattered glass, and the H&K was canted along the sill. Lyons hoped the attackers would respond to the movement and the general torso appearance of the dummy before they realized the threat was no more than a piece of furniture.

The Stony Man commando jumped back from the window and reached for his Colt Python. A salvo of full-auto rounds smashed the remaining glass and hammered the chair. Ragged holes appeared in the jacket fabric, and the furniture began to slide backward. Lyons barely noticed. His trick had worked, and he was too busy following with the next part of the plan.

He yanked open the door and thrust the .357 Magnum forward. Lyons spotted the guy with the subgun. Actually he packed an Ingram MAC-10 machine pistol, which explained why the man's marksmanship had been so poor when he tried to waste the Able Team warrior. The box-shaped, stubby-barreled Ingram was a close-quarters "room sweeper" with little range or accuracy at a distance.

The gunman's attention turned from the window to the door. He started to alter the aim of his MAC-10 when Lyons fired the big Colt revolver. The Magnum roared, and a 158-grain missile slammed into the killer's upper arm. The impact spun the man and sent the Ingram flying from useless fingers. He dropped to his knees, dazed and bloodied, his arm shattered.

The shotgunner started to swing his weapon toward Lyons. The Able Team captain hadn't forgotten the second man and had already shifted the aim of his Python to cover the thug. He chose an easier target, assuming the hired gun probably didn't wear a protective vest. Lyons pumped two .357 Magnum slugs into the man's chest and watched him collapse to the ground.

Suddenly a large figure with shaggy, uncombed red hair bolted from the shadows. The attacker's face was contorted with rage as he howled in bestial fury and pumped the action of his Winchester shotgun. Lyons didn't have time to aim and trigger his Magnum. He threw himself to the floor as buckshot tore into the door.

Lyons rolled clear of the doorway. Another burst of 12-gauge pellets smashed into the cabin entrance. He got to his feet, Magnum pointed at the door. The burly hardman appeared on the threshold, his hair swirling around his head like red tentacles. He was about to work the pump action to the shotgun when he spotted Lyons.

The Gunman lashed out with the shotgun in a backhand sweep. The tactic caught Lyons off guard, and the Winchester barrel slammed into the frame of the warrior's Python. Metal clanged and Lyons pulled the trigger. The big revolver bellowed, but the .357 round blasted a useless hole in the cabin wall. The Stony Man warrior felt the gun jerk from his fingers before he could retain his grasp.

The Colt clattered on the floor, and the hulking hoodlum quickly swung a butt stroke toward Lyons's head. The commando ducked, and the walnut stock slashed empty air. Lyons rammed his right fist into the hardman's solar plexus and followed through with a left hook to the side of the man's jaw.

Although Lyons was a large, powerful man and packed a punch most heavyweights would envy, his opponent was also big and strong, and charged with such frenzy the blows only rocked him.

Lyons grabbed the frame of the shotgun before his enemy could recover from the stunning impact of the punches and dropped backward, knees bent. The thug was pulled forward by the unexpected move. The big ex-cop's left buttock and thigh touched the floor, and he raised his right foot to meet his opponent's abdomen. Lyons's back met the floor as he swung his arms behind him, fists still clenched around the shotgun. The brute stubbornly held on, unaware of his mistake until Lyons straightened his right knee.

The combined motion and leverage of the judo circle throw sent the hardman hurtling head over heels to crash to the floor hard. He lost his grip on the shotgun. Lyons maintained his and swiftly rose, both hands wrapped around the steel barrel. The assassin had been dazed by the punishing fall and wasn't as quick to get to his feet. Lyons closed in and swung the shotgun like a baseball bat, the other man raising his arms to ward off the attack.

Yet Lyons's move was a feint. He launched the real attack at a lower, exposed target and chopped the walnut stock across the hardman's left kneecap. Cartilage crunched and the man's leg buckled. He staggered awkwardly on the dislocated joint. Lyons thrust a boot to the guy's chest, as if kicking in a door. The impact sent his opponent reeling backward into a wall.

Whatever else could be said about the beefy hood, he wasn't a quitter. Although battered and injured, the big man still lunged at Lyons one more time. The commando swung the shotgun and slammed the hardwood stock under the attacker's rib cage. The blow drove the wind from the man's lungs and knocked him off balance. Lyons tossed the shotgun aside and closed in to hit the guy, knocking him out cold with a hard blow to the left ear.

"And stay down," Lyons muttered, breathing hard from the exertion and stress of combat.

None of the enemy appeared at the back door. Lyons had been lucky. A gunner could have easily killed him while he was busy dealing with the brutish thug in hand-to-hand combat. Lyons knew better than to place his trust in luck and quickly retrieved the .357 Magnum and H&K submachine gun.

"What's going on out there?" Volkov's voice called from the bedroom.

Lyons heard the soft weeping of the Russian's wife and children. He hoped they were only frightened and hadn't been injured. As far as the Able Team warrior could tell, no concentrated gunfire had been directed at the portion of the cabin the Volkov family used for shelter.

"What's happening?" Volkov repeated.

"Stay put and stay down!" Lyons replied. "It's not over yet! Don't yell out again, either! You're lucky I was the one who heard you and not the assassins!"

The sound of gunfire warned that the battle was far from finished. Lyons wondered if his Able Team partners were all right, but didn't allow the thought more than fleeting consideration. Schwarz and Blancanales were as skilled and experienced in survival as Lyons himself. Of course, none of them were indestructible, and they always faced the risk of sudden, violent death. Worrying wouldn't save anyone and would only distract Lyons from the life-or-death struggle that required total concentration.

Without warning, an explosion erupted outside the cabin. The structure shook, and Lyons was nearly thrown off balance by the fierce tremor. Dust and tar pitch dribbled from cracks between the logs. The enemy had just escalated the level of attack. They were no longer simply trying to gun down Able Team and the Volkovs. The killers now intended to blast them into oblivion.

THE FIRST SHELL had been launched from the enemy vehicles. Lyons emerged from the cabin to discover the cars had drawn closer yet still remained almost five hundred yards away. He saw Blancanales crouched by the station wagon and headed for the Hispanic commando's position. Automatic fire barked from the vehicles. Slugs struck earth near Lyons's feet, loose dirt splattering his pant legs. The Able Team commander dived forward and rolled to the wagon. Blancanales moved to offer Lyons more space along the metal shelter.

"Fancy meeting you out here," Blancanales remarked.

Lyons grunted a sour reply. He glanced about but didn't see Schwarz. There was also no sign of attackers on foot.

"They bugged out," his companion informed him. "What was left of them. I'm not sure how many are dead, but some are still hiding in the trees and bushes— more afraid of getting killed by their so-called buddies in the cars than by us. A few others ran for the cars just before they fired that first grenade or rocket."

"Where's Gadgets?"

"I'm in the van," Schwarz's voice announced into Lyons's, ear. "Wanted to use the scope to scan the area, see what happened to the jolly foot soldiers and try to figure out what those other guys are throwing at us."

Lyons had forgotten he still wore the throat mike and earphone. He spoke directly to Schwarz. "What have they got?"

"Looks like one of them is loading an improvised grenade launcher right now. I'm watching him through the night scope. Real do-it-yourself job. Pipe bomb attached to the end of a stick. Can you believe that?"

"I'm not laughing," Lyons stated. "The first one came close enough to the cabin to rattle the logs loose. May not be state-of-the-art hardware, but they can still blow us to bits—"

"Incoming!" Schwarz announced.

Lyons and Blancanales ducked low, covered their heads and waited for the explosive round to arrive. When it exploded on impact, the mighty roar seemed to hammer the station wagon hard enough to threaten to tip it over on the two men. Obviously the improvised bomb-launcher wasn't terribly accurate. The second round had landed short of its target. Small comfort. The third might come closer.

Able Team didn't want to give them a chance to try again.

"They're about to reload," Schwarz told them. "Let's hit them before they can."

"Yeah," Blancanales agreed. "We're out of effective range of those automatic rifles unless they realize they'd have a better chance of hitting us if they switched to semiauto."

"Don't be a worrywart."

"Hey, you guys..." Lyons began, but he wasn't sure what to tell them.

"Stay put, Carl," Blancanales said. "Just sit this one out."

Lyons knew there was nothing he could do because his short-range MP-5 and Magnum revolver were useless against targets five hundred yards away. That knowledge was frustrating. He followed Blancanales's advice and remained by the station wagon as the Puerto Rican moved forward, his M-16 grasped in both hands.

Schwarz jumped from the back of the van. Both men aimed their weapons at the enemy vehicles and triggered the M-203 launchers attached to the rifle barrels. Twin 40 mm grenade shells streaked into the night sky.

Bullets struck the ground near the Able Team warriors' feet as they sprinted for cover. One stray round tugged at Blancanales's jacket and tore a hole in fabric near his left kidney. He was too busy staying alive to even notice how close the projectile came to causing serious injury. Lyons sucked in a tense breath, more worried about the safety of his partners than he had been about his own life when he had come close to stopping a bullet.

The grenades exploded. The enemy vehicles were shrouded in flames, metal twisted and mangled by the double blasts of 40 mm projectiles. The pair quickly reloaded, and fired two more explosive packages. The grenades resembled meteors of destruction as they sailed in a high arc and descended on the enemy position.

The hardmen no longer fired at Able Team. The first grenade blasts had pounded the fight out of the enemy attack force. The second salvo of M-203 rounds made certain the other side wouldn't be able to recover to resume their attack or even defend themselves. The battle was life or death, the stakes too high for Able Team to take any chances with the assassination unit.

The explosions scattered chunks of burning wreckage across the grassy knoll and dirt road. Yellow light illuminated ghastly remains of mutilated, dismembered corpses. Schwarz returned to the van to scan the area, but there was little doubt the battle was over. Only the grim chore of mopping up remained.

The sound of sirens announced they would have company. The flashing lights in the distance revealed at least half a dozen police cars were headed for the site. Lyons sighed. They would have to show the cops their Justice ID and give them a story with enough truth to satisfy the local law-and-order boys without blowing security. Obviously other people camped at the site had called the police when the shooting began. No way could they keep this out of the newspapers and other media. Television crews would probably arrive before the police could finish putting up the ribbons to restrict the area.

"Gadgets," Lyons said into the throat mike, "contact the Farm and give them a quick rundown on what happened—an abridged version. We have to get the Volkovs out of here. We'll need some help with the local police."

"Right," Schwarz replied. "Some of those guys are probably still alive out there. If nothing else, we'll want the cops to hold them until they can be picked up."

"That reminds me," Lyons said. "I left someone unconscious in the cabin. He might come to in a few minutes. Winged another one with a round in the arm. He's probably not in very good shape, but I figure he's still alive."

"Hopefully they can answer some questions," Blancanales remarked. "Maybe I should stay here with the police while you guys get the Volkovs out of here."

"Yeah," Lyons agreed. "You're better at appeasing folks with questions and answers than I am. They'll send Leo to take your place and give the cops whatever they need to get custody of the prisoners. Glad that's somebody else's job.''

"Seems like our job is tough enough at times," Schwarz's voice added.

"It has its moments," Lyons remarked. "Let's wrap it up here. The job isn't over yet."

CHAPTER SEVENTEEN

Stony Man Farm, Virginia
Wednesday, 0710 hours

"Cup of coffee?" Aaron Kurtzman asked.

"Surely you jest," Hal Brognola replied as he cast a distasteful glance at the Bear's coffeemaker. "Do you ever clean that thing?"

"You mean it doesn't clean itself?" Kurtzman asked with feigned surprise. "I just need some good strong brew in the morning. Sure felt good to sleep. You should try to get more, Hal."

"Later," the big Fed replied. "What's been coming in? Any more reports on Able Team and Volkov?"

"If anything had gone wrong, the emergency signal would have gone off to warn all of us and wake us," Kurtzman assured him. "They have to get the family to a safehouse before they can bring Volkov here."

"The killers might have a backup team."

"We got some of our security people to Lyons and Schwarz at the Ohio border," Kurtzman said as he checked an update report on the computer screen. "No incidents and no trouble. Apparently the bad guys in Kentucky threw everything they had at Able Team. Leo is going to head for Erlinger as soon as Jack can get his chopper fueled. Things are going better than they have since this mission began."

"Maybe," Brognola muttered.

"Hey, the computer logged the spot reports. Our guys in the field haven't come across a major crisis since the hit men in Russia wasted Khurumov and his family. They're making genuine progress, and the enemy hasn't launched another ACR attack. The other side might have been ahead on points, but we're catching up fast."

"Save the celebration for when this is finished."

Kurtzman shrugged and sipped some of the coffee no one else considered fit for human consumption. The transceiver unit began to blink frequency numerals, and a message appeared on the wall screen. A line of letters and numbers was followed by "Striker."

"We got Mack on the line," Kurtzman announced. "Not just a spot report, either. He wouldn't be using this access code for that."

"What kind of contact?" Brognola asked. "Verbal communication?"

"Yeah." Kurtzman keyed the machine as he spoke. "And visual. Striker rarely uses a monitor."

"I know. Wonder why he's doing it now."

Images flickered across the screen as dot-matrix patterns took moving form. The commanding figure of Mack Bolan appeared, four times larger than life. Dressed in black night-combat fatigues, shoulder holster rig with Beretta clearly visible, the Executioner sat behind a metal desk with a gooseneck lamp turned to one side. The light cast away from Bolan's neck and left his features in shadows. Only his lower jaw and strong mouth could be seen.

Bolan hadn't been a survivor of his one-man war against organized crime and the following campaigns in Stony Man by being careless. He seldom used visual monitors for this reason. If someone did tap into their transmissions, he didn't want his face revealed to the enemy.

"Hello, Striker," Brognola greeted. "Surprised to see you."

"I know what you're thinking," the warrior replied. "It's okay with me if anyone or everyone interested in what's going on catches this message. Even the other side."

"Really?" Kurtzman said with surprise. "Must be good."

"Our Persian friend did some investigating," Bolan stated. "His troops found the remains of the fishing boat along the southeast coast of Iran, near the Strait of Hormuz. The enemy tried to sink it, but an undercurrent pulled in our favor and brought it to the top. Came to shore with the tide."

"Thank you, Mother Nature," Kurtzman commented.

"You sure it's the right boat, Striker?" Brognola asked.

"Positive," the warrior replied. "They found a Soviet-made RPG launcher along with the wreckage. Apparently they tossed it overboard before they tried to sink the rig. However, some loose fishnetting snared the front sight when the boat went down. It towed in the RPG when the wreck drifted ashore."

"Fate really spit in their face this time," the big Fed remarked. "So we know how they started the sea battle when the satellites, radar, sonar and the other gadgets went haywire."

"Yeah," Bolan confirmed. "It wasn't the United States or the Iranians who started it. That's why I'll transmit this way and not give a damn who knows. Not if it can stop a war that shouldn't happen, a war some treacherous outsiders want to start."

"Sorry," Kurtzman said. "Nobody will see this but us. I understand your feelings, and we'll let the President know. Any idea how the Iranians will respond to this or don't they know yet?"

"Our friend tells me he's going to present a report to Tehran," Bolan replied, "tell them more or less the truth and urge them not to continue blaming the U.S., Armenia or Russia. He says it's sacrilege to declare a holy war when it's obviously the will of evil men, not God, that causes a war."

"Leadership in Iran hasn't always taken kindly to criticism," Brognola said grimly. "They've executed officers of higher rank just for disagreeing with their decision in the past."

Bolan frowned and said, "He knows that. He'll do it anyway. Our friend is a brave man and he loves his country enough to risk his life for it."

"That's what I call a true patriot," Brognola remarked. "A man willing to face possible execution by his own government to try to protect his country."

"You and our friend must have hit it off pretty well when you met," the Bear told Bolan. "Sounds like you made good impressions on each other."

"We came to an understanding," Bolan stated. "Our friend is a man who knows when to listen, and when he speaks others should pay attention. I hope they listen to him in Tehran."

"Hell," Brognola remarked, "I hope they'll listen to us in Washington. Some of the hawks in the administration want us to go to war immediately. The President is getting a lot of pressure to take that action. So is Congress. Since Iran can affect oil transportation through the gulf, there are some pretty powerful forces working behind the scene here—oil interests, Wall Street firms and some others who give a lot of financial support to candidates when they run for office. Those big-money sources support Republicans and Democrats. Regardless of what either party might say, they both want that backing when they run for reelection."

"Yeah," Bolan replied. "Let's just hope Washington gets bogged down with the usual debates and red tape long enough for us to find the real enemies and take care of them. Our Iranian friend says his people questioned villagers along the coast about any strangers in the area. A number of witnesses stated they saw a group of men. Some said nine or ten, others claimed it was twelve or more. Exact number isn't that important, but all witnesses seemed sure these guys got into two large trucks and headed north."

"I take it nobody has spotted the trucks yet."

"Not that I know of," Bolan replied. "They probably ditched the vehicles. Might have gotten different sets of wheels along the way. They might be on foot by now, or might have even left the country."

"Well, that hit team might have gotten away for now," the big Fed declared, "but one here didn't. Able Team stopped them cold in Kentucky when they tried to take out Volkov."

"Our guys okay?" Bolan asked.

"All three of them are fine."

"What about Volkov and his family?"

"Shook up a little, but not a scratch. Volkov is still with his wife and kids. When we're sure they're safe, we'll bring him in for his expert opinion to help us solve this mess."

"Sounds good," Bolan agreed, "but the other side is going to figure out what's happened pretty damn soon. When they realize things aren't going so well and their agents in the field haven't reported back because they've been taken out of the game, they'll do one of two things—either retreat or go on the offensive."

"Yeah," the Bear said. "Neither will be very good. If they decide to scrap operations, they'll separate and go into hiding. Be even harder to find them then and we might never catch up with the real leaders. Of course, they might start operations again in another year or two. Probably choose different targets and maybe different goals. That ACR technology would be perfect for sabotaging air-traffic operations. Could be blackmail for big bucks next time."

"One of the most frustrating parts of our current problem is we don't know what the hell they're trying to accomplish by what they're doing now," Brognola added. "What will they gain by starting a war?"

"That's something we'd better figure out quick," Bolan stated. "I don't think they'll retreat. Whoever these people are, they've been aggressive since this started. They don't seem to be very patient. They hit big and then hit bigger. Despite the fact they're well hidden, there's a certain desperation to their actions. Otherwise, they wouldn't have risked the second attack so soon after the first. My guess is they'll lash out if they feel threatened. That means the next hit will probably be even bigger than the sea battle in the gulf."

Barbara Price entered the computer room. She was surprised and pleased to see the familiar figure on the wall screen. Price joined Brognola and Kurtzman.

"Hello, Striker," she said. "How are things in Turkey?"

"Quiet," he replied. "And I really don't see there's much more for me to do here. The data I just sent in is probably the most information I can get here, and I can't do much that CIA and NSA can't do just as well on their own."

"I agree," Price stated. "That's why I think we should send you to Russia to join Phoenix as soon as possible. According to the computer assessments put together by the Bear, it's extremely unlikely the enemy base is in Turkey. There's a far greater probability it's in Russia or another CIS country. Of course, there are other possible sites in Syria, Iraq and other countries. When Volkov comes here, we might find out our guesses are based on flawed, outdated information and we'll have to start over again. Still, for now I think the best place for you is Russia."

"You heard our mission controller," Brognola remarked. "I'm going to contact that CIA wimp in Ankara. The one who's been crying to the President since this thing started. Willy Rolson?"

"Wesley Rollins," Price corrected.

"Yeah." The big Fed nodded. "Him. Rollins is going to make certain Striker's gear is packed in a diplomatic pouch and goes from the embassy in Turkey to the one in Russia PDQ. It had damn well better be there when Striker arrives. I don't care if Rollins has to take it there personally and carry it on his lap all the way. If Striker doesn't have his gear when he gets to Russia, Rollins won't have a career in the Company anymore."

"You sound a tad vindictive," Kurtzman remarked.

"Rollins was ordered to help Striker, but he just got in the way. It's time for him to do something useful. He either does it, or he can get used to asking people if they want some fries with their hamburgers."

"That's up to you, Hal," Bolan said. "I don't think the guy's worth the effort. Contact you when I get to Russia."

As the Executioner signed off, Brognola asked Kurtzman to put him through to the U.S. Embassy in Ankara.

Ural Mountains, Russia
Wednesday, 1320 hours

THE NEWS WAS VERY BAD, Valery Zhigalin decided. The former GRU communications and code expert hadn't received a message from Warner Muller's group in the United States, so he decided to attempt monitoring radio broadcasts in the general area of Ohio, Indiana, Kentucky and Pennsylvania. The international transceiver was very powerful, but the distance still presented problems. However, a news report of an "unconfirmed nature" alarmed Zhigalin.

Apparently police somewhere in Kentucky called Erlinger weren't commenting on the reports of a gun battle with explosions at an unnamed vacation spot near the Kentucky-Ohio border. The authorities wouldn't confirm or deny claims that a number of persons had been killed or injured during the incident, or that others had been taken into custody by the police. Hospital personnel at an Erlinger clinic also refused to answer questions about patients brought by ambulance or escorted by police vehicles. They wouldn't say whether these persons had been injured by gunshot wounds or explosions, or if any of them were dead on arrival. An official statement by the chief of police was expected within twenty-four hours.

Zhigalin knew this occurred in the general area Muller and his team were expected to deal with Volkov. After what happened to the hit team in Russia, Zhigalin feared Muller's people might have suffered a similar fate. He knew the former SSD agent had enlisted the aid of some local thugs in case they encountered opposition at the Russian's cabin retreat, but that might not have been enough. It might have simply increased the body count when the battle erupted.

Giessler's plan was coming apart. They had enjoyed early success with the aggressive concentrated radar and the actions carried out under its use, but the assassination units in both the United States and Russia had been stopped cold. Zhigalin assumed Muller's people were either dead or held by the authorities. He didn't know how much any of the prisoners could tell about the fortress at the Ural Mountains. It seemed to Zhigalin only a matter of time before the secret was discovered.

He cursed the day he'd agreed to participate in the scheme. Like many others, raised with the dogma of communism, Zhigalin had been emotionally crushed by the fall of the system in the former Soviet Union. He had also been afraid of what would happen to him as a former member of Soviet military Intelligence due to GRU's close connections with the KGB. Ceauşescu, his wife and other party leaders had been executed in Romania, following the overthrow of the government in that East European nation. There were stories of similar retributions in Czechoslovakia, Poland and East Germany.

Giessler had seemed to offer safe haven and a plan to regain power and privilege for the members of Intelligence networks formerly connected with the dethroned forces of communism. Although there was no evidence such individuals had been hunted down and slaughtered in the new CIS regime, Zhigalin remained with Giessler in the hope they could establish some new empire of their own, and "get even" with a world that had betrayed them.

This all seemed terribly absurd to Zhigalin now that the plan appeared to be going sour. All he wanted at this point was to get out alive and avoid the international dragnet he suspected would soon close around the covert base. They might not even get a chance to surrender if this happened. Bombing the site would be easy enough. Any survivors could expect little mercy from any court for their part in "crimes against the world." They were renegades. No nation would offer them shelter or immunity from prosecution. The whole world would want their revenge.

Zhigalin didn't report what he heard on the radio or log the information. When his shift ended, he quietly left the communications section and crossed the parade field to the billets. The Russian passed the grimfaced sentries, barely nodding to them. They were fellow countrymen, drawn into the conspiracy just as Zhigalin had been. He knew they wouldn't realize the folly of the scheme, and to talk to them would only cause his own destruction. Giessler would regard such criticism as treason, and the German mastermind would surely deal with traitors in a swift and brutal manner.

Two Arabs, clad in fatigues and well armed, stood by the quarters reserved for the visitors from the Middle East. Zhigalin didn't know if the men were Syrian, Libyan or Iraqi. It hardly made any difference. The bodyguards of Gahiz, Kadafadem and Mahdi were loyal only to their bosses. They regarded the Russians and Germans with suspicion.

Zhigalin shook his head, dismayed by his own foolishness at being part of Giessler's insane plot. Did they really want to be members of a new empire in the Middle East, ruled by the three hostile Arab potentates who obviously regarded Russians and Europeans with contempt? Zhigalin didn't understand Arabic or the customs of Syria, Libya or Iraq. He considered the Middle East to be a cesspool of fanatics and unstable political conditions. Who would want an empire in such a demented part of the world?

He entered the billets and found Leonid Sarkisov and Yuri Lyukshin playing chess in the recreation room. His friends greeted Zhigalin as he pulled a chair to their table.

"Look at the board," he whispered. "There are others present, and we don't want to draw attention."

Sarkisov shifted his eyes toward Zhigalin but didn't turn his head. He slowly reached for a bishop and used it to capture one of Lyukshin's pawns.

"What's this about?" he asked softly.

Zhigalin briefly told them about the radio broadcast and his concern that the base would soon be located and destroyed. The other two men listened quietly. Lyukshin started to move a rook in a diagonal pattern, realized what he was doing and returned it to the starting square. He stared at the board as if he had never seen a chess set before or suddenly forgot how to play the game.

"You're suggesting we desert?" Lyukshin asked, his voice barely loud enough for the other two to hear.

"I'm suggesting we've made a terrible mistake," Zhigalin replied. "If we stay here, we'll suffer with the rest when they come to tear this place down."

"You know what will happen if we're caught trying to leave here," Sarkisov remarked. It wasn't a question.

"And what will happen if we stay? I say our only chance is to get out of here as soon as possible."

"Let's not rush into anything," Lyukshin urged.

"There won't be much time when Giessler finds out what's happened," Zhigalin insisted. "He won't back down. He can't go back now. Those damn Arabs wouldn't let him if he wanted to."

"Nonsense," Sarkisov said. "The Arab leaders were foolish enough to come here to his place. Giessler can simply kill them and not worry about what they want."

"They weren't foolish enough to bring their money," Zhigalin reminded him. "Giessler has invested everything he has in this crazy dream of power. We'll all be stranded, with only a few rubles in our pockets. Giessler would rather die than face such a fate. He would rather die than accept failure."

"And he cares more for his own life than all of ours put together," Lyukshin agreed. "Perhaps we should leave."

"Exactly," Zhigalin stated. "And we should go now."

"You don't mean at this moment?" Sarkisov asked, his eyebrows raised. "We should plan the escape for a day or two."

"There won't be that much time," Zhigalin insisted. "I didn't report what I discovered, but someone else might pick up the same information and come to the same conclusion. When that happens, Giessler will tighten security and it will be more difficult to leave. No. We should leave immediately."

"At least wait for cover of darkness," Sarkisov advised.

"Why? The guards are more alert at night due to fear of mountain bandits and the possibility the enemy might come for us under cover of darkness. Besides, with the infrared detection devices they'd probably spot us anyway. That would only make us appear more suspicious."

"You realize those stories about hill bandits could be genuine," Lyukshin remarked. "We might be facing a serious threat from them, as well as Giessler and our own comrades here."

"I'd rather take my chances with bandits than that maniac," Zhigalin replied. "Let's just gather what supplies we can without drawing too much attention and go."

"No matter what we do," Lyukshin said, shaking his head in despair, "we probably won't survive."

"But there's only one way that offers us any chance at all," Zhigalin replied. "I'll get some rations for the trip. You two pack some blankets, flashlights and extra ammunition. Anything else you think you can stuff into a backpack or hide under your clothes without making the guards curious."

"All right," Sarkisov agreed with a reluctant sigh, "but this had better work."

"We'll soon find out," Zhigalin answered. "Meet me in one hour at the front of the billets."

THE THREE DESPERATE MEN left the billets at 1545 hours, choosing that time because the sentries on duty had only fifteen minutes left before they would be relieved. After standing watch without incident, they would be less inclined to fuss about something minor or to be so terribly interested in searching contents of backpacks so close to the end of their shift.

Zhigalin, Sarkisov and Lyukshin strolled across the parade field at a casual pace. They wore warm coats, gloves and fur caps, but that was standard protection against the chill. No one paid much notice to Lyukshin's AK-47 assault rifle or the side arms carried by the other two men. Many of the personnel at the base went armed. If anyone had questions about the backpacks they wore, no one had voiced them. Zhigalin felt hopeful the plan would work.

They walked to the perimeter of the base, flanked by walls of boulders. Two guards stood by the ridge of rocks. They watched the three men approach with more interest than shown by others in the camp. One sentry stepped forward.

"Where are you going?" he demanded.

"To gather some mushrooms and lentils," Zhigalin answered. "We saw some by the base of the mountain, on the shaded side at the east."

The sentry nodded. Several of the Russians at the compound collected mushrooms, lentils and other food found in the wild. Such supplement to their diet was a Slavic tradition, and it was a welcome addition to meals from cans and freeze-dried packets. Yet the guard didn't recall seeing these three men make such trips in the past.

"At the east side?" the sentry asked. "Are you sure you can tell good mushrooms from poisonous ones?"

"Of course," Zhigalin replied. "My grandmother taught me to tell the difference. I guess every Russian still has a bit of peasant in his blood."

"Yes," the guard agreed with a grin. "That's probably true. You know not to venture too far. Still, if you see a rabbit don't let it get away."

"We won't," Zhigalin assured him.

The sentries stepped aside to allow the trio to leave the base area. The three men moved forward, but stopped in midstride when a voice barked an order for them to wait. Zhigalin recognized the lightly accented Russian before he turned to see Giessler.

The former SSD agent approached the would-be fugitives, arms folded on his chest. He wore only a lightweight jacket and no headgear. Giessler hadn't taken time to bundle up in warmer clothing before seeking the trio. Ivan Suslev accompanied his superior. The stocky Russian carried a machine pistol in one hand, barrel pointed at the ground. Like the German, Suslev hadn't bothered to bundle up against the elements. The wind lashed at his hair, but his eyes remained fixed on the trio.

"I think we need to talk about radio-data procedure," Giessler declared. "You seemed to have failed to make an important log entry on your shift, Comrade Zhigalin."

"I . . . I don't know what you're talking about."

"Spare me the feeble denials," the German said. "You forget that I have radio conversations and reconnaissance monitored. Especially when our computer link detects a sudden and deliberate alteration in the frequency used. In fact, I listened to a tape recording of the matter you chose not to share with us, Comrade."

"I don't recall hearing anything that needed to be reported," Zhigalin stated, but he knew arguing with Giessler was hopeless.

"Then you and your friends won't mind coming with us to listen to the tape," the SSD veteran suggested. "Then you can tell us how you failed to hear it the first time."

"Suslev!" Lyukshin said. "You're Russian like us! Don't take sides with this filthy German pig against your own people!"

"My people don't run to the authorities to betray their comrades because a reward of fifty thousand rubles has been promised to anyone who can give information about the incident along the Iran-Armenia border," Suslev stated in a hard voice.

"Is that what Giessler told you?" Zhigalin asked. "He's a liar! I'll tell you what I heard—"

"Shut up, traitor!" Suslev ordered as he raised the machine pistol. "Save your fabrications for the court-martial. If we even waste time with a trial for you three scum!''

Lyukshin suddenly swung the AK-47 from his shoulder and tried to point the barrel at Suslev. The other man altered the aim of the machine pistol faster and squeezed the trigger. A 3-round burst drilled into Lyukshin's chest, punching him backward, blood splashed across his overcoat.

Zhigalin and Sarkisov decided they had no choice but to follow their friend's example. The two sentries had clearly been taken off guard by the unexpected confrontation. They didn't seem certain who was telling the truth and were slow to react even when shots were fired. If Zhigalin and Sarkisov could take down Giessler and Suslev, there was a chance they might be able to explain what had caused this incident and rally support among the others.

Thoughts blurred in Zhigalin's mind, and he drew his Makarov before he realized he had reached for the weapon. Sarkisov's reflexes were even faster. He pointed his pistol at Suslev. Both men opened fire. Sarkisov screamed and doubled up in agony with three slugs in his intestines and groin. Suslev dropped his weapon and clutched a crimson spider in the center of his chest.

The guards finally unslung their weapons, but didn't point the rifles at Zhigalin. Giessler had unfolded his arms, but raised both hands to the sides of his head. Zhigalin was startled by his good fortune and swung the Makarov toward the German. Giessler placed both hands at the back of his head as if to surrender.

Suddenly the German's arm descended. Orange flame burst from the diminutive .25-caliber Bauer automatic in his fist. Two tiny bullets slammed into Zhigalin's face. One split his left cheekbone, and the other pierced his eyeball. Blood poured from the socket as the Russian shrieked in agony and tried to trigger his pistol. Giessler's little Bauer didn't stop firing, and two more .25-caliber projectiles punched through Zhigalin's bleeding eye socket and drilled a hole at the bridge of his nose.

The Makarov roared, but Zhigalin's aim had been thrown off when the Bauer blasted his face into bloodied pulp and punctured his brain. The dying Russian's shot missed Giessler by fifteen centimeters—close enough to force the German to jump back, frightened by the high-velocity 9 mm Russian short round that sliced past the right side of his face.

"Colonel!" one of the guards exclaimed, as if suddenly awakened from a trance. "Are you all right?"

"Idiots!" Giessler snapped. "what were you waiting for? Those bastards could have killed Suslev and—"

He realized Suslev had been hit. Giessler knelt by his fallen aide. Blood still flowed from the bullet hole in Suslev's chest, but the Russian didn't stir. Giessler stared down at open, lifeless eyes. The German's face contorted with anger and grief.

A sickly whimpering drew his attention to Sarkisov. The gut-shot Russian twisted about in convulsions of agony, and blood pooled around him. Giessler glanced at Zhigalin and Lyukshin, satisfied both were dead. Only the man who killed Suslev remained.

"Should we get the medics?" a sentry asked.

"No," Giessler replied. "Let this bastard suffer. No medical treatment, and no one puts him out of his misery. He can serve as a warning to anyone else who contemplates betraying us."

The guards seemed uncomfortable with this command, but they realized their inaction had already put them in jeopardy with the German mastermind. Giessler slid the magazine from his .25-caliber pistol and reloaded as others rushed to the scene, drawn by the gunshots. He didn't return the Bauer to the covert holster rig at his nape. Giessler simply put it in a hip pocket instead.

Abdel Gahiz marched forward, accompanied by four bodyguards. Giessler met the man's stern gaze. The Arabs glanced down at the slain bodies and the moaning form of Sarkisov.

"What happened here?" Gahiz demanded.

"A discipline problem," Giessler answered in Arabic. "We'll have to strike camp and choose another site soon. Not before we use the ACR waves on another target. One I'm certain you'll appreciate."

Musa Kadafadem and Ahmed Mahdi also appeared. The Libyan and Syrian stood behind Gahiz, quietly waiting for Giessler's announcement.

A crowd had gathered. The majority were Russians with a few Germans recruited by Giessler for the mission. Few of them understood Arabic to any degree, which was fine by Giessler. He didn't particularly want the others to know what he told the Arabs anyway. Bukovsky was nowhere to be seen. Probably curled up with a bottle of vodka again, the German thought with contempt.

"What target do you have in mind?" Gahiz asked, annoyed by Giessler's long pause.

"One that will cause your nemesis Saddam Hussein some problems," the German replied. "We're going to see if it will be as easy to start a war between Iran and Iraq as it was in September of 1980."

CHAPTER EIGHTEEN

Moscow, Russia
Wednesday, 1555 hours

Yakov Katzenelenbogen smiled at the prisoner as he fired up a cigarette. He stepped closer to the sole surviving member of the assassination team at Ustinov. The captive was strapped to the chair and stared at the glowing tip of Katz's cigarette.

"Is something wrong, Sukhanov?" Katz asked. "Sometimes when you were in the KGB, lit cigarettes were used to extract confessions. Maybe that's why you seem nervous. Cigarettes make you uncomfortable?"

The prisoner didn't reply, but beads of sweat broke out across his forehead. Katz held his cigarette in the hooks of the prosthesis. The Israeli noticed the artificial limb also seemed to worry the captive.

"I know," Katz continued. "You probably think the scopolamine didn't work so now we'll resort to torture. Correct? Yet we know your name, so that posthypnosis conditioning wasn't as effective as you thought it would be."

Actually they had identified Sukhanov by running his description through the OO data banks on KGB and GRU personnel who had disappeared shortly before the fall of communism in the USSR or shortly after the collapse. Although Sukhanov had undergone some plastic surgery, they were able to make a ninety percent match. They were sure they had a positive ID.

However, Katz preferred to let Sukhanov think he had talked under the influence of truth serum. The guy might be more cooperative if he believed he had already told them most of what they wanted to know.

"I hope you don't mind if I smoke," Katz commented. "Bad habit, I know, but I haven't been able to kick it. Keep waiting for sometime when there isn't so much stress to deal with, and that time just never seems to come along."

"May I have a cigarette, please?" Sukhanov asked.

"Certainly," Katz replied and shook one from the pack.

"You speak Russian with a proper Moscow accent," Sukhanov remarked. "Are you Russian or American CIA?"

"Doesn't matter much," the Phoenix Force commander stated. "You're not in very good standing with East or West at this moment."

The prisoner took the cigarette in his lips, and Katz lighted it. Sukhanov nodded his thanks.

"The man who beat me in hand-to-hand combat," the Russian began. "The tall black American. He's a good fighter. Let him know I respect him for that."

"I'm certain he'll be glad to hear it," Katz replied. "Khurumov and his wife didn't get a chance to fight. I don't imagine her elderly parents could have offered much resistance, either, when you and your comrades murdered them."

Sukhanov frowned. "I was just following orders."

"I doubt that defense will work for a renegade Intelligence officer. You can't even claim to be working for a government agency when you carried out those murders."

"Markin and one of the others—I forget his name, but he called himself Ivan—they did the actual killing."

"As an accomplice, you're considered just as guilty. Besides, you're part of a conspiracy to start a war between the United States and Iran. You want to drag Armenia into the war, as well. Jamming those spy satellites with aggressive concentrated radar threatens the national security of the most powerful countries in the world. They're going to want your head for this, Sukhanov."

"It's all that damn German's fault," the Russian complained. "He is the one you should put on trial."

Katz's expression remained stoic and didn't betray his surprise or interest in this remark. He decided to play the information as if he had heard it before.

"The German again," he said with a sigh. "You rambled on about him while you were drugged. We asked you who he was and where we could find him, but you just spit out some obscenities. I thought he might be someone you were still angry about when you were stationed in Eastern Europe."

"That's where I first met him," Sukhanov stated. "He was some sort of superagent with the SSD. Called himself Wolfgang at the time. One uses so many false names in this business, it is hard to know when one is using the real one or not."

"Wolfgang the superagent?"

"Yes. Wolfgang spoke several languages, including Russian and English. Supposedly he worked as a go-between for some KGB-SSD operations. He also used to handle a lot of work in the Middle East. Maybe those stories were part of his cover. They claimed he'd been to Syria, Libya and Iraq back when those countries were regular clients of the Soviet Union."

"Syria, Libya and Iraq. Go on."

"We came across Wolfgang again after East Germany fell. It was already obvious communism was on its way out in the USSR. He already had this scheme involving aggressive concentrated radar. We'd never even heard of it before."

"And he met you in the Soviet Union five years ago?"

"Maybe four years ago. It took us a while to really believe the end had come. All our lives we'd been told the capitalists would be the ones that would lose. It was hard to accept."

"I'm sure it was, Sukhanov. So where is Wolfgang now?"

"I don't know. He basically left Markin in charge of us and told us to wait until he knew what he wanted us to do. We were paid, of course. Paid well, and there didn't seem many other prospects for us. Then we got word that he wanted some scientists terminated. Khurumov and some others we never got a chance to take care of. I don't know much more than that."

Katz considered what the man said. The Phoenix commander knew enough about Intelligence operations to realize more than four men would be used for assassination operations in a country the size of Russia.

"You mentioned other members in your cell," he began, "but you called them by code names. Who are they and where can we find them?"

"You mean the people who helped us get information? I'll tell you who they are if you'll agree to give me immunity."

"That's not up to me. Besides, you're talking about fish smaller than yourself. We need to know other members of the assassination unit."

"We were it. Just the four of us. If we lost anyone, Wolfgang said he could supply replacements. Maybe there was another team he never told us about."

"Maybe," Katz replied. "We'll talk later."

MAJOR FEDEYEV MET Katz outside the interrogation room. David McCarter was present, still surly and impatient from the lack of action. Gary Manning was also with him, clearly annoyed by the Briton's behavior. Katz briefed them about the conversation.

"You believe him?" Fedeyev inquired. "Maybe he made up Wolfgang and that business about getting replacements at the drop of a hat."

"I think he's telling the truth," Katz replied. "That means we need to search the computer data banks for anything on an SSD agent known as Wolfgang or one who fit the description."

"I wouldn't imagine they had many blokes in the SSD who could operate in the Soviet Union and the Middle East with equal ease," McCarter said. "Shouldn't be too hard to narrow down any list of possible suspects."

"Unfortunately," Fedeyev replied, "rioters stormed SSD headquarters and destroyed most of the records there about four months before East Germany ceased to exist."

"If Sukhanov told the truth," Manning stated, "KGB used Wolfgang for a fair number of missions. Probably worked under different code names and bogus ID. Still, his real name must be on file somewhere. OO ought to have something on the man."

"A superagent," Katz mused. "Speaks Russian and English. Probably Arabic, as well, since he carried out missions in Syria, Libya and Iraq. Also see what you have on record of visitors to Russia from any of those three countries. Better yet, scan visitors' data from any Arab nation. They might travel under false passports."

"You think there's a connection?" McCarter asked.

"Those are three countries that have tried to muscle into other lands in the past," Katz stated. "They've sent troops into other countries and attempted takeovers in the past. They are also countries with considerable oil wealth. If Wolfgang is behind the ACR conspiracy, he'd need financing. That's one way he could get it. An ambitious regime with lots of oil money but limited military resources would certainly be interested in ACR technology."

"Yeah," Manning agreed. "It sure would have helped Saddam if he could have blotted out spy satellites and radar during Operation Desert Storm. The antagonism between Iran and Iraq resulted in war in 1980 and lasted for eight years. Maybe this time they figure they'll see if they can get the United States to do the job for them."

"Maybe," Katz said, "but Saddam and his top people are under constant watch since the war. It wouldn't be easy for him to arrange something like this.

Let's not assume anything until we have more information."

"But why do you think Iraqis or Libyans or whoever would have come to Russia?" Fedeyev asked. "Wolfgang and his people could have set up their base in Syria or Iraq, according to your experts in the States."

"If Wolfgang really could supply the assassination team in Russia with replacements on short notice," the Israeli stated, "that suggests he has his base of operation here, somewhere in Russia."

"That would be lovely," McCarter said with a grin. "Then we could go get the bastards in person."

"I thought that would appeal to you," Katz said dryly. "If that is the case, I suspect any Arab investors would want to pay a visit or two to see what their money was buying. They might even have someone stationed at the base to keep an eye on what Wolfgang and company are doing."

"A lot of 'maybes' at this point," Manning commented. "Belasko is flying in from Turkey. Maybe he can help us solve this puzzle. He'll certainly be a welcome addition if we locate an enemy stronghold."

"This man is another American similar to you five?" Fedeyev asked without enthusiasm.

"We like to think so," McCarter replied.

"I meant no offense," the Russian major explained. "You gentlemen have certainly gotten more results than the OO would have done on its own. Yet I am not comfortable with some of your tactics. Gunfights in Ustinov. Truth serum given to prisoners. It reminds me too much of the methods favored by the KGB under the old Soviet regime."

"The old Soviet regime is what we're up against,"
Manning said. "At least some remnants of it. As well,
we might have a fugitive from East Germany's police
state involved in this. You can't deal with people like
these with kid gloves. They kill innocent people, and
we're trying to stop them. If you can't see the difference, I won't waste my breath trying to explain it to
you, Major."

"I realize that," Fedeyev insisted, "but our organization is trying to maintain an image. It is important
that we be different from the KGB and we don't use the
heavy-handed tactics they employed in the past."

"No one can accuse you of that," McCarter said
with a snort of disgust. "You've been afraid to make a
decision on anything since this whole business started."

"Go easy on the major," Katz said. "We should
appreciate the fact he's in a difficult position and he's
trying to do the best he can. The OO has basically been
cooperative with us. We really can't ask more than
that."

"If you say so," the Briton muttered as he reached
for a pack of Player's cigarettes. "I just want to find
those bloody bastards and shut them down."

"We will," the Phoenix commander assured him.
"We're getting closer. It won't be much longer."

Stony Man Farm, Virginia
Wednesday, 1219 hours

JACK GRIMALDI LANDED the helicopter at the field.
Nikolai Volkov sat in the back of the chopper, sand-
wiched between Carl Lyons and Gadgets Schwarz. The
Russian scientist wore a blindfold, a standard security

precaution to maintain the secret location of the Stony Man operation. He hadn't protested or attempted to remove the blindfold.

After the assassination team had struck at the cabin resort, Volkov realized the danger to himself and his family was all too real. He also appreciated the fact they had survived only because the three mysterious commandos had been present to deal with the assault force. The Russian had no choice but to place his life and the lives of his wife and children in the hands of Able Team and Stony Man personnel.

Volkov's family had been moved to a safehouse somewhere in Maryland. Even Lyons and Schwarz didn't know the exact location. That information pleased Volkov. He recalled a quote by the famous American Benjamin Franklin: "Three people can keep a secret, if two of them are dead." The fewer people who knew about the whereabouts of his wife and children, the safer they would be.

He allowed himself to be led from the helicopter, the Able Team commandos still beside him. Volkov shuffled forward, unable to see and virtually deaf from the roar of the rotor blades.

"Mr. Volkov!" a woman's voice announced. She spoke loudly to be heard above the helicopter. "You are standing by a Jeep! Please be careful as you get into the vehicle!"

Hands assisted the Russian to gently pull and push as he climbed into the Jeep. Volkov sat and two forms crowded next to him, one on each side. The familiar position suggested Lyons and Schwarz remained his close companions.

"We're almost there," Lyons assured him. "Just a little bit farther."

Volkov nodded. He had no choice but to accept the conditions and did so in silence. The Russian feared the ride would be long, but his travel in darkness lasted only a few minutes. The Jeep came to a halt, and he was guided from the rig to something large and motionless. Although the blindfold prevented him from seeing the massive object, he still detected the increased shade that made the darkness over his eyes even deeper and he didn't feel a breeze in front of him. Something stood in the path of the wind. He guessed this to be a building.

"Mind the steps," Lyons's voice advised, confirming Volkov's suspicions.

They mounted the risers. Electronic beeps sounded. Volkov recognized the sounds. He had been to high-security installations in the past and recalled coded access doors that could be opened only by punching in a certain series of numbers. These numbers would probably be changed from time to time to ensure no one with a keen ear and natural pitch could detect the tone pattern and determine the correct series for the code.

He was guided through a doorway and inside the building. At least three figures escorted him across a floor. They stayed close to Volkov, and he couldn't tell if he walked across a spacious room or a narrow corridor. These people didn't intend to give him any information about where he was that he wouldn't need to help them, Volkov realized. They were very good, very careful.

The Russian passed through another doorway. The hum of machinery and air-conditioning announced a different environment. At last the blindfold was removed. The Russian blinked his eyes to adjust to the sudden light. The room wasn't painfully bright, but light reflected on plastic and metal all around him.

"Sorry if our precautions caused you any discomfort, Mr. Volkov," a deep male voice said.

Two strangers faced the scientist. A big man, approaching middle age and clearly burdened by stress, took an unlit cigar from his mouth. The other man also seemed large, although he sat in a wheelchair. The first extended his hand.

"Glad to finally meet you," Hal Brognola declared. "We looked for you pretty hard."

Volkov shook hands with the big Fed.

"Since others were looking for me, as well," he replied, "I am glad your people found me first."

"You got a good idea why we brought you here," Aaron Kurtzman said as he shook Volkov's hand. "Got one hell of a situation here. National security threatened, only need a little shove to get us into war, assassination teams running around and a strong possibility this is just the beginning of what the enemy has planned."

"Who is the enemy?" Volkov asked, a trace of suspicion in his tone.

"That's still one of the problems we're trying to deal with," Brognola replied. "We know who some of the players are, but we still don't know who's behind it, what they want or where to find them."

"But we do think we're making progress," the woman said.

Volkov turned to face Barbara Price. He was surprised to see such a beautiful blond lady working with these grizzled veterans. The woman offered him a slight smile.

"Let me rephrase that," she said. "We *are* making progress."

"You are?" Volkov asked with raised eyebrows. "I'm glad of that. I'm not sure how much help I can be since someone has obviously taken ACR even further than we had in the Soviet Union when I worked with Professor Bukovsky."

"You're still the expert in the field," Kurtzman said. "As far as we can tell, you're the only real expert left who isn't working for the other side. Maybe you can take a look at my computer graphics based on what we've got so far and give us your opinion."

Volkov nodded. He watched Kurtzman wheel himself to the horseshoe-shaped cockpit of the computer center. The Russian expected Kurtzman would need some time to access the computer, key in the necessary data, summon the graphics from the memory banks and display them on the screen. However, the Stony Man teraflops computer system was faster and more efficient than anything Volkov had encountered in the past—especially with Aaron Kurtzman at the keyboard.

The stark 3-D images suddenly appeared on the wall screen. Volkov was startled by the unexpected detail and quality of the computer graphics. Brognola and Price had seen it before, but they were clearly impressed, as well. Volkov watched with amazement as Kurtzman programmed the colored tracking patterns of the area covered by the ACR wave during the sea battle in the Persian Gulf.

"Okay," Kurtzman began, "we figure the aggressive concentrated radar reflected across the spy satellites in the area. By area, I mean quite a patch of territory. Yet we've reduced the affected area to within roughly two thousand square miles."

"*Da,*" the Russian began. "Yes. I see what you mean. The radar equipment on the satellites actually assisted the ACR and bounced it down to the gulf. The radar and sonar aboard the vessels transmitted it farther on ground and sea level. It functioned like a current of electricity, moving from one conduit to another conduit without any diminishment of its power. Incredible. Bukovsky had claimed this could be done, but he never got the opportunity to prove it."

"Did you know it affected the computers and other electronic systems on the ships and tracking stations?" Brognola asked.

"I'm not really too surprised to hear that," Volkov said. "ACR is a deliberately forceful wavelength. It will cause electromagnetic disturbances, just as created in nature by sunspots. I can see how ACR could affect radio, telephone or even telegraph communications."

"None of the other people associated with ACR development that we were able to contact said anything about those sort of side effects," Kurtzman remarked. "I don't recall coming across anything like that when we researched the stuff on file about the research, either."

"They probably didn't work with it long enough to appreciate the potential," Volkov explained. "Or they might have deliberately left such 'side effects' out of their reports. Bear in mind, the military was basically interested in ACR as a way to cloak fighter jets from enemy radar. They didn't want something that would cause chaos for both sides during a battle.''

"So you can turn it loose," Brognola said, "but you can't really control what it will do. The waves cover a wide pattern, but it doesn't discriminate one side from the other."

"Exactly," the scientist confirmed. "That's why if the Iranians used it in this sea battle, they were quite foolish. It would have put their forces at as great or even greater disadvantage as the American ships."

"We don't think the Iranians are responsible," Brognola said. "Somebody might want us to believe that, and they damn sure want Iran to go to war. We think it might be a scheme carried out by some sort of independent outfit that isn't part of a government of any country."

"That's hard to believe," Volkov remarked.

"Just before you arrived," Price stated, "we received information from the FBI in Kentucky, Ohio and Indiana. They identified some of the men involved in the attack on your cabin. Turns out they were petty criminals, each with a history of crimes of violence. Yet none were members of organized crime or any sort of political extremist group."

"Just like the hoods who tried to take out our guy in Turkey," Brognola added. "That suggests whoever is responsible doesn't have a limitless supply of trained, professional agents or commandos. They have to hire free-lancers to make up for the lack of manpower. Any government with military and intelligence agencies wouldn't have that problem. An independent would."

"There are other possible reasons for hiring locals," Price admitted. "If the enemy would have too much difficulty operating in certain parts of the United States without attracting attention, they might hire somebody who wouldn't have that problem. A group of Asians or Arabs or even Europeans who spoke little English or with a pronounced accent, would probably stick out in Kentucky or Georgia. People would remember them. Or they might have hired street thugs so in case anything went wrong, they could try to make it appear to be actions of common criminals."

"Yet if they're carrying out operations in America, Russia and Turkey, as well as responsible for the ACR sabotage," Volkov said, "they must be very large, well organized and well financed."

"If they were a bunch of punks, we would have nailed them by now," the big Fed stated. "Just because they're independent doesn't mean they'll be easy to locate."

"Speaking of locations," Kurtzman said. "Let me show Mr. Volkov the general sites of where the enemy stronghold might be based on our information about ACR."

Another display of brilliant computer graphics appeared on the wall screen. Volkov's eyes widened at the precise detail of the map. The mountains were illuminated with pale blue and bright orange to enhance the sites.

"So what do you think?" Price asked.

"I think you have a remarkable computer system," the Russian replied. "You are correct to assume the conspirators would need an elevated station to effectively use ACR against satellite targets."

"The orange lights are the areas considered most likely for choices by the enemy," Kurtzman explained. "The blue areas are still possible, but unlikely due to the estimated range for ACR wavelengths based on the information available to us. Since we suspect Iran is being set up, we also figure the enemy wouldn't have a base there or the small Arab countries in the gulf region. Not much mountain range in those little countries anyway."

"I'm inclined to agree with what you've done here," Volkov stated. "Of course it is possible whoever is doing this has also found a way to increase the effective range of ACR. Still, I doubt they'd try to use it at the very limit of estimated accuracy. Your map is probably correct. The enemy is somewhere in this area, among the orange mountain ranges."

"Okay," Brognola said, "but that still covers a hell of a lot of territory in five or six different countries. How do we whittle that down to the most likely spot?"

"That's a good question," Volkov replied. "They would need a fairly large platform for the equipment, and the reflector disk or dish is fairly large. Roughly the size of a big radar dish for standard satellite communication. In fact, that's what it would appear to be from a distance."

"Yeah," Kurtzman said, "we know. We've seen pictures and diagrams of them. Are you sure somebody couldn't have developed a more compact model? Maybe a system that could be mobile, perhaps carried around in the back of a truck?"

"I doubt that," Volkov said. "A large reflector disk would be necessary to use any form of radar to cover such a large area. ACR is no different in that respect. Also, it would require a power source. Fairly powerful and consistent.''

"Figure they couldn't do that with diesel engines?'' Brognola inquired.

"I wouldn't rule out the possibility, but it seems more likely they'd use a hydroelectric source or perhaps solar-energy cells. If they had effective storage cells, the power from the sun could still be used to produce electricity at night or during cloudy days. Generators could be used to backup such a system and perhaps during prolonged periods of rain or snow.''

"So they need a fairly large setup and it would probably be stationary,'' Price commented. "I doubt they'd leave it unprotected. That means there's probably an armed security force, as well. Weather on mountains tends to be harsh. Cold or exposure to the sun would both be concerns. They'd need dwellings. At the very least they'd need tents. Maybe more permanent structures. Heated billets, for example.''

"Yeah,'' Brognola agreed. "And that means a bunch of guys must have spent some time putting that base together, setting up equipment and hauling in supplies. Somebody must have noticed something.''

"I know one source to check,'' Kurtzman informed them. "Maybe these bastards can block SIGINT spy satellites with their ACR, but they had to get their gear ready to be able to do it. Even if they can hide from us now, they might have been observed by recon satellites while the base was under construction. Hell, if we're really lucky, we might be able to locate it by observing videotape from SIGINT satellites currently in orbit.''

"Sounds like you need to spend some more time at the keyboard, buddy," Brognola said. "The computer can scan that data faster than we could do on our own. Patch through to NSA, ONI, CIA and any other sources that might have satellite recon material on file."

Kurtzman was already punching keys to summon up a list of access codes and passwords to get the necessary information. Even as he worked, another computer screen came alive with a flashing amber light to be certain it wouldn't be ignored. Price headed for the terminal. She saw a password blink on the screen and gain access as a preamble to the message that followed.

"It's from the Justice Department," Price announced. It was the same as saying it was from Leo Turrin, but she didn't want to use his name with Volkov in the room. "Some of the assassination team in Kentucky aren't on file with the FBI. The American branch of Interpol is with the Justice Department. They've run a check on those men. Apparently they carried Austrian or Swiss passports, but those governments have no record of citizens by the names those men used."

"You said apparently they carried such passports?" Volkov inquired, confused by her choice of words.

"Some of the bodies and evidence was destroyed by the grenade blasts and burning gasoline used during the fight between our three commandos and the assassins," Price explained. "Anyway, Austrian and Swiss passports were found."

"But they were forged passports," Brognola remarked. "That probably means those guys weren't really Austrian or Swiss. When somebody pretends to be from a different country, they usually choose one with a language they speak fluently. Austrians speak German, and I think the official languages in Switzerland are both German and French."

"Switzerland has four official languages," Kurtzman said without looking up from his computer terminal. "French, German, Italian and Romansh."

Brognola glanced at the Bear. He didn't know how Kurtzman happened to know this information, but he was certain it was accurate. Kurtzman didn't refer to anything as a fact unless he was sure of it.

"The point is," the big Fed said, "German is probably their native language. Has Interpol made a positive ID on any of these guys based on photos, fingerprints, dental records?"

"Not yet," Price answered as she watched Turrin's message continue across the screen. "They have notified European offices, including the BND in Germany. Should have some word as to the success of these efforts in an hour or two. A few of the would-be assassins are still alive, but they're hospitalized with injuries and can't be interrogated yet."

"How long do you think I'll have to stay here?" Volkov asked. "I realize this is important, but I do have a family."

"Wish we could give you an answer," Brognola replied. "We might need you for a couple of days, or this could drag on for weeks. Sorry, Mr. Volkov. That's just the way it is."

"Please," the Russian said, "call me Nikolai or just Nick. What should I call you?"

"Uh ... Smith, Brown and Jones," the big Fed answered.

"I see," Volkov said with a sigh. "Which of you is which?"

"Take your pick," Brognola said with a shrug.

CHAPTER NINETEEN

Above the Caspian Sea
Wednesday, 1911 hours

Fog rose to meet the small fleet of gliders. The windscreen to Sadek Nimeri's aircraft was covered by thick gray mist. The Iraqi clenched his teeth and gripped the bar in helpless rage and fear. Some of the Syrians in his unit had convinced him motorized gliders would be a superb method of transportation for their mission. The Syrians were experienced with such aircraft and had received extensive training during their time in the military. Apparently some genius in the Syrian army decided motorized gliders would be an ideal method of invading Israel.

Nimeri wished he hadn't listened to those idiots. He had found the gliders easy to operate, pleasant to use and lightweight for mobility. However, that was when the Syrians taught him how to operate a glider. The training sessions had been conducted in daylight with good weather. In dense fog and increasing darkness, the gliders no longer seemed safe. Nimeri became painfully aware of the flimsy construction, the limited power of the compact motors and the extreme risks involved in using the gliders.

Of course, to remain in Iran presented enormous risk, as well. Nimeri and his men had discovered the

Iranian military was combing the area between Kerman and Zahedan, searching for a group of men fitting the general description of the commando unit. Apparently a lieutenant colonel had become suspicious about reports of a fishing boat sighted during the sea battle in the gulf. They had to have found the vessel because the officer managed to convince his superiors to order an intensive search for "possible fugitives, disguised as nomadic merchants or similar travelers, who might have been involved in a conspiracy to plunge Iran into war."

That was what Nimeri heard on a radio broadcast intercepted by his transceiver unit. Who was Colonel Sabzeh and why was he being such a pest? How had he become suspicious and why had he been so determined to convince his commanders the sea battle had been started by outside forces? Under different circumstances, Nimeri would have appreciated Sabzeh's competence and courage. Contradicting the Iranian government's official version of events had been extremely dangerous, and Sabzeh could easily have paid for it with his life for daring to do so. However, he had to have made quite an impression to be able to get the officials to accept the possibility they might be wrong.

At that moment Nimeri didn't feel any admiration for Colonel Sabzeh. He felt nothing but fear, anger and the burning desire to survive. Staying alive seemed almost impossible as he rode the glider across the Caspian Sea.

The motor puttered like a moped within the wooden hull of the fragile craft. One of the Syrians actually piloted the glider in the cockpit behind Nimeri. The man kept assuring the Iraqi everything was all right and not to worry. Nimeri couldn't remember the Syrian's name at the time. It hardly mattered. He hated all Syrians for being fond of gliders. Nimeri also hated the Iranians for being difficult, the Americans because they had failed to declare war when they were supposed to, the Armenians for not getting Russia to back them in an invasion of Iran, which would have saved Nimeri and his troops a lot of trouble.

He also hated Abdel Gahiz for sending him on the insane mission to Iran. Damn that German Giessler for convincing Gahiz the scheme to start a war with Iran could help Gazhi seize power in Iraq. Curse Bukovsky for coming up with aggressive concentrated radar. To hell with everyone except Nimeri and the men under his command. At that moment they were the only lives in the entire world Nimeri cared about.

At least two of his men had already been lost during the flight across the Caspian Sea. Nimeri had seen one glider suddenly plunge from the sky to the merciless waters below. They didn't carry parachutes. Due to the cramped space within the gliders, there was no room for such devices. Besides, the gliders cruised at a slow rate, low in the sky to avoid Iranian and Russian radar. They probably wouldn't have time to bail out with parachutes anyway. There simply wouldn't be enough time before a glider went down.

Nimeri knew the men wouldn't survive the crash landing in the sea. The gliders weren't sturdy enough to hold together from such a nosedive. The poor bastards could do nothing but ask God to receive their souls with mercy before the craft smashed into the waves. Nimeri was an atheist and wouldn't even have the comfort of a final prayer if his glider went out of control and delivered him to a violent, wet death.

The sense of helplessness and frustration was maddening. Nimeri couldn't see where they were headed through the dense fog cover. The size and simplicity of the gliders prevented any radio contact aside from the use of small two-way hand-held units, which failed to pick up anything but static. Nimeri saw the tail of a glider in front of his craft. At least one other of them remained aloft, he thought with relief.

The fog swallowed the tail of the lead glider, robbing Nimeri of what slender confidence he had clung to that somehow they would successfully reach Russian soil. They might indeed face new dangers then, but Nimeri would welcome a confrontation with human opponents after the harrowing flight. Combat with men was different. Nimeri was familiar with life and death on the battlefield. At least a man had a chance against something that could be shot, stabbed or blown to bits with a grenade. There was no way to fight the pull of gravity if the glider suddenly fell from the sky.

Suddenly a shape appeared amid the fog. The huge gray mass resembled a massive hunched back. For a terrible, fearful instant Nimeri thought it might be a whale. Perhaps the glider had drifted too low in the fog and they were skimming the surface of the Caspian Sea. However, he soon recognized the formation to be a hill or small mountain. The glider had reached Russia.

"Not much longer," the Syrian announced. "That weather gave me some concern back there, but we made it. Praise to God!"

"I'd be more thankful if God had allowed us all to survive the trip," Nimeri bitterly replied.

He knew he shouldn't voice such sacrilege because the Syrian might be a devout Muslim, but Nimeri had glanced out the Plexiglas windscreen to discover only two gliders trailed behind his craft. Another was ahead. Four total. Two had gone down over the Caspian. Four of his men had perished in the sea below, and the number of his unit had been reduced to eight men. Less than half the original troop strength. Considering the high-risk mission, it was incredible any of them escaped from Iran alive.

"We're approaching the landing area," the Syrian pilot announced. "Someone will be there to meet us?"

"I radioed ahead," Nimeri replied. "Someone had better be there, or I'll march all the way to the base in the Ural and personally shoot Heinz Giessler in the face."

Ural Mountains, Russia
Wednesday, 2112 hours

HEINZ GIESSLER BANGED his fist on his desk. "Who gave Nimeri authorization to leave Iran? We need his commando team in-country to move them into position by the Iran-Iraq border!"

"I'm not certain what happened, sir," Gruber, a fellow German and a communications expert, replied. "I just know Nimeri decided the Iranian authorities were getting closer, and he needed to pull out. Maybe they were at risk of being captured."

"And they doubled that risk by flying over the Caspian Sea to Russia. It's a minor miracle they weren't spotted by Russian military observation posts in the area.''

"Technically they used gliders and didn't fly—"

"I don't need to hear that now, Gruber," Giessler said in a sharp, hard voice. "Nimeri's actions will cause us quite a delay. We'll have to get a team into position by some other method."

He turned to face a wall map of the Middle East. Perhaps the best route would be across the border into Turkey, he thought. From there a commando team could reach the junction that connected the borders of Turkey, Iran and Iraq. It could be done, but it would take days to accomplish. Giessler wasn't certain they could afford to remain at the base that long. His assassination teams had been killed or captured in the United States and Russia. It was difficult to say how much the Americans and Russians might know about his operation, but he couldn't risk staying at the base in case they had somehow discovered its location.

"Gahiz is in the corridor," Gruber said, almost afraid to mention the Iraqi at the moment. "I believe he wants to talk to you."

"We don't always get what we want," Giessler replied, his tone filled with caustic anger. "Do we?"

"No, sir."

"Personally I want to watch Gahiz and Nimeri both choke to death on camel dung," Giessler growled, "but I guess I won't get that wish. Will I, Gruber?"

"I don't think so . . ."

"Go back to your post," Giessler said with a sigh, "and tell Gahiz to come in."

The German communications man quickly left his superior's office. Abdel Gahiz entered, looking grim.

The Iraqi never seemed very happy, but his expression suggested doomsday had arrived.

"I know about Nimeri's decision to flee," Gahiz said. "I am frankly shocked by his cowardice. He is a disgrace to the Arab people and the nation of Iraq. When he arrives, I will personally execute him and the other Iraqis under his command."

"Really?" Giessler said with surprise.

"Of course," Gahiz replied. "I will also advise Mahdi and Kadafadem to deal with the Syrian and Libyan traitors in the same manner. That should discourage any of our other personnel from running away from their duty."

"It will encourage them to run away from us," the German declared. "I know you're angry. I'm angry, too, but we can't respond to this setback like barbarian lunatics. That's the sort of thing Saddam Hussein would do. Did you forget how quickly Iraqi soldiers surrendered to U.S. ground troops during the Gulf War?"

"You're not suggesting we reward disloyalty and cowardice?"

Giessler snorted with disgust. "Nimeri is not a coward. He already proved his courage. So have the others with him. They accomplished their mission when ordered to start a border conflict between Iran and Armenia. They were even more successful in the Persian Gulf."

"They still had no right to retreat without permission to do so," Gahiz insisted.

"I'm certain Nimeri didn't make that decision without good reason," Giessler said, surprised that he found himself defending the commando's actions.

"Gruber tells me Nimeri believed the Iranian authorities were getting close to finding his team. Nothing would be accomplished if Nimeri and his men got captured by the Iranians. You're aware of the interrogation tactics often employed in Tehran? They could make Nimeri and the others talk."

"They should kill themselves rather than be taken prisoner."

"I'm sure they would have if it came to that," Giessler commented. "A self-inflicted bullet in the brain is better than suffering in a torture chamber. However, Nimeri chose to get out. We really can't fault a man for wanting to stay alive or to protect the lives of his men."

Gahiz smiled. "You advocate mercy? That surprises me. I did not think forgiveness was part of your beliefs. You certainly showed little mercy toward those Russians who tried to leave the base. Why so generous toward Nimeri's disobedience?"

"Do you have another man with his qualifications to replace Nimeri?" Giessler asked. "A trained commando, familiar with Iran, its geography, culture and language? One who has already earned the respect and loyalty of fellow commando soldiers? If so, fine. That we won't need Nimeri, and you can do with him as you like."

Gahiz considered the German's words for a moment.

"So you want to send him back to Iran?" Gahiz mused. "I suppose you have a point. Nimeri does have special qualifications. Of course, he might refuse."

"So we can execute him if he doesn't agree," Giessler said with a shrug. "Don't misunderstand me. I'm not happy with Nimeri and I really don't care if he lives or dies, but it doesn't make much sense to kill the man if we can still use his talents. He's the best man for the job, and we really don't have a replacement for the mission."

"But if it's true the authorities were hunting Nimeri and his team in Iran..."

"They were supposedly looking for the commandos along the Persian Gulf or toward the central eastern part of Iran," Giessler said. "They won't be expecting us to send a team to the western border area."

"How long will it take for commandos to reach this site?"

"A day or more. When Nimeri arrives, we'll give him his new assignment and send him on his way. Then we'll see about striking base and moving to a new location. Simply as a precaution. I'm still confident our operation will succeed."

"It better," Gahiz warned. "Your life depends on it."

Giessler nodded, but didn't voice his thoughts. If he had to die, he'd take all of them with him.

CHAPTER TWENTY

Moscow, Russia
Wednesday, 2235 hours

Mack Bolan listened intently as Phoenix Force briefed him on the progress made by the commando team. The Executioner had said little on the trip from the airport to OO headquarters. Based on what he knew about the new Russian Defense service, the Intelligence agency didn't deserve any merit badges for competence. Realizing the limo might be bugged, the warrior waited until he could meet with Phoenix Force in person to discuss the mission.

"Your theory about the base being here in Russia because Wolfgang seemed confident he could get reinforcements for the assassin team on short notice may be right, Yakov," Bolan remarked. "Any luck trying to identify who Wolfgang really is or what might have happened to him?"

The warrior sat at a conference table with the five-man army. The room was soundproof, and they had swept for bugs to be certain they could talk in total privacy. This also gave Bolan an opportunity to inspect the weapons and other gear delivered by the diplomatic pouch to the American Embassy. Hal Brognola had to have chewed out Wesley Rollins thoroughly, the soldier guessed. The CIA case officer had personally taken the package to Moscow to make certain it would be there when Bolan arrived.

"Unfortunately," Katzenelenbogen said, "most of the SSD files were destroyed, either deliberately or by anti-Communist protesters who stormed the headquarters in East Berlin. A lot of KGB records about covert activities were also destroyed or altered when they realized communism was going down the drain. We haven't been able to get much from the OO computer system, but we're patching through a few names of possible suspects to the Bear. Maybe he has more details about these SSD agents or can access it from CIA or NSA."

"The good news is there were only four guys in the SSD who fit the description of Wolfgang," Gary Manning added. "One of them is living in Switzerland, in charge of bank security at a major firm. There's no evidence to suggest he left the country in over a year. Another guy had spent some time in Saudi Arabia, but there's nothing on the files we could get to suggest he was ever in Iraq, Libya or Syria."

"Bear in mind," Encizo said, "that Wolfgang might not have told the truth about his background. What our prisoner said about the man may be sheer fabrication."

"True," Bolan agreed, "but if we find someone with a history similar to that alleged to be Wolfgang's background, it'll sure increase the probability we're after the right guy."

"Well," Manning stated, "judging from what little we've been able to gather, I'm inclined to think there are only two men who could possibly be Wolfgang. One is a guy named Umbert Hauser who is currently believed to be working freelance in Central Africa. The other is Heinz Giessler. KGB figured he was a genius at languages and strategy. He damn sure worked as a go-between for Soviet–East German operations and probably even commanded KGB operatives in the Middle East from time to time. Both Hauser and Giessler speak Russian, English and Arabic.''

"Let's not spin our wheels trying to guess something when we really don't have enough information," Bolan said. "Maybe Kurtzman will come up with something. Even if he does, it won't help us much unless it gives us a clue where to find the enemy base. You also said you think it's possible an Arab government or possibly a renegade faction is bankrolling the ACR conspiracy?''

"Just a suspicion based on the claim Wolfgang spent some time in that part of the world," Katz replied with a shrug. "Rafael may be right and we could be chasing a phantom. Still, Major Fedeyev has his people looking into the records of recent visitors to Russia from the Middle East. Especially persons with Arab passports.''

"Don't know what's taking him so bloody long," David McCarter complained. "Can't be too many visitors from that part of the world here in Russia. Not much reason for them to come here since the good old days of Soviet support for Marxist and military socialist regimes is officially over.''

"Fedeyev and his people might be taking longer because they're looking for something they aren't going to find," Calvin James remarked. "We don't know there is an Arab connection, and if there is, the parties from the Middle East could have entered the country by covert methods. If they sneaked across the border, the OO can search passports and airport surveillance-camera footage until the year 2000 and not find a thing."

"And I admit there's a very good chance no Arabs were sent to oversee operations," Katz added. "I just suggested it because it seemed likely whoever financed the conspiracy would want firsthand knowledge as to how it was going."

"Better we bark up a couple wrong trees than leave the forest," Bolan commented. He frowned and added, "I feel that we've all overlooked something that could make all the pieces of the puzzle fall into place. I just wish I had some idea what the hell it might be."

"Maybe we're looking in the wrong direction," Encizo suggested. "Like a stage magician gets the audience to look at his right hand while the left makes the card disappear."

"A distraction," Bolan said thoughtfully.

Electrical beeps announced someone at the coded access panel to the door. It slid open and Major Fedeyev entered. The OO officer's expression was difficult to determine. Although stress lines pulled down the corners of his mouth and long hours of research left his eyes tinted red and puffy, his manner seemed more energetic than Phoenix Force had previously observed. It seemed Fedeyev might be excited, but his body was too tired to display this unfamiliar emotion with gusto.

"I trust you've finished briefing Mr. Belasko," the Russian said. "If so, you might want to hear what we found by consulting airport security surveillance, customs and the Moscow police."

"We can use all the encouraging news we can get," James replied. "Shoot, Major."

"Shoot?" Fedeyev repeated with a frown. "Oh, yes. Slang for 'talk.' Like the expression 'shoot your mouth off.' When I first heard that I thought it was a vicious remark to urge someone to commit suicide—"

"Will you tell us what you found out before I'm tempted to shoot *your* mouth off?" McCarter snapped with impatient anger.

Fedeyev stared at the Briton, startled by the vehemence expressed by the threat. Katz kicked McCarter in the shin, the action concealed by the table. Manning glared at the sharp-tongued Englishman and shook his head. Bolan looked up at Fedeyev and shrugged.

"Just another slang expression," he explained. "We would like to hear what you discovered, Major."

"We looked into information about recent visitors from the Middle East," Fedeyev told them. "Not surprisingly we didn't find many from Libya, Iraq or Syria who weren't directly connected with their embassies or other diplomatic efforts. However, we did find a number of persons claiming to be from Saudi Arabia or Jordan. There were also five individuals with Egyptian passports who flew to Moscow from Riyadh.

"At first," the Russian continued, "we were only mildly suspicious, but the Moscow police have been able to locate a number of these visitors. They haven't returned to their hotel rooms for almost two weeks. So we checked with customs to discover all the suspicious Arab 'tourists' had nothing to declare and brought little in their luggage aside from some warm-weather clothing. However, the three men clearly in charge of each group—the alleged Saudi, Jordanian and Egyptian entourage—all carried an unusually large amount of money—U.S. dollars and British pounds, not Russian or any type of currency from Arab countries."

"Interesting," Katz agreed, "but not exactly damning evidence."

"Yet it was enough for us to continue investigating their background," the Russian said. "We were especially interested in the three leaders of these groups. Fortunately customs and airport security were also suspicious and kept records and videotapes of these individuals. With everything that's happened recently, they suspected these might have been Iranians pretending to be Arabs to carry out some sort of sabotage."

"But they arrived prior to the border clash between Iran and Armenia," Encizo commented. "Do they usually make and keep surveillance tapes of foreign visitors?"

"If they feel one might seem suspicious," Fedeyev answered. "They took the tapes and logged the information as a precaution, but they kept them because of events over the past few days. Since you'll probably find out this embarrassing fact anyway, I might as well tell you customs had tried to contact us about this matter on Monday. Unfortunately communication and cooperation between different departments within our government isn't very good."

"The same thing happens in the United States," Bolan assured him. "Maybe that's a sign your democratic reforms are really working and you're getting the same sort of headaches America has had for decades."

"That's something I would have rather avoided, Mr. Belasko," the major said. "However, we do have photographs and video footage of these individuals, as well as information about their passports. We might need your help to go much farther."

"How's that?" Manning inquired.

"The United States has better relations with Egypt, Saudi Arabia and Jordan than Russia has at this time," Fedeyev admitted. "It will be considerably more difficult for us to get those countries to give us information about their citizens than if your department in America requested this data."

"Right," Bolan said. "Time to make another high-tech computer phone call."

Stony Man Farm, Virginia
Wednesday, 1806 hours

AARON KURTZMAN RECOGNIZED the access numbers and password on the screen. He didn't have to consult the computer menu to respond and keyed Mack Bolan into the system. The warrior was using the visual monitor again. Kurtzman punched the intercom alert button to signal Hal Brognola and Barbara Price to either access their terminals to the mainframe or head for the computer room.

"Is this important?" Volkov asked as the screen announced that audio visual contact had been established. "Should I leave the room?"

"Stay here, Nick," Kurtzman replied. "Got someone we want you to meet."

The images took shape on the wall screen. Mack Bolan appeared, once again partially hidden in the shadows as he sat behind a desk.

"Hello, Mike," Kurtzman greeted. "Mr. Smith wants to know if your package arrived okay at the embassy."

"It arrived," the Executioner replied. "You must have someone with limited authorization present to be using bogus names."

The Bear waved Volkov to the screen. The Russian stepped forward and nodded to the magnified figure on the wall. Kurtzman gave brief introductions.

"Glad you made it, Mr. Volkov," Bolan said, then addressed the Bear.

"What am I suppose to call you? Chairman?"

"Oh," Kurtzman replied, "I'm Jones today."

"You guys aren't straining your brains to be original. I have some other names and passports that might be phony, as well. Already sent it by fax. Need the info on them PDQ."

"Everybody is in such a rush these days," the Bear remarked. "The fellas with you in Russia asked for some data on a couple of former East German Intelligence officers."

"Yeah. Hauser and Giessler."

"You can forget about Hauser. He was arrested in Zaire last week, and he's in a prison cell awaiting trial. Apparently he sided with the wrong bunch of would-be revolutionaries. Heinz Giessler is Wolfgang. I'm pretty convinced of that."

"You sound sure of that," Bolan remarked.

Brognola suddenly entered the computer room. An unlit cigar stump jutted from the corner of his mouth as he looked up at the screen.

"Did Rollins get that package to you when you reached Moscow?" he asked.

"I got it," Bolan replied. "I was talking with Mr. Jones about Giessler."

"Right," Kurtzman said as he rolled his wheelchair to a stack of printout sheets and fax copies of photographs. "You know a bunch of assassins tried to kill Nick Volkov and his family, but they were stopped by three guys who you know quite well. Most of those killers are now lying on marble slabs with tags on their toes. A few wound up in a hospital. The majority were hired thugs, but some were foreign agents with fake passports. Interpol and CIA managed to ID all but one of them. There wasn't enough left of that guy to figure out who he was."

"And they turned out to be German citizens," Brognola added. "East Germans who disappeared when the wall came down."

"Did they also happen to be members of the SSD?" Bolan asked.

"You got it," Kurtzman confirmed. "And one of the dudes in the hospital was also an East German agent. A .357 Magnum slug chewed up his arm pretty bad, but his mouth still worked. He told us the merry band of assassins was led by a fella named Warner Muller. The guy got blown to bits when a grenade hit his car, but CIA discovered Herr Muller used to work with another SSD agent back in Eastern Europe during the cold war."

"Giessler," Bolan stated.

"That's right," Brognola said. "According to the information we found on Giessler, he was a real ball of fire. KGB thought he was terrific. SSD figured he was the best man they ever had. He would have been a shoo-in to be promoted to director of SSD if East Germany hadn't gone the way of the dinosaurs."

"He probably would care to have all that power and influence go down the drain," Bolan agreed. "Sure sounds like we got positive ID on Wolfgang."

"I'm faxing you a couple of photos of the guy just in case you come across him," Kurtzman announced as he waved some file folders with pictures attached. "And if you do, remember Giessler is one shrewd son of a bitch."

"May I see that, please?" Volkov asked, staring at the folder in the Bear's hand.

Kurtzman handed it over. Volkov studied the photograph and nodded grimly.

"I've seen this man before. He knew Professor Bukovsky fairly well. I saw them together from time to time, but Bukovsky never introduced him to me. I assumed the man was a high-ranking party member or KGB. I didn't know he was German, either. Seemed to speak Russian fluently."

"Wait a minute," Bolan said. "Bukovsky was the Russian scientist who supposedly died in a fishing accident. 'Listed as dead' was the term used. That means they didn't find his body."

"And he knew Giessler," Brognola added. "The man staged his death so he could work with Giessler on this scheme."

"You know Bukovsky," Kurtzman said as he turned to Volkov. "You figure he'd be willing to participate in a conspiracy as ruthless and ambitious as this ACR sabotage?''

"Yes," Volkov answered without hesitation. "Bukovsky was a very ambitious, selfish man. He enjoyed the power and status he held under the Communist regime and certainly wouldn't want to see that end. He was very upset when the Kremlin cut funding for his research. Bukovsky was probably the leading expert in aggressive concentrated radar in the world, and he was certain he could prove ACR had far greater potential than the Soviet military appreciated."

"I think he *has* proved it," Bolan stated. "That was a missing piece. We knew the enemy used ACR, but we didn't know how they got the necessary expertise in a field that seemed to have damn few experts. We overlooked a dead man who wasn't really dead."

"Hell," Brognola muttered, "we even thought Bukovsky might have been murdered by the enemy. Turns out he's one of them. Sneaky bastards."

"Not sneaky enough," Bolan said. "Mr. Volkov, you knew Bukovsky fairly well. Where would he set up a base for ACR operations? Bear in mind, he feels he can do this without anyone suspecting he's involved because everybody thinks he's dead."

"The Ural Mountains," Volkov replied. "Bukovsky was originally from a village in the area. The state recognized his extraordinary intellect when he was a boy and shipped him off to advanced science schools when he was still quite young, but he still spoke of the Ural Mountains frequently. More than once he said it would be an ideal site for an ACR dish. In fact, I have an idea where it might be along the mountain range."

"Do tell," Bolan said with interest. "How's that?"

"I've been studying satellite recon information try-ing to find evidence of possible construction of an ACR base at an elevated position," Volkov stated. "I came across several possibilities. There's a radar sta-tion in northern Iraq, an apparent weather observa-tion post in Syria, that sort of thing. Now, several months ago there was some construction carried out near a mountain peak in the Urals. Nothing definite, but there were armed troops present and they did have what might have been large photovoltaic cells, used to harness solar energy from the sun to create electricity. However, there was no satellite data on the finished station. I had assumed the project was simply termi-nated for some reason."

"But you said there wasn't further recon made by the satellites..." Brognola began. He stopped in midsen-tence when he realized what Volkov suspected. "You think the bastards might be using the ACR to hide their position from spy satellites?"

"ACR would render laser camera or radio waves, as well as radio-radar surveillance, useless," the Russian said. "This could be accomplished by simply leaving the dish at a constant low level of transmission. Not enough to overtly affect the observation satellites, but adequate to deflect their recon efforts."

"So the base would seem to disappear," Bolan mused. "It is virtually invisible to satellite recon. How about more conventional aerial recon? Planes could fly over the area and photograph it using plain old long-range lens and video cameras. No fancy high-tech stuff. Does it have any defenses for that?"

"No," Volkov replied, "but I imagine Giessler would consider that. The site must be well camouflaged."

"But we have an idea of what we're looking for now," Bolan said. "Something else occurred to me. Fell told me that they couldn't get any sort of radar or radio wavelengths at Mountain Balloon when the satellites failed to transmit over Armenia and Iran, but they picked up some ham radio operators. What about shortwave radio waves? Would those be affected by ACR?"

"Probably not," Volkov replied, surprised by the question and his own deduction. "It wasn't designed to deal with shortwave radio because that's such an outdated method of communication no one even considered it in our research."

"Okay," Bolan said, "I'm sure we can put together some sort of two-way radio unit that uses shortwave. If we can get the waves to bounce back when they encounter ACR wavelengths, we can judge the distance. That would let us find the location and let us know when we get closer."

"A type of shortwave radar system," Volkov remarked. "Incredible. We never considered something like that. Imagine ACR being vulnerable to such a crude type of device."

"Sometimes that's the sort of thing that's overlooked," Bolan stated. "A man in a bullet-resistant vest might be safe if he's shot in the chest by a .38 Special, but an icepick can pierce between the fibers of the vest to stab him in the heart. No armor makes a person totally safe from attack, and no system provides protection that can't be penetrated one way or the other.''

"Okay," Brognola said. "You guys get to work on this, and we'll see what else we can do at this end. Good work, Mike. I think we're really closing in now.''

"It's not over yet," the Executioner replied. "I'll let you know when we're ready to move. Hang tough.''

"You, too," Brognola urged as Bolan signed off.

CHAPTER TWENTY-ONE

Ural Mountains, Russia
Thursday, 0107 hours

Professor Bukovsky no longer had any vodka to soothe his nerves and repress the terrible fear that gnawed at his stomach. The scientist wondered if he could find some alcohol somewhere at the base. Of course, many of the other men there had some liquor hidden, but their reserves would also be running low. Methyl alcohol was used as a solvent for many purposes, yet Bukovsky was neither stupid enough nor desperate enough to seriously consider drinking wood alcohol.

Ethyl alcohol was what he needed. Bukovsky wasn't aware of any supply of this item at the base. He considered his plight as he washed down some aspirin with a glass of water. He could only hope that they would be able to stock up on liquor at the new base and none of the Muslim teetotalers would accompany them.

Bukovsky wished he had never allowed Giessler to talk him into this insane scheme. In truth, he had been a willing accomplice and had even given the German many of the ideas they had used during the conspiracy, but Bukovsky preferred to think of himself as an innocent victim who had been duped into participating in the plan.

He hadn't expected the stress and fear to be so difficult to deal with. The idea of limitless wealth and power had lured him into the plot, but he suspected they would never succeed. Too many things had gone wrong within the past few days. Less than a week had passed, and already they were being forced to flee from the site that was supposed to be secure. How long could they hope to avoid the international search before they were hunted down and captured?

Bukovsky had also been surprised to discover he genuinely missed his wife and son. Giessler had been right when he reminded the Russian of his unfaithful conduct and neglect. He had been a terrible husband and father. The isolation at the secret base had given him time to contemplate his behavior. Guilt and a sense of loss badgered him night and day. Bukovsky had enjoyed a good life and probably could have continued to do so under the new Russian government. Perhaps his status would have declined, his influence and income fallen a bit. Yet he would have still been employed and received a better salary, a better standard of living, than the vast majority of Russian citizens.

There was no point dwelling on what could have been. Bukovsky had helped carry out actions that caused dozens, perhaps hundreds of deaths. No one would forgive and forget such crimes. They would never stop looking for him. He would never know a moment of peace....

Heinz Giessler marched into the scientist's control center. The German saw Bukovsky's troubled expression. He was tired of Bukovsky's constant fretting and complaining. The Russian had occasionally felt excitement and satisfaction that his theories proved correct. He had been thrilled by the first successful use of ACR technology, and his confidence had boosted to exaggerated heights. However, Bukovsky had clearly abandoned any belief the plan would work in the long run after the series of setbacks occurred.

What they faced were more serious than setbacks, Giessler had to admit. The CIA, or whoever was after them, might have already identified him. Muller was one of the few agents who knew Giessler by his real name, and Muller was either dead or captured. Even his old code name "Wolfgang" might have betrayed him. There was no way to know what the enemy might suspect or what they might know to be fact.

Yet Giessler didn't believe the situation to be hopeless. Far from it. The other side might know he was involved, but that wouldn't help them unless they knew about the base in the Ural Mountains. By the time they learned about it, Giessler and his coconspirators would be in another country, a new base once more in operation.

"I see you're sober," Giessler remarked. "Good. I want you to keep a clear head. We'll be pulling out after Nimeri arrives and we assign him a new mission to Iran."

"Do you really think this can still work?" Bukovsky asked. He shook his head sadly. "Everything has already gone wrong."

"If that was true, fighter jets would have already blasted this place to bits and all of us with it. Your problem is you've had everything too easy your entire life. You didn't want to lose your soft life-style so you agreed to this."

"I made a mistake," Bukovsky said in a soft voice.

"If you thought this would be easy," Giessler agreed. "Nothing is being handed to you this time, Anatoly. You help us take what we want, and you'll share the rewards along with the rest of us. If we fail, you'll go down with the rest of us, too. So stop acting as if you're a condemned prisoner waiting to be executed. I can't afford to have you come apart at the seams. We already have a serious morale problem. I don't regret killing those three deserters, but it didn't make the rest of the men here any happier about this situation. Those traitors had to be stopped and used as an example to the others. That inspired fear, but not confidence. We can't command these men effectively if they don't believe in what we're doing. Fear alone won't be enough. Not if the majority decide to turn against us."

"I'm sorry about Suslev," Bukovsky remarked.

Giessler glanced down at the floor and said, "Suslev was a good man. I could trust him. I have to be able to trust you, too. This is a stressful situation. That's why those three deserters tried to run. Those of us in command can't fold under the pressure or we're all dead."

"I understand," Bukovsky said with a sigh. "How much longer will we be here?"

"Another day or two," Giessler replied. "We don't want to disassemble the ACR equipment until we're ready to go. We still need the shield to keep recon satellites from detecting our presence. Gahiz will almost certainly return to Iraq in order to prepare his revolution against Saddam Hussein. The Iraqi military should be preoccupied with Iran. An ideal time for the overthrow of Saddam."

"That might be more difficult than Gahiz believes," Bukovsky remarked. "Mahdi's plan to remove Assad and take over Syria won't be a simple matter, either. There will certainly be others who want to be president there."

"He has a good idea who most of them are," Giessler replied with a shrug. "After Assad is gone, the competition will also be removed."

"What about Kadafadem's plan in Libya?"

"How they carry out the coup attempts isn't our problem, Anatoly," Giessler said. "All we have to do is deliver what we promised. We'll accomplish that soon enough. Then we'll need to stay out of sight while our Arab friends make their plays for power. If they succeed, we'll be part of the most powerful force in the Middle East."

"Do you really think we can trust them?" Bukovsky asked, his tone suggesting his personal doubts.

"We can trust them to do what's in their best interest," the German answered. "They'll want ACR technology to protect them from satellite observation of weapons systems and troops. They're worried about threats from Israel and fellow Arab nations. Your ACR will give them a strong advantage by blotting out the radar and sonar of enemy forces."

"I still think their plans for taking over those countries are farfetched, foolish dreams," the Russian remarked.

"The fact it seems unlikely they'd try anything this bold is in their favor," Giessler replied. "Actually they have a pretty fair chance of succeeding as long as no one suspects they're involved in any sort of conspiracy."

Moscow, Russia
Thursday, 0115 hours

"WE JUST RECEIVED this information by fax from our headquarters back in the U.S.A.," Yakov Katzenelenbogen began. "Positive identification of the three leaders of the visiting groups recorded by customs and airport security. Turns out they are not Jordanian, Saudi Arabian and Egyptian, but Iraqi, Syrian and Libyan."

The one-armed Israeli placed a stack of computer printout sheets and dot-matrix photos on the table. Mack Bolan picked up the top photo and studied the hawkish face of a man in his midforties. He grunted as he scanned the file on the guy.

"I thought this guy looked vaguely familiar," the warrior remarked. "Can't say I remembered his name. Ahmed Mahdi doesn't exactly roll off my tongue or stay that well in my memory, but I remember a mission a few years ago that concerned covert assistance to Palestinian terrorist groups by a faction of the Syrian military. This guy was part of it."

"Yes," Katz said, "but you'll notice recently he's been on poor terms with President Assad. Apparently he left the country last year because he was regarded as an enemy of the state. The fact he stole approximately nine million dollars from the Syrian treasury certainly didn't help his standing with Assad."

"Don't politicians call that sort of thing an 'accidental withdrawl beyond authorized restrictions'?" Calvin James inquired.

"They might try that in the States," Bolan replied. "Someone does that in a country like Syria, and it probably means a firing squad."

Rafael Encizo examined material about Abdel Gahiz. The man seemed to work hard at imitating Saddam Hussein. Probably because Gahiz wanted to take the strongman's place as leader in Iraq. He had formerly been a supporter of Saddam before Desert Storm, but recently he was believed to be plotting against the Iraqi boss. He had also violated the trust of his government by dipping into the hidden financial resources Saddam had deposited in banks around the world. Gahiz definitely knew how to dip. He might have grabbed close to fourteen million dollars before he disappeared.

"I am impressed by how quickly your organization responds," Major Fedeyev remarked. "The OO computer-research section hadn't even confirmed the passports were false by the time this information arrived with complete details about these men."

"You'll notice that all three of these Arab schemers are renegades," Katz said. "Musa Kadafadem is the only one who isn't officially considered a traitor by the current government of his country."

"The Libyan," David McCarter said as he examined Kadafadem's record. "Looks like he's been close friends with Khaddafi in the past, but they haven't been getting along so well lately. Apparently Kadafadem disagreed with his leader's rather lukewarm support of Saddam's invasion of Kuwait and had been urging Libya to establish closer ties with moderate Arab nations like Saudi Arabia and Oman."

"Doesn't sound so bad to me," James commented. "Still, he must be up to something shady to be traveling with an Egyptian passport and hanging out with these other dudes. Did he rip off his government's treasury, too?"

"Didn't have to," Katz answered. "Musa Kadafadem is independently wealthy. Worth roughly one billion dollars and smart enough to put most of his holdings in Swiss bank accounts."

"Well," Manning stated, "I'd say we found the persons who are financing Giessler's and Bukovsky's ACR operations. Any idea why they're doing it?"

"Or why they came personally to supervise the use of the aggressive concentrated radar instead of sending somebody else," McCarter added. "Seems bloody careless to me."

"Since they're operating on their own, they probably didn't really have anyone they trusted who they figured could command any authority with Giessler," Encizo replied. "That SSD vet isn't the type to be intimidated or bossed around easily. They probably assumed they could get through Russian security without raising any suspicion because this country has a lot of internal problems, but hasn't had much trouble from foreign terrorists."

"Fortunately," Fedeyev said, "they underestimated us."

The Russian officer seemed delighted to prove the OO and other security agencies of his nation weren't as incompetent as the Americans might have thought from previous incidents. Katz appreciated this and nodded in agreement.

"The reason three Arabs with considerable money, influence and ambition would join forces seems obvious," Bolan began. "They all have the same or similar goals, and they're working together to achieve what they want. Good chance Giessler knew all of them from his time in the Middle East and helped to form this union so he could make a deal with them."

"But why do they want to start a war with Iran?" Fedeyev asked. "Do they plan to take over the country after Iran is pounded down by allied forces that consist of Americans, Russians and whoever else could be called in?"

"That doesn't seem very likely," Bolan admitted. "Maybe this is a stage-magician trick, a distraction."

"I don't see what the distraction would be for," Encizo commented.

"If world attention is focused on Iran," the Executioner replied, "no one will be that interested in what happens in the rest of the Middle East. Especially if Iran is at war with Russia and most of the Western world—and if the governments being toppled aren't very popular anyway."

"Hell, yes," McCarter said. "Sammad Hussein isn't very well liked by anyone. He's managed to stay in power just by terror tactics. Assad might have established better relations with the West, but nobody really trusts him and a lot of people say he's similar to Saddam, but more subtle and smarter."

"Of course the United States and Western Europe have been on shaky terms with Khaddafi for almost two decades," Katz remarked, "but Khaddafi does have popular support in Libya. Saddam Hussein has plenty of enemies within Iraq, and Assad probably does in Syria, as well. The majority of Libyans appear to like Khaddafi. It's difficult to carry out a successful revolution under those conditions.''

"So Kadafadem doesn't plan to storm the winter palace,'' Bolan replied. "He could still take power by having Khaddafi assassinated and killing off the other contenders for his throne. Kadafadem isn't regarded as an enemy of Khaddafi. He could 'inherit' the leadership of Libya without appearing to be involved in having the present government wiped out.''

"And after they all take power, they can continue to join forces to create a powerful force of military might, oil and shipping,'' Manning remarked. "There have been attempts for almost a century to unite Arab countries, but distrust and internal problems have always stood in the way. If these three men can appear to form a successful trio of working states, they could start getting support from other factions in other Arab nations that want unity.''

"Who knows what kind of government could take power in Jordan if King Hussein and members of the current regime were removed,'' James mused. "Egypt has always been active in efforts to form Arab unity. They might be lured into joining these guys without realizing what they're getting into. They could form kind of a modern-day gerrymander across part of the Middle East and Africa.''

"A gerrymander?'' Fedeyev asked, unfamiliar with the word.

"It's a term used for creating voting districts in a manner to benefit a ruling political party,'' James explained. "First used when Governor Gerry was accused of doing this in Massachusetts back in 1812.

Critics said the pattern of voting districts on the map looked like a sailamander, and somebody came up with the 'gerrymander' expression."

"You do remember high school history class," McCarter commented.

"I think they taught us that in junior high," James replied. "The gerrymander our enemies are trying to create could consist of more than voting districts. They could put together a genuine power structure with the potential of growing even larger."

"And they'd still have the ACR technology to help conceal any nasty business they wanted to keep secret," Katz added. "Things like nuclear power plants, missile silos, chemical-warfare production centers and so forth. We've seen how much trouble a single ACR dish can do. Imagine what they can accomplish if Bukovsky has limitless access to research and development, expense no limitation. He could produce dozens of the devices and possibly find a way to concentrate the wavelength to only affect the equipment of an enemy during a confrontation."

"Incredible," Fedeyev remarked. "We've got to put an end to this before this madness goes any further. We do know where to find the enemy base now, don't we?"

"We have a good general idea," Bolan replied. "We've got the shortwave radio transceiver unit, which hopefully will help us find the ACR transmissions and the base. All that's left is to head for the Ural Mountains and start looking for it."

"I still wish we could just find the stronghold and blast it to pieces with bombs and missiles from a MiG fighter jet attack," Fedeyev said. "Unfortunately my government wants us to bring back the ACR device. They finally believe that it has military potential."

"The U.S. military wants it, too," Bolan said. "I'm not too concerned with that one way or the other. The main reason we have to go to the base and launch a raid on ground level is because we can't simply destroy it and everyone there. We need evidence to convince the rest of the world what happened. Otherwise, a war with Iran could still occur. If nothing else, distrust and resentment would fester between nations over something this gang of high-tech power mongers are responsible for."

"Oh," Katz interjected, "speaking about trust between Americans and Iranians, a note was included with the faxed data about the Arab conspirators. You met a Lieutenant-Colonel Sabzeh recently, Belasko? I understand you two had an agreeable conversation."

"Yeah," Bolan replied. "Last I heard he was going to the Iranian authorities to try to convince them outsiders might have started the sea battle at the Persian Gulf. Pretty gutsy, since the authorities in Tehran have been known to execute officers of higher rank for questioning the official version of events."

"He made a good impression with you and he also managed to make one with the Iranian leaders," Katz explained. "They listened to him and looked at evidence he discovered along the gulf. Sabzeh has been promoted to general, and he's going to France with a diplomatic corps to meet with the U.S. Secretary of State to discuss recent events."

"Good," Bolan said, relieved. "There's a little sanity left in the world after all."

"But we still have a batch of madmen to take care of," McCarter said with a trace of impatience. "What are we waiting for? Let's go find them."

"As much as I hate to admit it," Gary Manning said, "he does have a point. We've got most of our weapons and gear ready, and we can probably get some rest on our way to the Urals."

"I'd rather we got a larger assembly of troops for this target," Fedeyev admitted. "Twenty commandos doesn't seem adequate to accompany you on this mission."

"If we use more troops, the enemy will certainly see us coming," Bolan replied. "If we need reinforcements, we'll call them in."

"Providing the ACR waves don't jam our radio communications," Encizo remarked.

"Now, why the hell did you have to say something like that?" James asked, sighing.

CHAPTER TWENTY-TWO

Ural Mountains, Russia
Thursday, 0632 hours

Dawn broke across the pale sky, golden rays extended across white clouds to herald a new day. The sun wasn't a comforting sight for Mack Bolan and the twenty-five men in his command. Darkness had offered concealment or at least an illusion of cover from enemy eyes. The enemy would almost certainly have night-vision gear anyway, Bolan thought. In fact, they might be less alert during daylight hours than after sundown.

The group consisted of Bolan, Phoenix Force, Major Fedeyev and nineteen members of the Independent Airborne Force. The latter consisted of an elite fighting unit of paratroopers. Formerly a Soviet military outfit, the Airborne Force had made some changes in training and uniform. Their jump badges still bore a white parachute, but the red star had been removed. The troops still wore the light blue berets and striped T-shirts under fatigue uniforms.

Few of the Russian commandos had seen actual combat. Some had participated in the Soviet invasion of Afghanistan, but the majority had never fired a weapon beyond a training range. However, all were well-trained in a tradition that extended to the Red Army parachute units of World War II. The Russians carried AKS-74 assault rifles. Similar to the AK-47, the AKS featured modifications in the muzzle design and extractor to improve accuracy, control of the weapon and reduce jamming in the chamber. Not as heavy as the elder Kalashnikov model, the AKS fired 5.45 mm ammo, and the recoil was less than that of an AK-47 for additional control while firing on full-auto mode.

The Executioner recalled most of these details as he glanced at the Russian assault rifles. He had studied Soviet weaponry when the USSR was still "the enemy." Not long ago he wouldn't have turned his back to a group of well-armed Russian soldiers. Bolan wondered if they also felt odd to be working with former enemies. Probably more so, he realized, because the Soviet military had basically taught that the Western democracies were the root of all evil, just as their counterparts in the West regarded Communists as aggressors who threatened to enslave the entire world.

It was ironic these elite Russian paratroopers had been trained to fight "capitalist war mongers" and now found themselves allies with a special group from the United States to hunt down an enemy base. Fellow Russians would be among the enemy forces. Yet any apprehension felt by the soldiers didn't appear on their faces. They seemed ready for action and gave no sign of hesitation about fighting opponents who shared their nationality.

Bolan was prepared for war. In addition to the Beretta 93-R in shoulder leather, he also carried the big .44 Magnum Desert Eagle in a hip holster. His choice for a primary assault weapon was an M-16 with an M-203 grenade launcher mounted under the barrel. Phoenix Force was armed with micro-Uzis, the machine-pistol version of the larger SMG model. Gary Manning carried an FAL rifle instead of an Uzi and a pack of special explosives at the small of his back. David McCarter also brought a Barnett Commando crossbow, as well as his Uzi and Browning. Calvin James wore a medic kit among his gear.

All members of the special strike force wore bullet-resistant vests. They carried both fragmentation and tear-gas grenades, protective masks in canvas cases and plenty of magazine pouches with spare ammo. Most packed garrotes and knives. Rafael Encizo carried a Gerber Mark I dagger in a boot sheath, as well as a big Cold Steel Tanto combat knife. Canteens, helmets, rations, entrenching tools and other gear contributed to their burden as they marched across the rugged terrain.

The area of the Ural Mountains was rocky and uninviting. There were more hospitable portions of the region that served peasant farmers. However, there appeared to be little vegetation among the great stony giants that surrounded the commandos. Rock formations and boulders threatened to block their progress as they moved through a natural passage between the mountains. Climbing around these barriers consumed more time than expected.

Major Fedeyev gasped for breath after scaling a huge cluster of fallen rocks. The OO officer wasn't accustomed to such physical effort. He slumped against a boulder and wiped a sleeve across his sweaty brow. Bolan approached as the major opened his canteen.

"I know what you're going to say," Fedeyev began, struggling for enough break to speak. "I'm not in peak condition for this sort of thing."

"We did warn you this would be difficult, Major," Bolan replied. "It wasn't necessary for you to come along. You might just get in the way."

"Your one-armed friend is older than I am," Fedeyev stated. "You didn't object to his participation."

"He's a tough combat veteran and can take care of himself better than most men half his age," Bolan said. "I'm not worried about him. But anyone who can't keep up will have to be left behind. We'll pick up the person or persons later on the way back."

"Assuming you come back," Fedeyev remarked. "Hill bandits might get anyone left here alone."

"Hill bandits? The commander of the paratroopers thinks they're just local folklore, and there haven't been any real bands of outlaws in the Urals for fifty years."

"Captain Leotiev is entitled to his opinion," the major stated, "but I wouldn't be so quick to dismiss those stories. A lot of people have reported seeing bandits here."

"Well, a lot of people claim to have seen Big Foot and the Abominable Snowman, too."

"You mean the yeti of the Himalayas?" Fedeyev asked. "You know there are stories about an ape-man creature in the Caucasus Mountains called a *kaptar?* I don't recall any sightings in the Urals."

Bolan grunted. He had heard tales about hairy wildmen in several other countries around the world, but he had never seen one or any evidence there was any truth to the stories. The Executioner didn't really care if the Abominable Snowman, the *kaptar* or the

Ural bandits existed as long as they didn't get in the way of one of his missions.

Manning and Encizo headed for Bolan. The warrior noticed the others had assumed they were supposed to rest because he had stopped to talk to Fedeyev. It was time for a break, anyway, Bolan decided.

"The ACR detector unit has registered a wavelength about thirty kilometers northeast," Encizo announced as he handed Bolan the unit. "Looks like we've found them."

The Executioner took the black plastic-and-metal contraption. A column of tiny lights flashed across the top of the detector above a distance gauge that estimated how far the ACR wave operated. Communications engineers in the OO had done a good job putting the detector together on short notice. That would make Fedeyev happy, Bolan thought.

"The location fits the area where Volkov says construction had formerly begun at a mountaintop," Manning added, and showed Bolan a map. A red circle marked the area he referred to.

"All right," the warrior said, "we'll split into two groups. If the topography is correct on this map, we should be able to approach the mountain from two different directions. If we're lucky and time this correctly, we should all reach the target area about dusk."

"Why is dusk a good time to arrive?" Fedeyev asked. "Even if the enemy has night-vision equipment, I still think an assault in the middle of the night would be better."

"Guards tend to be careless at dusk," Bolan explained. "They're usually bored if they've been on duty very long, and they're apt to watch the sunset rather than the area they're supposed to be protecting. Even sentries who are fresh tend to be relaxed at dusk because they think there won't be any threat until it gets dark. Like the middle of the night."

The Russian major shrugged, somewhat embarrassed. "I suppose you gentlemen know more about this sort of thing," he remarked.

"The problem is Giessler or whoever he put in charge of security might be aware of this, as well," Manning said. "They might increase security, double the guards on duty and pay extra attention at twilight."

"That's possible," Bolan agreed, "but Giessler and most of the others appear to be ex-Intelligence operatives, accustomed to carrying out covert missions that involved espionage rather than actual combat. Most of their experience has probably been in cities and towns. That can be in our favor."

"I hope you're right," Encizo commented. "We don't know who we'll find up there or what sort of experience they have. Those bodyguards who arrived with the three Arab leaders are probably veterans with military and extensive security backgrounds. Giessler isn't stupid, and he'll listen to somebody who knows more about a subject than he does."

"Maybe the bodyguards will assume the security people at the base know what they're doing and just concentrate on looking after their clients," Bolan replied. "We can speculate for hours and still guess wrong. We'll find out when we get there."

Katz, McCarter and James joined them. Captain Leotiev also noticed a conference was in progress and approached. He seemed quite willing to accept Bolan and Katz as leaders, but he obviously had little respect for Fedeyev despite the OO officer's field-grade rank. A guy like Leotiev wouldn't consider the OO to be "real military" and would figure Fedeyev ought to stay behind a desk and let the real soldiers do their job.

Unfortunately Bolan also noticed Leotiev seemed to ignore James and Encizo. Racism is a universal sickness, and a fair number of Russians regarded blacks and Hispanics as inferior. Bolan didn't like this sort of bigotry in Russians any more than he did in Americans. However, there was nothing he could do about Leotiev's prejudices except hope they didn't cause problems during the mission.

"We were discussing dividing the attack force," Bolan explained. "I'll take one group, and you take the other, Mr. Gray."

"That's not my cover name for this operation," Katz said with a smile, "but I understand."

"Okay, but I'll just call you Gray. Old habits die hard. You speak Russian fluently, so you shouldn't have a problem commanding the captain's troops. They'll follow orders without any problems of accepting his authority, Captain?"

"They'll follow orders form Mr. Gray," Leotiev replied. "I'm not certain they'll be eager to listen to a couple of the others in your group."

"They'd better be," James remarked. "We don't want any shit from them when this thing comes down."

Leotiev barely glanced at the tall Afro-American and turned his attention to Bolan and Katz. They didn't need any friction within the unit, but Bolan had to divide the forces in the manner best suited for the assignment.

"Okay," he said. "Captain, you'll come with me. I need a translator. I'll also take Mr. Black."

"Black?" Leotiev asked, a trace of alarm in his tone.

"Relax," James said. "I'm Mr. Blue. Like singing the blues? That's 'cause there are so many dumb cracker assholes around—"

"Cultural exchange can wait for a better time," Katz stated. "Perhaps Mr. Blue should accompany me. Do you want Green? He can help remove sentries at long distance with his FAL and plant charges for explosives."

"You'll be as likely to need him as I will," the Executioner replied. "Besides, Black can take out guards just as well and even more silently with his crossbow at a distance."

"Black is the Briton?" Fedeyev asked with a frown.

"Yeah," Bolan said. "I know the guy can be a real pain at times, but don't let that short temper and sarcastic tongue throw you off. He's a different person on the battlefield.

"Thank you very much," McCarter said with a grin. "See, Major? I have some redeeming qualities after all."

"Not enough to brag about," Manning muttered.

"Let's give Fedeyev a break," Bolan said. "He'll go with Gray's group. Brown will come with me."

"Right," Encizo said with a nod. He cast a mock salute at Captain Leotiev. "Guess we'll be working together, amigo."

The paratrooper officer was obviously less than pleased, but he didn't protest. Bolan checked a two-way radio unit and hooked it to his belt.

"Radio contact has to be extremely limited because we don't know what sort of monitor system the other side is using," he explained. "The ACR also affects most communications, so we'll be using these compact shortwave units. We can't risk conversations in case they're using receivers to pick up shortwave radio."

"Our only contact will be short beeps," Katz said. "A single beep means we're making progress as planned. Two beeps mean we've been delayed. When we get into position, we press the button three times to let the other team know. Correct?"

"It's simple so there's less that can go wrong," Bolan stated. "That's the way we want it. When we reach the mountain, we'll send a signal to the forces stationed at Serov. They'll send the planes, and we just have to hope they arrive in time. The shortwave radio transmission should help them locate the right area."

"They won't need to know the exact site unless it's necessary for the MiGs to launch an air attack on the base," Leotiev remarked. "Unfortunately if that happens, it will mean most of us are probably dead and those that are alive will have a good chance of getting killed along with the enemy."

"What a pleasant thought," Manning commented. "We'll just have to avoid getting into that situation."

"I hope we can manage that," Bolan replied. "Break is just about over, gentlemen. We've still got a lot of territory to cover before the day is finished."

CHAPTER TWENTY-THREE

Ural Mountains, Russia
Thursday, 0821 hours

The transport helicopter landed at a flat area between giant rocks. Heinz Giessler watched the passengers climb from the big chopper. A pair of binoculars allowed him to see the men well enough to identify the first one to step from the rig. Sadek Nimeri and what remained of his commando team had arrived.

The German mastermind was relieved to see Nimeri and his crew had finally reached the stronghold. He regretted the need to use the helicopter. It was strictly for emergencies or when time was too limited to wait for something to be delivered by truck across the vast Ural region. Indeed, time could be running out, and Giessler wanted to leave the mountain range and find a new base of operations as soon as possible.

First, they had to set into motion the new phase of their plan. Giessler glanced at the stern face of Abdel Gahiz. The Iraqi stood near the edge of the cliff, watching Nimeri's group below. Ahmed Mahdi was also present, along with Syrian and Iraqi bodyguards. Musa Kadafadem apparently felt no need to be on hand when the commando unit returned to the base.

"Don't let anger block wisdom," Giessler advised, speaking to the Arabs in their language. "We need Nimeri and his men."

"We've discussed this already," Gahiz replied. "Nimeri gets to live only because he is still useful to us."

"Just don't left him know that's how you feel," the German warned. "And none of that Islamic holy-war rhetoric or telling him this is the will of God. You and I both know that won't mean anything to him."

"Damn atheist," Mahdi hissed with contempt.

Giessler knew Mahdi and Gahiz had less respect for religion than a rabid badger. Their pretending to be devout Muslims offended by Nimeri's lack of faith was probably for the benefit of their bodyguards—who probably realized their act was a farce. The former SSD agent expected this sort of masquerade from men who aspired to become leaders of Arab nations.

However, he would be extremely suspicious of Nimeri if the commando started to claim to be a soldier of God or willing to die for the holy war. That would mean he was just saying what he figured the Arab leaders wanted to hear so he could grab his money, pretend to accept the next assignment and then disappear.

Giessler didn't intend to let that happen. If he suspected Nimeri might betray them, he would kill the Iraqi commando himself. The German packed a Makarov pistol on his hip, and the little .25 Bauer was once again in the hidden holster at his nape. Giessler had nothing against Nimeri, even respected the soldier's ability and courage, but he wouldn't hesitate to take the man's life if this could help him preserve his own.

Nimeri and his companions had no trouble scaling the rock face of the mountain. Due to the complex construction efforts previously performed at the summit, stone had been chiseled into several series of crude steps. These had allowed the builders to haul up material for putting together the base. The steps let the commandos climb the mountain with ease. Nimeri noticed the two box-shaped metal devices with stout vented barrels, located among rocks on natural ledges. Red disks on the contraptions suggested heat or motion detectors. Perhaps infrared, as well, Nimeri thought. The gun barrels warned these mechanical sentries didn't only register intruders. They could also terminate unwanted visitors with machine-gun fire.

The commando leader felt only slight reluctance as he approached the robot guns. Yet he realized the deadly security devices had been shut off or the guns would have already opened fire. Besides, Giessler wouldn't be that careless. If Nimeri and his men died that day, it wouldn't be by accident.

They reached the top. Nimeri wasn't surprised by the reception committee or the less-than-happy expressions. Gahiz seemed especially hostile, his brow wrinkled, shaggy eyebrows nearly touching and his mouth drawn down at the corners. Mahdi's face was almost as unpleasant, and their bodyguards appeared ready to open fire at any second. Giessler's features revealed nothing of his thoughts or emotions.

"Welcome back," the German said with a curt nod. "We're glad to see you arrived from your hazardous journey in good health."

"Except more than half my men didn't survive the mission," Nimeri replied. He turned to Gahiz. "I wish to report it was necessary for us to make a tactical retreat due to unexpected efforts by the Iranian military to search for us."

"And you have no idea how they came to suspect the sea battle had been started by outside actions?" Gahiz asked.

"Not really. We accomplished every portion of the mission until we were forced to retreat or face the risk of capture. You certainly didn't want that to happen."

"You could take your life rather than talk," Mahdi remarked.

"Personally I'd rather shoot myself in the mouth than go to an Iranian torture chamber," Nimeri replied, "but I'm not going to order my men to kill themselves. The decision would have to be made by each individual. We weren't going to commit suicide as long as there was a way to survive and escape."

"A very risky method," Gahiz commented. "Those gliders could have been reported by ground forces and shot down or tracked."

"Anything we did would be risky. I lost four men over the Caspian Sea, but we flew under radar and no aircraft followed us."

"We appreciate that," Giessler said, "but you weren't ordered to come here. You violated security. Your actions could jeopardize our entire operation."

"I suspect you already plan to break down this base and move to a new location," Nimeri stated. "That would be the intelligent thing to do under the circumstances. You are all intelligent men. I'm not stupid, either. If you'll just pay my men and myself the money we earned, supply us with transportation to the Turkish border, we'll part company."

"That's not possible," Giessler explained. "The money isn't here. You certainly don't think we keep millions of American dollars and British pound notes here."

"I'll settle for a bank draft," Nimeri stated, "made out to a certain bank in Istanbul where Mr. Gahiz has an account of more than five million U.S. dollars."

"Actually we're all going to Turkey," Giessler told him. "The new site will be there. You'll receive half your payment when we arrive."

"What about the other half?" Nimeri asked. He knew he wouldn't like the answer.

"That will depend on whether you complete your mission. That was the agreement. If you don't like the terms, you can settle for partial payment and we'll say goodbye in Turkey."

Nimeri considered the offer. Perhaps he couldn't retire on half the promised amount, but he could certainly use it for a nest egg to support himself for some years. It would be enough to let him move to Singapore and seek new employment as a mercenary or gunrunner. Yet the fact they still wanted him to return to Iran suggested they didn't have anyone else with his qualifications for the mission.

That could be the only reason they allowed him to return to the base instead of ordering Nimeri and his men executed while they were traveling to the Ural Mountains. Gahiz was the sort of man who would want someone to die for disobeying orders, and Giessler wasn't the type to care enough to stand in the way of such an order unless Nimeri was more valuable alive.

If Nimeri refused to complete his mission, they would kill him and the remaining commandos under his command.

He never should have accepted the mission, Nimeri thought bitterly. When it went sour, he should have headed for the Turkish border or perhaps Afghanistan rather than return to Russia and the mountain base. Looking back on his options, Nimeri realized he could have taken his men to Tehran, mixed among the dense population at the capital and stowed away on a train to head back to the Persian Gulf. It would be unlikely the Iranian authorities would have expected that. They could have gone along the north coast to Kuwait or even Saudi Arabia. Of course, they would have had to forget about the money and only concentrated on staying alive.

Now, Nimeri thought, there was no choice. What he should have done no longer mattered. He had to accept the reality of the situation and do what he could to survive and possibly profit.

"You find this arrangement agreeable?" Giessler asked.

"Certainly," Nimeri said, lying.

The German smiled and nodded, yet his expression revealed he knew what Nimeri truly felt.

CAPTAIN LEOTIEV LOWERED his binoculars and frowned. The Russian officer had tried to determine where the helicopter had gone. The big transport ship was an unusual aircraft in that region, and it immediately aroused suspicions. Mack Bolan had ordered the men to seek cover and conceal themselves in case the chopper belonged to the enemy.

Rafael Encizo consulted the ACR detector unit. The gauge revealed the wavelength of aggressive concentrated radar to be approximately twenty-three kilometers from their position. The helicopter had headed in the direction of the enemy transmission.

"What's the verdict?" McCarter inquired.

"Looks like that helicopter went to the hidden stronghold," the Cuban replied. "That's probably where it vanished from view."

"Not likely they built a heliport on a mountaintop," the Briton commented. "Maybe cleared an area in a passage between mountains. Gives us an idea what to look for. Especially if that whirlybird is still parked and waiting for us."

The Executioner glanced up at the morning sky. It was still quite early, and he had little doubt they would reach the base before dusk. Travel was slow due to the rock rubble and boulders, but he didn't have to ask Encizo for a distance update. Bolan's trained eye allowed him to estimate the range based on where the helicopter descended.

However, he was concerned about approaching the base unobserved. The enemy would have the advantage of an elevated position, which would make it easier for them to peer down at the commandos. They had to take greater care when they got closer. Any high-tech base that employed an advance form of forceful radar would certainly appreciate the need for recon and security. Reaching the site might not be difficult, but catching everyone off guard could be a different matter.

The radio transceiver on his belt beeped once. Katz and the rest of the commando party were making progress as planned. Bolan responded to the signal with a single press of the transmit key. A Russian trooper took point and led the way as they marched toward a natural archway of curved stone, flanked by clusters of boulders.

Bolan heard the shuffle of stone fragments against rock. He instantly braced his back against the boulders, M-16 held close to his chest, in response to a possible threat. David McCarter and Rafael Encizo reacted in a similar manner. The Briton rolled across the surface of a slab of stone that resembled a table. He dropped in a crouched position behind the rock as Encizo slipped between two large conical stony formations.

"What are you—" Leotiev began.

A scream instantly arrested the captain's attention. He turned to see the trooper at point had cried out because a figure had attacked without warning. The ambusher had waited behind some rocks by the arch and lunged with a bayonet attached to a rifle barrel. The blade struck the soldier's chest, but deflected against the flak vest he wore. Both men were startled, but the attacker recovered form his surprise faster and quickly whipped the wooden stock of his weapon into the side of the trooper's skull.

Bolan barely glimpsed the ambusher, yet realized the man was not a member of a military or paramilitary outfit. Bearded, clad in filthy greatcoat and ratty-looking fur cap, the guy resembled a crazed mountain man rather than a soldier. His rifle appeared to be a relic from World War II. Bolan wasn't sure of the make or model, but it was designed similar to an old Mauser.

The Executioner turned his attention to the rocks surrounding them, aware a single opponent wouldn't attack thirteen heavily armed men unless he was completely insane. At least two AKS-74 assault rifles spit bursts of automatic fire to blast the life from the ambusher. Bolan knew his Russian companions would deal with the guy. He was more concerned about how many others were left to continue the attack.

A partial answer appeared among the rock formations above Bolan. More shapes, dressed in raggy attire, slithered closer. They moved with practiced silence and confidence among the rocks. The bandits weren't soldiers, and their weapons were outdated, but they obviously knew the terrain and had experience in this kind of attack.

Bolan braced the stock of the M-16 against his hip, raised the barrel and selected a target. He triggered a 3-round burst and saw a bandit's head recoil from the impact of the 5.56 mm slugs. Blood and brains spewed from the exit wounds and tore bits of fabric from the guy's hat.

Another bandit swung a sawed-off shotgun toward Bolan, but the Executioner had already altered the aim of his rifle and fired at the would-be assassin. Bullets ripped into the gunner's throat and face. The shotgun fell from lifeless fingers and clattered among the rocks. Its slain owner slipped from view as two more bandits tried to avenge him.

One outlaw slid from cover to try to gain a more favorable position for attack. He didn't realize he had moved directly into the line of fire for Encizo until the Cuban fired his Uzi. The burst of 9 mm rounds slammed into the bandit's chest and sent his body hurtling across the rocks in a graceless somersault. Bones crunched as the man hit stone, but his heart had already been stopped by the parabellum rounds. He was dead by the time the body crashed to earth.

Another bandit stayed behind an oval hump of rock as he aimed an old revolver at the commandos. He barely exposed the top of his head, part of his forehead and one eye to peer down at the targets below. Not much of a target, but enough for a marksman with Mack Bolan's skill. The Executioner opened fire and nailed the gunman just above the exposed eye. Frontal bone split, and 5.56 mm missiles tore through the man's brain.

More ambushers attacked from the boulders at the opposite side of the gorge. A shotgun roared and a paratrooper caught a burst of buckshot. The force threw him backward into unyielding stone. The soldier slumped to the ground, but two other Russian commandos responded with AKS fury. Automatic fire took out the enemy shotgunner and sent another bandit tumbling from the rock wall, torso torn and bleeding.

An opponent raised an arm with a bottle clenched in his fist, a flaming rag stuffed in its neck. The bandit was about to toss a Molotov cocktail. Something shot from the Briton's table-rock position like a bolt of blurred lighting. The man with the gasoline bomb cried out and stared at the fiberglass shaft of a crossbow bolt that skewered his biceps. The bottle fell from his grasp and shattered. Burning gasoline spilled across the rocky cover of two unlucky bandits. They shrieked and broke cover, their bodies draped in angry yellow flames.

David McCarter quickly exchanged the crossbow for his Uzi and opened fire. Two bursts of 9 mm slugs raked the fiery forms to terminate their suffering. If the bandits appreciated this act of mercy, they didn't express it. Instead, the enemy returned fire with an assortment of shotguns, rifles and handguns.

Bullets and buckshot pelted the rocky cover used by the three Stony Man commandos and the Russian paratroopers. Another soldier fell in a crumpled, bloodied heap before he could reach shelter. Leotiev's men replied with wild sprays of automatic fire. Bolan, Encizo and McCarter were more conservative with their ammo, seldom triggering a weapon unless they had a definite target.

Yet the frenzied firepower of the paratroopers claimed at least two more bandits. Mangled bodies toppled down the rocks to join the collection of dead in the passage. Some of the mountain outlaws became bold enough to charge the commandos' position. One lunatic triggered both barrels of his sawed-off shotgun as he descended the rock walls. Buckshot scored bits of stone near Bolan's position and even forced the Executioner to stay down as the man closed in.

The shaggy outlaw tossed the empty shotgun aside and reached for the bone handle of a knife on his belt. Bolan snap-aimed the M-16 and squeezed the trigger. A single shot rang out, and the bullet struck the madman in the chest. Yet he barely grunted in response and continued to charge toward the warrior.

Bolan had exhausted the ammo in the M-16, and he didn't have time to reload or draw a pistol. The burly bandit waved a long-bladed knife, his eyes ablaze with rage. Crimson drool on his beard revealed the bullet had probably punctured a lung, but the attacker's demented frenzy was greater than his pain. He seemed determined to take Bolan with him if he was going to die.

The bandit shuffled behind the rock cover and lunged with the long, sharp steel. Bolan lashed out his rifle barrel and chopped it across the wrist above the knife. The blow deflected the thrust and drove the fist and knife into solid rock. The warrior followed with another stroke and smashed the frame of the M-16 into the man's forearm. Bone cracked and the knife slipped from trembling fingers.

With a bellow of pain and anger, the bandit swung his other fist. Bolan whipped the hard plastic stock of the M-16 to block the other man's forearm, then swung a boot hard between the outlaw's legs. The brute wheezed in agony as the kick crushed his testicles. Bolan didn't give him a chance to summon up more reserves of superhuman strength. The Executioner slashed the rifle barrel across the side of the man's jaw and hooked a butt stroke to his solar plexus.

The man's knees buckled, and he staggered from the rain of punishing blows. Bolan cracked the rifle stock across the opponent's skull, and the man slipped to the ground.

Three bandits attempted a suicide charge against McCarter's position, probably enraged by the fiery deaths of two of their comrades. The Briton blasted the last rounds from his Uzi machine pistol into two men, terminating their attack and their lives. The third kept coming, firing a revolver as he advanced.

McCarter dropped sideways behind his shelter. Bullets ricocheted along the stone. Chips showered down on the Briton, but he barely noticed as he drew the Browning Hi-Power. McCarter held the pistol in both hands and swung it around the edge of the shelter. He peered up at the bandit's furious face. Their eyes met as McCarter squeezed the trigger. A 9 mm parabellum round punched the bridge of the bandit's nose and knifed through his skull. Literally dead on his feet, the outlaw simply fell over to join his lifeless friends on the ground.

Bolan didn't see the British ace deal with his opponents. The Executioner still had problems of his own. Two bandits scrambled for the warrior's position. They had probably seen his fight with the burly lunatic and decided he had to have run out of ammo to take on the big opponent in such an up-close and personal manner.

They found out they were dead wrong when Bolan drew the .44 Magnum Desert Eagle. The first shot hit the closer bandit in the center of the chest. He was lifted off his feet by the big Magnum round and pitched backward into some jagged rocks. The man's skull cracked open on stone, verifying his death.

The second attacker dropped to one knee to try to present a smaller target as he tried to return fire with an old Tokarev pistol. The trick might have worked against a less experienced opponent, but Bolan adjusted the aim of his Desert Eagle without the need for conscious thought. Reflex and instinct guided his actions. He triggered the Magnum, and a .44 slug crashed into the man's face to splash his brains across the rock wall.

The firepower and skill of the commandos was obviously more than the bandits anticipated. Most of the

surviving members of the outlaw band decided to retreat. They bolted over the summits of the rock formations, away from their intended targets. One bandit
literally ran across the natural stone arch in an effort to
escape. Captain Leotiev didn't feel generous or merciful as he spotted the fleeing figure. The officer fired a
spray of AKS-74 rounds at the bandit. Bullets plowed
into the man's lower legs and knees. He cried out as he
toppled from the arch and plunged to the ground below.

A figure seemed to materialize in front of Leotiev.
The officer swung his rifle to confront the attacker, but
the angry bandit fired a revolver point-blank at the
captain's chest. The slugs hammered Leotiev's flak vest
and knocked him off his feet. His elbow struck rock,
and the impact jarred the AKS rifle from his hand. The
captain stared up as the bandit stepped closer to point
the revolver at the fallen officer's face.

Suddenly another shape appeared beside the gunman, clutching a large knife in its fist. The blade struck
with enough force to knock the gun hand higher and
simultaneously cut deep into the bottom of the bandit's wrist. The trigger finger managed to fire another
round before the gun slipped from the hand. The bullet pinged along stone to ricochet above Leotiev's head.

Rafael Encizo delivered another vicious stroke with
his Cold Steel Tanto combat knife. He slashed the
blade across the wounded bandit's exposed throat.
Blood spurted from a sliced carotid as the man staggered backward, his eyes wide with pain and terror.
Encizo's empty hand slammed a heel-of-the-palm
stroke to the side of the outlaw's head and rammed the
thug's skull into a boulder. The dying man slumped

unconscious, mercifully unaware his life spilled from the terrible slit in his throat.

"You all right, Captain?" Encizo asked.

"Yes," Leotiev said, nodding. "Yes. I would be dead if...if you had not..."

"Just part of the service, Captain," the Cuban assured him with a slight grin.

The battle ended abruptly. What remained of the bandit gang disappeared, but Bolan warned the others to stay put in case the outlaws decided to regroup, plan a quick strategy and launch another attack. He didn't consider this likely, but it was wiser to remain in a defensive posture than risk another ambush in the open.

"For the record, Mr. Belasko," McCarter called out, "I think we can now report that those stories about bandits in the Ural Mountains are true after all."

"Yeah," Bolan replied. "How many men did we lose?"

"Two dead and three wounded," Leotiev answered. "One is serious. I don't think he can go on."

"Then we have to make a litter and carry him," Bolan said. "We can't leave him behind. Those bandits would take out a lot of frustrations on a lone wounded soldier."

He glanced at the battlefield. Bodies were sprawled across the gorge. Bloodstains and discarded weapons marked several rocky spots. Bolan could only guess how many bandits attempted the ambush, but at least a dozen had been killed during the encounter.

"I think the *bandito* bastards have had enough," Encizo commented. "I'm more worried about Giessler and his men. Sound travels quite a distance here. There's a pretty good chance they know somebody was setting off some fireworks here. They'll probably recognize the sound of automatic rifles and realize this wasn't a shoot-out between rival bandits.''

"It's not going to make our job any easier," Bolan agreed as he removed the transceiver from his belt.

He keyed two beeps to let Katz know they had a delay. The Israeli had certainly heard the gunshots. At least he would know Bolan's team hadn't been wiped out. Katz would also realize what this meant for their mission. The assignment was now even more dangerous because the enemy would now expect trouble.

CHAPTER TWENTY-FOUR

Yakov Katzenelenbogen scratched his jaw with the steel hooks of his prosthesis as he crouched low behind some boulders. The Phoenix Force commander didn't attempt to look over the rocks as the roar of the rotor blades drew closer. The helicopter was searching the area, and Katz guessed what they were looking for.

The commando unit led by the Israeli had heard the gun battle. They assumed Bolan's group had been involved, although they weren't certain who their opponents had been. The chopper, however, had come from the direction of the enemy base. They heard it approach before the craft was even a dot in the sky. Katz had ordered his men to hide among the rocks by the passage. The chopper hovered overhead, its shadow cast across the boulders like that of a great bird of prey.

"I wonder if bandits attacked Belasko's group," Major Fedeyev remarked as he knelt by Katz.

"He signaled a delay shortly after we heard the shooting," the Israeli replied. "That means Belasko and his team won, but they certainly left dead bodies behind. The helicopter probably already spotted the corpses of the bandits or whoever. Now they're trying to locate who killed them."

"They must not have spotted Belasko's team or they wouldn't be clear over here," Calvin James remarked.

"Anybody see that whirlybird well enough to guess what kind of arms it might be packing?"

"I didn't really recognize it in the distance," Gary Manning admitted. "At least that means it's not a Hind Mi-24. That's one Soviet-made gunship I'll damn sure remember after we tangled with some of them in Afghanistan a few years ago."

"The Hind is a very formidable gunship," Katz agreed, "but we'd better not assume the helicopter out there isn't well armed with machine guns and possibly rockets, as well."

"Must not have heat sensors or they probably would have already found Belasko's group before they headed this way," James commented. "Or maybe that fancy computer surveillance shit doesn't work so well with that ACR wave in the area."

"Nice thought," Manning agreed. "Might even cut them off from radio contact with home base. Could be a plus in our favor."

"Best thing we can hope for is they'll decide to return to the stronghold after they fail to find anyone responsible for the bodies they came across," Katz said. "Just in case, I'd like to have at least one RPG loaded and ready. Two of the paratroopers have rocket launchers?"

"I only noticed one," Fedeyev replied. "I believe Belasko's group has the other RPG."

Katz grunted. He and the twelve other men were crammed into narrow gaps between boulders and the rock wall. The one-armed commando couldn't slip past the others to speak with the Russian soldiers or send Fedeyev to deliver the order. There was no way to do this without risking exposure to the helicopter near their position. Neither James nor Manning spoke Russian, so they couldn't pass the command down the line.

Maybe the man with the RPG would have enough sense to load the launcher without being told to do so, Katz thought. He wondered how much longer the helicopter would circle the area. The fact it hadn't left worried him. For some reason, the pilot seemed suspicious.

A sudden burst of machine-gun fire confirmed his fears. Bullets raked the boulders; chips of rock pelted the commandos; ricochets burned air near the huddled figures. One stray slug recoiled off stone and struck Katz in the center of the chest. He hissed in startled reaction, but the bullet had already lost most of its velocity and the Kevlar vest reduced the impact to a mere tap.

The paratroopers responded to the attack with hasty volleys of AKS rifle fire. One trooper immediately fell back, slumped between the rocks, his face and skull pulped by large-caliber bullets. Another man cried out and dropped his assault rifle. His right hand spouted streams of blood. The index finger had been abruptly amputated at the second knuckle.

Katz carefully peered between boulders and saw the helicopter. The aircraft was a large rig, but designed primarily for troop transport rather than direct combat. Katz didn't see any rockets or bombs attached to the hull. Two machine-gun barrels jutted from the nose of the chopper, but the strafing fire came from a weapon mounted by the open sliding doors on one side of the chopper.

"Get the RPG ready!" Katz shouted in English. He quickly switched to Russian and added, "We'll try to draw their fire long enough to launch a rocket into the hull of the helicopter!"

"We're going to do what?" Fedeyev asked, stunned by the statement.

"Draw the enemy fire," Katz replied in English for the sake of his fellow Phoenix Force commandos.

James responded immediately and poked the stubby barrel of his micro-Uzi between two cone-shaped rocks. He triggered a long burst of 9 mm rounds in the general direction of the chopper, unable to see the rig well enough to have a definite target.

Katz stuck his Uzi around the edge of a rock and fired without benefit of his prosthesis for support. He had been an amputee for nearly three decades, and his left arm had developed exceptional strength to compensate for the missing limb. He had no trouble with the violent recoil of the full-auto weapon in his single fist.

Manning had more trouble attempting to use his FAL assault rifle because the long barrel was difficult to bring into play in the tight quarters between boulders and rock wall. Fedeyev didn't even try to shoot at the chopper. The OO major just concentrated on staying down and out of the way of the veteran fighting men in the group.

A torrent of machine-gun fire hammered the boulders used by the three Phoenix commandos and Major Fedeyev for cover. They ducked low and clenched their teeth as stone chips and stray bullets slashed the air around them. Fragments tore cloth and bit into skin. James was in the best position to see the Russian paratroopers. He watched a soldier attempt to brace an RPG across a boulder. The trooper placed his shoulder to the bazooka-style weapon and started to rise. He suddenly fell into a seated position, his head slumped forward. Blood streamed down the dead soldier's face.

"Shit," James announced. "They wasted our guy with the RPG. Must have more than one gun going now. Bastards can cover any area we try to pop up at."

"So much for drawing enemy fire," Katz rasped. "We have to counterattack regardless of the risk. We can't stay boxed in here much longer. If they don't have rockets, they certainly have some grenades in that chopper. If they can pin us down long enough to fly over us, all they need do is drop a couple of F-1 frags in our laps."

James slithered along the space between rocks to reach the RPG. He tried to stay as low as possible, but he had to move quickly. Bullets seemed to tear at his pack and scrape his helmet every inch of the nerve-racking crawl.

Manning braced his back against the rock wall, the rifle barrel along a boulder. He unscrewed the retainer to the telescope mount and removed it from the FAL. The Canadian marksman realized the scope was fine for a target that was more or less fixed and allowed adequate time to aim. However, he needed to find his target instantly and fire just as fast. The iron sights to the rifle were better suited for this than the scope.

The big Canadian noticed that James had reached the RPG. The Afro-American had to literally sit on the corpse of the slain paratrooper in order to grab the rocket launcher. Manning knew his partner could use a distraction before trying to aim and fire the weapon.

Manning could use one himself, but he didn't have time to wait for a more favorable situation that might not arrive.

He sucked in a tense breath and put the buttstock to his shoulder. Manning rose swiftly, his eye level with the rear sight of the FAL rifle. The Canadian saw the chopper and a figure stationed by the open doors at the carriage. Secured by a harness, the man gripped a machine gun that was mounted on a tripod near the threshold.

Manning didn't hesitate. He pointed the FAL at the gunner and squeezed the trigger. A 3-round burst spit from the rifle. The Phoenix Force commando saw the enemy jackknife from impact of 7.62 mm NATO slugs drilling into his upper torso. The chopper turned in a gliding circle as both gun barrels at the nose swung toward Manning.

"Damn," he muttered as he ducked behind the rocks once more.

James made the most of the half second of opportunity Manning had provided. He aimed the RPG and fired. The grenade streaked from the boulders to crash into the windscreen of the enemy aircraft. It exploded on impact, tearing the hull apart and igniting the fuel tank.

Gasoline burst in a second explosion that sent burning debris across the face of the mountain opposite the commandos' position. Metal and plastic chunks rained from the sky.

Manning slowly raised his head and saw the burning wreckage of the helicopter. Pieces were scattered across the summit of the mountain, along ledges to the rock wall and the passage. Smoke carried the obvious stench of burned rubber and charred human flesh. James looked at the debris and set down the RPG. Fedeyev sighed with relief and tried to rise. He discovered his legs were shaking too much to support him.

"Good work, gentlemen," Katz declared. "Mr. Blue, check on our people. We've got at least one wounded and probably one or two dead among the paratroopers."

"Right," James replied as he reached for his medic kit.

"No need to check for survivors from that helicopter," Manning remarked. "Nobody could walk away from an explosion like that."

"No," Katz said, "but unfortunately there are more where they came from."

CHAPTER TWENTY-FIVE

Abdel Gahiz lowered the binoculars. The Iraqi frowned, narrowing his dark eyes. Gahiz glanced about for Giessler, but the German had disappeared, probably retreating into one of the buildings. The Iraqi placed a hand on the button-flap holster on his hip.

"Don't do anything rash," Ahmed Mahdi warned as he stepped closer. "The damn Europeans are watching us."

Russian and German guards formed a semicircle near the smaller group of Arabs. Gahiz, Mahdi and their bodyguards were outnumbered by Giessler's security force. Drawing a weapon would probably cause the guards to open fire and blast the Arabs off the edge of the cliff.

Gahiz held his temper in check and moved his hand from the pistol. The idiots were still willing to follow Giessler although they could see smoke rising from the wreckage of the helicopter. Some had even seen the craft literally burst apart in midair.

The Arabs and security forces stood by the edge of the base, neither side certain what would happen or what action to take. Sending the helicopter to search the area had been a mistake, yet Gahiz and Madhi had insisted upon it. Of course, the aggressive concentrated radar had prevented radio contact with the craft.

Giessler had even warned them before he sent the helicopter to investigate.

Radio communication to and from the base had to be timed precisely according to the orbits of spy satellites that were blocked by the ACR waves. An American satellite was at the perigee, or lowest level into the atmosphere, of orbit over the Urals. They couldn't risk shutting down the ACR shield. The troopers in the helicopter had taken it upon themselves to start shooting at whomever they found out there, and they were blown out of the sky for their effort.

"This place might be under attack soon," Mahdi told the Iraqi. "Even if we survive a gun battle with Giessler's people, we'll still be forced to fight whoever might be coming here. Obviously we need every man possible if that happens. If we fight among ourselves, we'll just make it easier for the enemy to finish us all."

Gahiz nodded. He didn't like to admit the Syrian had a point. Gahiz felt Giessler had failed them and ought to pay for it with his life. Yet killing the German wouldn't help them deal with any attack force headed for the stronghold.

Musa Kadafadem approached. Dressed in white robe and kaffiyeh, the Libyan looked as if he were headed for a costume ball among the figures clad in fatigues. Yet Kadafadem conducted himself with quiet dignity that seemed to fit his choice of traditional attire.

"My brothers," the Libyan began, "I suggest we should get our prayer rugs, face Mecca and pray for the protection and wisdom we'll need in this crisis."

Gahiz was in no mood for religious ritual. Although he spoke of Islam as the true faith and condemned the infidels every chance he got, Gahiz considered religion to be nothing more than superstitions turned into dogma by past leaders clever enough to realize the masses were always seeking guidance. The carrot-and-stick principle worked best. What carrot could be greater than the promise of spending eternity in paradise, what stick more threatening than to face eternity in the fiery pits of hell?

However, Kadafadem's suggestion gave them a reason to move away from the lip of the cliff and the glaring guards. Gahiz and Mahdi joined the Libyan, followed by their bodyguards. The Arabs walked away from the others. Kadafadem stepped between Gahiz and Mahdi, lowered his head and spoke softly to avoid being heard by the others.

"We have to get out of here," the Libyan whispered. "That helicopter might have come across a well-armed scouting party, but whoever sent them must have reinforcements ready."

"You might be right," Mahdi replied. "But how do we leave here without alerting Giessler and his men?"

"They'll probably be more concerned with the possibility of attack than what we might do," Kadafadem stated. "We'll wait for our chance to leave. When that might be will depend on what these dolts decide to do."

Gahiz was startled by the Libyan's cool, cunning intelligence in the face of danger. He had underestimated Kadafadem as an eccentric, religious zealot. No doubt this act had kept the Libyan from being regarded as a serious political opponent in his country, and explained why Gahiz and Mahdi were wanted men in Iraq and Syria.

"So you don't really want us to pray?" Gahiz asked. "That was just an excuse to get us away from those surly infidels?"

"Prayer wouldn't hurt," Kadafadem replied, "but I doubt either of you remembers how to do it and God might not be terribly interested in listening to your pleas at this point. Better we count on our own abilities to stay alive."

Giessler emerged from the billets, accompanied by two officers of base security and Professor Bukovsky. Only the scientist was unarmed and apparently on the brink of a nervous breakdown.

"How can we get out of here without the helicopter?" Bukovsky asked, his lower lip trembling with fear. "It was our only way out of here."

"The transport chopper wasn't big enough to take us all out at once," Giessler answered without bothering to look at the Russian scientist. "We still have trucks concealed in the caves at the rim of the mountain range. We can get there on foot. It'll be a tough trek, but it can be done. Originally we had planned to use the helicopter to move everything to the trucks. Now we'll just have to take what we can carry and leave the rest."

"That's insane," Bukovsky complained. "Those bastards will get here before we can get clear of the mountain. Even if they don't stop us, we'll never reach the trucks."

Giessler suddenly whirled and swatted the back of his hand across Bukovsky's face. The unexpected blow staggered the scientist and sent him reeling back several steps.

"Go back to your machines and start packing the mainframe for the ACR," the German ordered.

"Eventually we'll get another dish to use at our new base. For now just do what I say and stay out of the way of the rest of us. We have work to do, and we don't need to listen to you whine."

Bukovsky placed a hand to his face and stared at Giessler with astonishment. He headed back to the main building with a stumbling stride. Giessler shook his head with disgust.

The former SSD agent had donned a flak vest and helmet. He carried a Russian-made submachine gun, although the weapon felt unfamiliar. Giessler had spent most of his life as an espionage operative, not a combat soldier.

However, Boris Trusov and Viktor Polyakov were veterans of the conflict in Afghanistan and several military "police actions" within the Soviet Union before the fall of communism. Giessler's security commanders cast suspicious glances at the Arabs on the parade field.

"Ignore them," Giessler urged. "We have more-serious matters to worry about. How well can we defend the base and strike camp at the same time?"

"We'll use most of our security personnel to stand guard while the rest of the force helps with equipment and supplies we'll need for the trip," Trusov replied. "If we're lucky, the group out there is a scouting party. Well armed and professional, to be sure. Taking out the helicopter was proof of that. However, it must be a fairly small unit, or we would be able to see them advance."

"So you don't think they'll attack us?" Giessler asked.

"The most they'd have in a scouting unit would be twenty or thirty men," Polyakov answered. He was a big, grizzled infantry commander who had seen action in numerous bleak battlefields in Afghanistan. "If they have any idea of how many men we've got here or what our defenses might be, they won't attempt to hit us on their own."

"And the ACR will prevent them from radio contact with any reinforcements," Giessler said, hoping to find some reason for optimism. "What if we just send more troops to hunt them down and wipe them out before we disconnect the ACR?"

"I have to vote against that," Trusov stated. "They obviously have a general idea where we're located. If the recon unit doesn't return or establish contact somehow, they'll send reinforcements anyway. Probably air support. Too hard to get tanks through the passage between mountains, but they can set up artillery guns a hundred kilometers from here and still shell our position as soon as the pilots of attack jets or gunships can establish radio contact. Artillery cannons can hit a target even if the gunners can't see it. All they'll need are accurate coordinates to hit us."

"Besides," Polyakov added, "trying to hunt down the recon unit would be time-consuming and cost the lives of many of our people. The terrain is similar to what we faced in Afghanistan. Whoever those men are out there, they're damn good. They'll know how to hide among the rocks and lie in wait for us. The mujahedeen used those sort of tactics. We could lose a lot of men and still not manage to get all the enemy."

Giessler considered their situation. He gazed at the wisps of black smoke in the distance. The German guessed the helicopter had been shot down more than two kilometers from their position. He knew the passages between mountains were difficult to travel due to the boulders and rock rubble blocking the pathways. It might take the enemy some time to either reach the mountain base or go back to report to a larger unit beyond the mountain range.

"Reinforce our base defenses," Giessler announced. "Everyone not involved in protecting the base will help us pack what we'll need for the journey."

The roar of engines suddenly drew their attention to the sky. A trio of fighter jets appeared above the southern mountain peaks. The planes rose higher, trails of white steam marking their path. With easy grace, the jets streaked forward. Trusov raised his binoculars to examine the craft.

"MiG fighter jets," he announced in a grim voice. "Probably MiG-27s. Very fine aircraft. Fast, agile and armed with an impressive arsenal. Machine guns, bombs and missiles."

"How the hell could this happen?" Giessler asked, aware no one would answer him. "They couldn't have learned our exact location."

"Those questions hardly matter at this point," Trusov said in a hard tone. "The fact is, it's too late to run now."

MACK BOLAN SAW the MiGs roar through the blue firmament. He had been expecting them, because he had personally pressed the five long beeps on the shortwave transceiver to signal the planes to advance. Of course, the MiGs had no definite target and weren't to open fire unless fired upon. The enemy base wouldn't know this or suspect the planes were acting only as a distraction.

The warrior was confident the enemy didn't realize he and his team were hidden among the rocks less than a quarter of a mile from their mountain stronghold. They were certainly aware of Katz's team because the helicopter had been shot down some distance away. This gave Bolan's group an advantage of surprise.

Unfortunately the disadvantages they faced were far greater. Katz's team had been delayed by the helicopter attack and his group was probably at least a mile from the base. The distraction wouldn't work for long, and Bolan couldn't wait for the Israeli's group to catch up. This meant they would have to launch the raid with less than half the number of men originally planned for the job.

The Executioner could only guess how many opponents were stationed at the mountain base, but there was no doubt his team would be badly outnumbered. The battle with the bandits had reduced Bolan's group to nine men fit for combat. Two had been killed and two had been wounded badly. At least one injured man was still able to walk, but he didn't have full use of a bullet-torn arm. He would stay with the soldier who lay on a litter, only semiconscious.

"Nice of them to cut those steps in the rock wall," Encizo remarked. "It'll make climbing that mountain easier."

"Don't count on any of this being easy," Bolan warned.

He screwed a long silencer onto the threaded muzzle of his Beretta 93-R. David McCarter loaded a bolt into his Barnett crossbow. Bolan knew the Briton used bolts with cyanide in the hollow shafts. The crossbow was quieter than a silenced firearm, and the poisoned ammo killed faster than a bullet.

"We'll be awful lucky if we can manage to climb up there without being noticed," the British ace commented.

"Maybe we'll get lucky," Encizo said as he attached a silencer to his Uzi machine pistol.

"The fact we've gotten this far has been remarkable," Captain Leotiev stated. "I just hope we haven't exhausted our share of good fortune."

"Men make their own luck," the Executioner told him. "Good or bad. Mr. Brown and I will take point. Mr. Black and you will follow, Captain. We need to fan out enough to avoid being a clustered target that can be taken out by a quick sweep of automatic fire and a couple of grenades, but I don't want the men spread out too far to be unable to see commands by hand gesture or unable to assist one another if needed."

"I understand, Mr. Belasko," Leotiev assured him.

"Also have your best marksmen and the guy with the RPG bring up the rear," Bolan continued. "They're to hold their fire until we can get into position—if we can manage to reach the base undetected to get into position. If they spot us before we reach the top, we'll need accurate rifle fire to deal with the enemy or at least keep them busy long enough for us to go on to the top."

"We'll do our job," the captain promised.

"That's it, gentlemen," Bolan announced as he slid the sling to his M-16 across a shoulder. "If there are no questions, let's do it."

No one had any questions. Bolan glanced at Encizo. The Cuban nodded, and both men moved from the cover of the rocks. They headed for the base of the mountain quickly, backs arched and knees bent to present a smaller target. Yet no shots were fired as they dashed for the rock rubble at the foot of the stony wall.

Bolan held the Beretta close to his chest as he gazed up at the rock wall. It seemed taller, more formidable at that angle. The mountain wasn't particularly large, Bolan realized, perhaps two hundred yards high. Yet scaling it would be a stressful and potentially dangerous task with a mob of armed opponents at the summit.

The Stony Man commandos separated, Bolan heading left and Encizo to the right. The crude steps constructed in the rock wall did make the climb easy. Almost too easy, the Executioner thought as he mounted the wall with only occasional need for a handhold.

Bolan spotted it. The squat metal figure on a rock ledge could easily be dismissed as an unusual stone formation. It would have been even harder to spot at night. The warrior flattened himself against the rock wall as best as possible. He noticed the vented barrel below the dull circle.

"Rafael!" he rasped, voice as loud as he dared under the circumstances.

The Cuban had also frozen in position along the stony surface. He had seen another robot sentry stationed on another rock ledge. It was impossible to estimate how sophisticated the security devices might be, though they were probably designed to detect heat or motion by anything larger than a small goat, Bolan guessed. The gun barrel warned that the miniature robot guards would start shooting as soon as a target had been detected.

Bolan extended his arms, hands clenched in a Weaver's grip on the Beretta. He didn't know how solid the robot might be, and he couldn't dwell on whether the metal shell was hard enough to withstand a 9 mm parabellum round. Shooting the damn thing might set it off and send a salvo of full-auto slugs screaming across the face of the mountain. The robot could be wired to an alarm system. Even if it was destroyed, the device might alert the enemy to their presence.

The Executioner squeezed the trigger. A 3-round burst of 9 mm missiles hissed from the muzzle of the silencer. Metal sparked on metal when the high-velocity slugs hit the robot. Bolan saw the circle collapse from the impact. He held his breath, half expecting the gun barrel to respond with a stream of rapid-fire bullets.

The robot didn't open fire. The barrel didn't stir. Bolan sighed with relief and turned to Encizo. The Cuban had seen how Bolan had taken out the first mechanical sentry. He followed the Executioner's example and blasted the second robot with a silenced volley of Uzi rounds.

The commandos approached slowly, unsure if alarms had sounded within the base to announce them. The roar of the MiGs seemed to fill the mountain range. The planes soared and swooped over the area again and again, as if searching for something they couldn't find. Bolan wondered how long the enemy in the base would concentrate on the fighter jet air show. Wouldn't at least one person up there suspect the aircraft could be a distraction? How long would it take before someone looked over the cliff just in case?

Bolan and Encizo couldn't afford to dwell on such notions. They kept climbing. The Executioner recalled his own claim that men make their own luck, but he was counting on being lucky at that moment. Fate hadn't spit on them so far, and he hoped they would remain in the good graces of destiny.

The Executioner had less than three yards of stone left to the top. A shadow appeared at the lip of the cliff. Bolan pressed himself against the rock wall, arm extended with the 93-R in his fist, his other hand clasped to a stone ledge. He remained still, aware the M-16 might rattle against stone if he moved.

The shape moved from the edge. Bolan waited almost a minute before he resumed the climb. He raised his head and Beretta to the top. A sentry stood near the edge, his back turned to the warrior. The guard's attention was on the circling planes. Bolan saw no other sentries within the immediate area.

He climbed onto the lip of stone and started to rise, his silenced pistol aimed at the guard's spine. Suddenly the sentry turned. Perhaps he heard the slight rustle of cloth on cloth or otherwise sensed danger. Whatever the reason, he whirled with his AK-47 in his grasp, mouth open to shout to his comrades.

Bolan triggered the Beretta, and a 9 mm round drilled into the man's open mouth, punching through the roof of his mouth to burrow into his brain. The man dropped his rifle and fell to both knees. His mouth remained open as his eyes stared with lifeless accusation at the Executioner. Then he slumped sideways in a dead heap.

The Stony Man warrior dragged the slain sentry to a boulder to conceal the corpse. He knelt by the cover and scoped the enemy stronghold. Structures of sheet metal, aluminum and plastic stood in the clearing. More than two dozen men were on the parade field, most still watching the MiGs. The big radar dish was mounted on one of the buildings.

Bolan nodded with grim satisfaction. He had found the ACR device responsible for so many deaths and driving the world to the brink of war. Yet the aggressive concentrated radar technology wasn't to blame. The men who had used it for this evil purpose were at fault, and it was time for them to pay.

The Executioner had arrived to pass judgment on the enemy.

CHAPTER TWENTY-SIX

Mack Bolan triggered the M-203 attachment to fire another 40 mm shell into the enemy base. The grenades were loaded with tear gear. The noxious fumes caused the opponents to weep, cough, vomit and stagger about in a sickly, disoriented condition. The Executioner and his men needed an edge to compensate for the greater number of foes at the stronghold. The element of surprise and the tear gas served that need.

Bolan and Encizo had helped pave the way for the others. The four sentries closest to the cliff had been silently dispatched by the Stony Man commandos. With knife and garrote, they took care of the guards without alerting the base. The Executioner waited for the rest of his group to climb to the top and move into position before he started the fireworks.

A large burly man nearly beat him to the punch. The guy saw something at the perimeter of the camp, swung his AK-47 toward some of Leotiev's troops and almost triggered the rifle. A poisoned bolt from McCarter's crossbow slammed into the man's chest, left of center. With a dose of cyanide in his heart, the gunner collapsed without firing a shot.

There was no time to waste. Bolan launched the first tear-gas round into the center of the parade field. He hastily donned his protective mask, aware the others would do likewise. The rubber face gear, with bug-eye lenses and plastic filters, would not only spare them the effects of the gas, but also help identify friend from foe during the frantic confusion that was bound to occur on the battlefield.

Automatic-rifle fire and the machine pistols of the two Phoenix Force warriors ripped into the enemy troops. Bullet-torn bodies dropped rapidly. A few baffled hardmen raised their weapons to fire at the MiGs, believing the attack had come from the jets. The circling fighters were safely beyond the range of small arms, but the same couldn't be said about the Executioner and his assault team.

The destruction ratio increased quickly. A round from the rocket launcher crashed into the main billets. The rocket blasted apart the flimsy aluminum walls and collapsed the entire structure. Leotiev's paratroopers lobbed F-1 fragmentation grenades at the enemy, while Encizo and McCarter tossed both M-26 fraggers and tear-gas canisters. The explosions sent debris and ravaged corpses hurtling in all directions.

Bolan's hand moved from the M-203 to the trigger of the M-16 as two gunners charged his position. They were half blind and fired their weapons wildly as they advanced. The warrior stopped them with two 3-round bursts. He pumped the M-203, ejected a spent casing and fed another cartridge grenade into the breech.

He selected a shell loaded with heavy explosives for the new target and lobbed the projectile at the structure next to the ACR dish. The HE blast demolished the front of the building and caused part of the roof to cave in. Smoke and flames among the ruins revealed the damage was even greater than first impressions suggested.

Two figures appeared from behind some boulders near a water silo. Bolan whirled, saw they wore gas masks and hesitated, concerned about opening fire on his own people. However, his keen eye quickly noticed they wore different model masks and carried AK-47 rifles instead of the AKS-74s used by the Russian paratroopers. The weapons were already pointed at Bolan when he dropped to the ground.

Twin streams of 7.62 mm rounds cut the air above the warrior's prone form. He replied with the M-16. A short salvo caught one opponent in the chest and hurled him back into the rocks. The man slumped in a seated position while his companion retreated for cover. A third figure poked a rifle barrel around the edge of the boulders to fire at the Executioner.

Bolan rolled to a stack of crates for shelter as the bullets dug into the ground near his tumbling body. He triggered another trio of 5.56 mm rounds at the gunmen to force them back behind the rocks. Quickly he took an M-26 grenade from his belt, pulled the pin and popped the spoon.

The warrior fired the M-16 with one hand fisted on the pistol grip. The other held the grenade for two tense seconds, then hurled it at the boulders. The M-26 landed behind the rocks and exploded a moment later. The force of the blast tossed a decapitated shape into view.

Bolan rose from the cover of the crates and glanced at the boulders to see a figure close in rapidly. It was the guy he previously shot in the chest. The man had obviously been wearing a flak vest.

SADEK NIMERI GLARED at the mysterious and deadly invader through the lenses of his gas mask. The Iraqi commando and the soldiers in his elite team had quickly donned the masks from their gear when the battle began. Although more combat savvy than the bulk of the forces at the base, most of Nimeri's comrades had been cut down by the deadly hail of bullets and shrapnel.

The tall man armed with the American-made assault rifle had taken out the last two survivors of Nimeri's proud unit. The Iraqi was furious and determined to kill the man who had blown his comrades to pieces. The Iraqi had lost his rifle when he fell against the rocks, dazed by the force of the M-16 rounds to the vest. He hadn't wasted time looking for the AK-47. Nimeri drew a double-edged combat knife as he charged. This was one opponent he wanted to kill at close quarters and see the man's blood on his blade.

Bolan swung the rifle toward the Iraqi as Nimeri threw a high roundhouse kick. The boot slammed forcibly into the M-16 and sent the weapon spinning from the Executioner's grasp. Nimeri slashed at Bolan's arm to try to cut the artery at the crook of his elbow. When the Executioner jumped back to avoid the blade, Nimeri lunged for his opponent's chest.

The warrior sidestepped the attack. The knife missed its mark, and the blade barely scraped the Kevlar armor around Bolan's torso. The Executioner swiftly grabbed the wrist above the knife with one hand and the rubber snout of Nimeri's mask with the other. He pulled hard and swept a boot to the back of the Iraqi's ankle. The judo trip sent Nimeri to the ground. He landed on his back. Bolan held on to his opponent and dropped on top of him.

Suddenly both his hands grasped Nimeri's wrist. The Iraqi had been stunned by the fall and failed to react fast enough to prevent Bolan from shoving the captive wrist forward. Nimeri's own fist and knife jammed under his chin. The double-edged steel pierced the hollow of his throat, severed vertebrae and snapped the spinal cord before it pinned his neck to the ground. Bolan felt the man's body twitch in a brief death throe before he rose to retrieve his rifle.

ABDEL GAHIZ LED Mahdi and Kadafadem down the mountain, accompanied by fifteen bodyguards. They had planned to slip away before the MiGs appeared or the strike force hit the base. Gahiz couldn't understand how anyone had managed to simply climb up the mountain unobserved in the afternoon daylight. Yet as he descended the rock face, he realized the mountain was quite easy to scale due to the stairs built into the stone surface. The planes had acted as a diversion.

It was a simple tactic, but a very bold one. Gahiz had to give the raiders credit for courage. However, the assault force had failed to cover every side of the mountain. The Arabs discovered no resistance as they fled the base. The battle raged within the stronghold above, but no one seemed to notice they had escaped during the pandemonium.

Gahiz tried to act as if he had taken command to lead the others to safety. He didn't want them to s pect that he simply wanted to get away as fast as possible, and by taking the lead he reduced his chances of stopping a bullet because they were closer to the conflict. The five Iraqi bodyguards hurried to keep pace with the man they were paid to protect. None of them noticed the stocky metal sentries stationed on the rock shelves.

The robot guards had been designed to detect invaders attempting to climb the rock wall. The sensors didn't spot Gahiz and his men until they passed. Unable to distinguish which direction the shapes were headed, the detectors registered heat and motion and activated the firing mechanism, and the gun mounts opened fire.

Volleys of full-auto rounds spit from the gun barrels. Gahiz screamed as bullets struck his lower back and tore his spine apart. A bodyguard took three slugs through the rib cage and right forearm. A third swung about with his Kalashnikov to face the attackers. He didn't realize the hydrant-shaped object was a threat until the barrel rotated toward him and shot him through both lungs.

One Iraqi bodyguard managed to bolt uphill to avoid the spray of bullets. The others tumbled down the rock wall, wounded or already dead. The Syrian and Libyan protectors urged their employers to stay back as they aimed weapons at the robots and fired a volley of rounds. Moments later the mechanical sentries had been put out of action.

"Damn Giessler," Mahdi rasped as he stared down at the motionless form of Gahiz. "Why didn't he tell us about these things?"

"Maybe he thought we might try to slip away for some reason," Kadafadem replied dryly. "Watch for any more surprises the German might have left here."

The remaining members of the group slowly descended the mountain, watchful of any sign of booby traps. Gahiz and the four luckless bodyguards lay at the foot of the mountain. Ripped by bullets, bones broken and flesh pulped by the punishing fall, there was no life left in any of their bodies.

"May God receive them with mercy," Kadafadem said in a solemn voice.

Mahdi barely glanced at the corpses. He had never cared much for Gahiz when the man was alive and had no intention of mourning his death. There was no time to spare on such matters anyway. Mahdi headed for the passage that bisected the bases of two small mountains. He allowed his bodyguards to venture ahead in case a new threat lurked among the heaps of rock rubble and boulders.

Kadafadem and the other guards followed with haste, not eager to be separated from the Syrians. The mounds of stone shapes seemed ominous, yet the sounds of gunfire and explosions reminded them of the danger they had fled. Imagined terrors paled compared to the small-scale war in progress at Giessler's base.

"I hope they kill that infidel German pig," Mahdi remarked. "May his death be slow and painful."

"And may peace be with you," a voice announced in fluent Arabic.

The group stopped abruptly, startled by the remark. They looked at one another, confused, wondering who had uttered the traditional greeting. Kadafadem was particularly puzzled because he recognized the accent of a Cairo Arabic. None of them were Egyptians or had reason to impersonate such an accent.

"You may live in peace if you drop your weapons and raise your hands in surrender," the voice said again. "Otherwise, you will suffer a violent death."

A bodyguard swung his AK-47 toward the sound of the voice. The speaker was hidden behind a heap of rocks, but he decided to open fire although he had no genuine target. The guard pulled the trigger.

His head exploded as a rifle slug drilled through one temple and exited the other. A short burst of full-auto fire sputtered from the dead man's weapon as his finger held the trigger for a split second.

Firearms rattled on the ground, and the Arabs raised their arms. Yakov Katzenelenbogen emerged from the rocks, an Uzi machine pistol braced across his prosthesis. Gary Manning appeared by some boulders sixty meters from the Arabs. Smoke curled from the muzzle of his FAL rifle. Calvin James also stepped forward, micro-Uzi held ready. Katz addressed the Arabs in their language once more.

"I knew you gentlemen would be reasonable if we made everything perfectly clear," he stated. "Now, sit down and keep your hands in clear view."

Major Fedeyev and the paratroopers in their group joined the three Phoenix Force commandos. Mahdi, Kadafadem and their companions followed orders and sat on the ground, hands placed in front of them. Fedeyev stared at the prisoners with amazement.

"We have two of the ringleaders here," the major remarked. "Good. They can stand trial as soon as the countries involved decide who wants to execute the bastards."

"I want you and two of the paratroopers to stand guard," Katz said. "If any of them try to move, shoot them in the legs. We can't afford to let them get away."

"I understand," Fedeyev replied. "Where are you going?"

"We arrived a bit late," Katz answered, "but they still have a battle in progress on the hill. Our friends might need a hand."

He glanced at his single fist on the pistol grip of the Uzi and smiled at the unintended pun. James and Manning didn't wait for an invitation. They were already headed for the mountain. Katz didn't waste any time on further conversation and jogged after his partners.

GIESSLER CURSED under his breath as he slammed a knee on a jagged rock. The German had slid into a crevasse along the side of the mountain. He had previously considered the gap in the stone wall as a possible hiding place in an emergency. What happened at the base was worse than an emergency. It was a total disaster.

The ex-SSD agent set down his submachine gun, removed his helmet and opened a canteen. He poured water in his palm and splashed it across his eyes and nose to wash out the traces of tear gas. The sounds of battle seemed to gradually decline, but he felt no optimism about the outcome. Despite being half blinded by the gas, Giessler had witnessed enough of the conflict to realize the attack force had gained the upper hand and pressed this advantage. He had little doubt his forces had been defeated.

Giessler wasn't sure what went wrong. They had tried to do too much too soon and failed to move fast enough when needed. Maybe the whole plan had been too outrageous and ambitious from the start. It was over now. Everything was finished, and all that remained was personal survival.

An aluminum briefcase lay next to Giessler. It contained five hundred thousand Swiss francs and forged documents to identify Giessler as Horst Richter. If he could make his way to the trucks, there was still a chance he could escape, melt into the shadowy underground and decide what to do in the future.

He reached for the barrel of the submachine gun. A bullet struck, chipping rock bare centimeters from his fingers. Giessler drew back his hand and glanced at the gap in the stone as big as his thumb. He raised his hands to shoulder level and slowly turned. His ears throbbed form the painful ringing caused by a large-caliber weapon fired into the enclosed fissure of stone.

Mack Bolan stood by the mouth of the crevasse, the big .44 Magnum Desert Eagle in his fists. The Executioner had exhausted the ammo for the M-16 during the battle and discarded the rifle when he saw Giessler attempt to escape. He aimed the Desert Eagle at the German's chest, noticed the guy's flak vest and raised the pistol slightly.

"Leave the gun," Bolan instructed. "Raise your hands higher and come forward slowly."

Giessler noticed the tall stranger spoke English with an American accent, but he couldn't place the region.

"Hey," Giessler began, "what the fuck is wrong with you, buddy? Don't you know who's in your own goddamn unit?"

"Nice try," Bolan replied, "but I *do* know everyone in my unit. You're not one of them. You speak good English and came up with that bluff pretty quick. I assume you're Heinz Giessler."

The German was startled by the question. How could they have found out about him? Giessler had thought he covered his tracks very well, but obviously not well enough.

However, one thing wasn't in his file—the little .25 Bauer holstered at his nape. He slowly placed his hands to the back of his head, closer to the hidden weapon.

"You seem to have me at a disadvantage," Giessler stated.

"Yeah," the warrior answered. "I have a gun pointed at your head. You coming or do you want to die in this hole?"

"Take it easy," the German urged. "The shooting stopped. The fight must be over. Wonder which side won?"

"You lost," Bolan stated. "You coming? It's okay with me if you choose to be a corpse."

Giessler slid his fingers to the back of his neck.

"I have a large sum of money in this case," he began. "You and I could split it fifty-fifty—you still use that expression in the United States?"

"Forget it," Bolan said. "You can't buy your way out of this."

Giessler touched the butt of the .25 auto.

"No," he remarked. "I guess not."

The German yanked the Bauer from the holster. A big .44 Magnum round drilled into Giessler's forehead. The exit wound blew open the back of his skull and plastered the man's brains across the rocks. His corpse collapsed, the unfired Bauer pistol still in his fist.

Bolan lowered the Desert Eagle and shook his head.

"I've seen that trick before," he told the dead man.

The Executioner climbed from the crevasse. The fighting had ended. The enemy base lay in ruins, the majority of Giessler's followers dead. The few survivors had been rounded up and held at gunpoint by Leotiev and his troops. Bolan was glad to see that Encizo and McCarter had both survived the encounter without injury. They still wore the protective masks, but Bolan had no trouble recognizing the commandos.

"We were looking for you," Encizo remarked.

"Had a little unfinished business to take care of," Bolan replied. "I just took out Giessler. Gave him a chance to surrender, but he didn't take it."

"I wouldn't be too choked up over that," McCarter said. "Bloke deserved what he got. By the way, our mates showed up for the tail end of the battle. Turns out the Arabs involved in this business managed to climb down the hill and ran right into them. Most of them are still alive and being held prisoner by Fedeyev and a couple of Russian soldiers."

"How did our people hold up?" Bolan asked.

"Lost two paratroopers," Encizo answered. "That's not good, but considering the odds it could have been a lot worse."

The Executioner grunted. The loss of a single good man was one too many. He understood the Cuban's point and felt relieved that they hadn't suffered greater losses. Bolan noticed the three other members of Phoenix Force were gathered by the wreckage of the aggressive concentrated radar dish and the structure that had stood next to the device.

A crushed figure lay among the debris. The portly, middle-aged man had apparently been killed when the heavy radar dish crashed down on him, the rim jammed at the base of his broken neck. Blood streaked the dead man's face, but Bolan recognized it from photographs.

"Professor Bukovsky," Katz remarked, confirming Bolan's observation. "They'll need to update the report of his death."

"Yeah," Bolan agreed, "but that's somebody else's job. We've done ours. Let's wrap it up and head for home. We're finished here."

U.S. Justice takes a bloodbath...

DON PENDLETON's

MACK BOLAN.

Former Nazi Bernhardt Ensslin reigns rich and untouchable over the largest cocaine manufacturing empire in South America. Now his "corporation" has extended its payroll to an army of seasoned terrorists hired to massacre U.S. judges. His agenda: force a U.S. retreat in the Drug War.

**Blazing a perilous trail through the
heart of darkness**

JAMES AXLER

Road Wars

A cryptic message sends Ryan Cawdor and the Armorer on an
odyssey to the Pacific Northwest, away from their band of warrior
survivalists. As the endless miles come between them, the odds for
survival are not in their favor.

In the Deathlands, fate and chance are clashing with
frightening force.

DON PENDLETON'S THE EXECUTIONER ®

NEW COVER
COMING IN
JANUARY 1995

The Mack Bolan team will be coming your way with new eye-catching cover graphics.

We're bringing you an exciting new cover design, but Gold Eagle is still committed to bringing you action adventure heroes who confront danger head-on. We are dedicated to action adventure at its best—now in a bright, new package!

Don't miss the new look of THE EXECUTIONER— available in January 1995.

In the quest for great adventure, watch for the new Executioner cover from Gold Eagle books.